Praise for Kathryn Magendie's Bestselling Series, The Graces

Tender Graces
Secret Graces

"This message is for guys: It may have a soft, pink cover but it ain't that kind of book. Kathryn Magendie's Virginia Kate has plenty of what my grandmother called "brass," treats us to earfuls of authentic dialogue, and gradually reveals a story not easily forgotten. We will soon read more, I hope, from Magendie's pen. She's real."
—*Wayne Caldwell,* Author of Cataloochee and Requiem by Fire

"A prodigal daughter story . . . exuberant.
—Asheville (N.C.) Citizen-Times

"Lilting . . . well-told."
—Baton Rouge (LA.) Advocate

"Kathryn Magendie's TENDER GRACES is a powerful, moving and beautifully written debut. With rich detail, vivid imagery and finely drawn characters who leap off the page, drag you into their lives and make you root for them, this book will command your attention all the way to the final page...and leave you wishing for more."
—*Danielle Younge-Ullman,* author of FALLING UNDER

Sweetie

Kathryn Magendie

Bell Bridge Books

Bell Bridge Books
PO BOX 300921
Memphis, TN 38130
ISBN: 978-1-935661-91-7
Bell Bridge Books is an Imprint of BelleBooks, Inc.

We at BelleBooks enjoy hearing from readers. You can contact us at the address above or at BelleBooks@BelleBooks.com and www.BellBridgeBooks.com.

10 9 8 7 6 5 4 3 2

Cover design: Debra Dixon
Interior design: Hank Smith
Photo credits:
Girl holding flower Haneck@dreamstime.com
Texture Dimitriy Gool@dreamstime.com
Forest scene Idrutu@dreamstime.com

:L2:01:

Dedication:

To the little ones: Norah Kathryn, Nicholas, Amelia, Sabastyn, Maddison

Acknowledgements

Thank you to my friends and family; you mean everything to me. And to my long-suffering novel-widower GMR, who puts up with my strange ways and my distant mind and my leaving him (synaptically and brainwavingly) for long eons of time as I write, for the days I talk about some person and he suddenly realizes I am speaking about a character and not a real, living, person so no wonder he doesn't remember them, and for all the times he's cooked for me so I'll "Please eat something," and how he has to shuffle about the house among all the ghosts and spirits I call forth—even the ghost dog of my Kayla-Girl and the mysterious Shadowman for whom I woke to see watching me sleep.

And big huge heartfelt thanks to Sweetie's "first readers:" Mikell Web here in Western North Carolina and to my bound-sister Angie Ledbetter in South Louisiana—you both helped to bring clarity where I saw cloudity.

Thank you, lovely Mary Ann Ledbetter, for coming through again with a brilliant Reader's Guide.

Bellebooks/Bell Bridge Books—the Debs—Deb Smith the coolest editor ever and Deb Dixon who creates book covers that make me go *Oh!*—and all the staff who make my dreams a tangible reality I can hold in my hands: thank you!

I must mention Deena at Drollerie Press, who encouraged me after she read an earlier version of Sweetie and saw something good in my work.

And to Haywood County—if I didn't get something right, please forgive me, for I tried my best to honor the place I live and love; as did Melissa, who is really the voice and storyteller here.

And always, to readers: my words are a love-letter to you; thank you for your support.

SWEETIE

*Let me tell you I am better acquainted with you for a long absence,
as men are with themselves for a long affliction: absence does but
hold off a friend, to make one see him the truer.*
— Ovid

*Sadly we sing and with tremulous breath, as we stand by the
mystical stream,
in the valley and by the dark river of death, and yet 'tis no more
than a dream*
—old mountain song

ONE

This is not the beginning . . .

Wake up.

I smoothed my thumb over the tiny wood-carved bird lying in my palm, closed my hand around it, and recalled the day Sweetie became my friend.

She stood, feet rooted in the grass as she gazed down at her cupped hands held against her chest. Her blonde hair blew in the mountain wind, pieces of it whipping across a tough face. The intensity was only a reflex of preparation, a bracing against her secrets. She wore a cotton dress of faded yellow, scattered with once-bright roses that had turned the color of old blood.

I held my Big Chief ruled tablet at eye level, pretending to study my homework, and secretly watched her by peeking over the top. She brought her hands to her right eye and peered inside them, and I wondered what was there, a butterfly, or a wish? I shuffled by inches to stand closer to her.

When she looked at me full on, I was captured by her eyes—cat's eye marble eyes. A bright burning flared in them, then was gone. She held out her hands to me. I hesitated, for I had been tricked before. What society of children could resist tormenting the walking cliché from daytime movies?—I was always the awkward new girl in town. One would hope I brought that cliché to the limit, somehow growing to be beautiful and showing them all, but I was at best unremarkable, average; though Sweetie would say, "Not nothing average about you, Miss-Lissa."

Sweetie, herself born with moonbeams in her eyes that, when the veil was lifted, sparked and raged with a burning bright light of mystery and knowledge beyond anything I'd ever known.

In the schoolyard that day, in that little Haywood County town of Western North Carolina, I stood watching a girl who wore her strange beauty like an afterthought, beauty that defied the scars mottling her body. There had been no one in my life like Sweetie before, and no one like Sweetie since.

She kept her hands held out, enticing me to her, not hurrying my shy hesitation. My feet took me to her, as if they were independent of my body, as if I were pulled to her by the force of those strange compelling eyes. When I at last stood by her side, I smelled mint and moist earth smells.

"See here what I got?" Sweetie thrust her hands to my face.

I put my right eye to the tiny hole she made between her thumbs, closed my left eye, and squinted through my glasses. She opened the backside of her hands a bit to let light filter through. A baby bird nestled in her palms.

"This here bird fell out its nest, and I got to put it back so its mama'll take care of it." She eyed me up and down, as if trying to make up her mind about me.

I stared at the scabs marching across her knees, the puckered skin racing up her right arm, the reddened zigzag that ran from her ankle, up her thigh, to disappear under her dress. She didn't try to hide her imperfections, as I would have.

"You want to watch me give this here bird back to Mama-bird, or just stand there gawking?"

I tore my eyes from her hurts, tried, "N-n-no. I mean, y-y-yes. I . . . " and then tried a shrug to show I didn't care how I sounded or looked or was or had ever been or would ever be.

She narrowed her eyes. Then a grin lit her mouth, as if she then did make up her mind about me. She tossed her head to a herd of girls on the playground. "Them girls would keep it, like a pet." She then asked, "It belongs where it belongs, right? And where something belongs is where it's got to stay, right?" Without waiting for my answer, she pulled up the hem of her dress, gently placed the bird in a fold, tucked the ends into the cut-off dungarees she wore underneath, and climbed up the tree. When she was to the nest and had placed the baby bird inside, she waved to me, and then scuttled down as swift as an animal.

I looked up at the nest, hoped the little bird wouldn't die, hoped it'd stay where it belonged, whispered, "Don't d-die little one. You're s-safe now."

Sweetie stood again by my side. "Little Bird might be sickly, or busted up inside, and Mama-bird pushed it out the nest to spare it from dying slow." She shrugged. "Or, it might grow up and old and live forever and ever and ever."

"Y-y-you saved its l-life."

"You got to breathe, Miss-Lissa." She inhaled through her nose, filling her thin chest, and then blew out through slightly parted lips.

"It's *Me*lissa, n-n-not *Miss*-Lissa."

"Just try what I said, Miss Stubborn-brain."

I breathed in and out as she'd done.

"That's right. Stop getting in a hurry with your words and your thoughts." Sweetie looked hard at me, then looked up to the nest. "All a person can do is give it all they's got. Right?"

There was no turning back from Sweetie then, and I knew I'd follow her to the ends of her earth that summer. She was a mountain creature who could not be contained, and when they wanted to take her from her home, she fell away so they would not find her.

She said she would wait forever. She said she would wait for me. How could it be so?

I squeezed the wooden bird and its beak cut into my palm. When I opened my hand, a spot of blood beaded there. Another memory pierced me sharp with sound and image—the crowd of shouting people, the white robe with Sweetie's bloody handprint, and Sweetie asking for her mother's healing even though it meant she sacrificed her own unique gifts.

I would find what I needed there among the magic Smoky Mountains, at our meeting place—Whale Back Rock. The big rock rose up out of the mountainside with its back full of moss and lichens, appearing like a great humpback whale curving back into the ocean after its breath released from its blowhole. There were natural signs to lead me: Bear Claw Rock, Turtlehead, Jabbering Creek, Triplet Tree, all the places we'd roamed on the mountain with its coves and secret places. And there were Sweetie's maps. And there were whispers calling, unseen.

I pushed the bird deep into a pocket of my backpack, and walked up the blacktop road, which used to be a dirt and graveled road. The road led to the old log trails, only two miles or so from my old neighborhood where I'd lived that summer before Father and Mother took me away from the mountains, before the long deep sleep of denial.

I'd happened upon it. The Pandora's Box of our memories. When opened, old dust and voices rushed, charging about my white-walled, antiseptic, scientific room made perfect for a scientific woman; where tiny microscopic universes came from microscopic big bangs; where germs became colonies marching to new words only to be foiled by antibiotics; where white coverings and masks and intense purposeful looks, or dreaming hopeful ones, made all of us look the same the same the same, where outside traffic rushed by, people clomped on purposeful shoes, mothers or fathers rushed their children to school and day care; where when spiraling out, suburban neighborhoods held family units with two-point-five kids, a collie or German Shepherd, Sunday dinners and Sunday drives; and all around and out of that Pandora's Box the dust and voices slammed against the walls, to the ceiling, out the door and opened window, in my hair, through my pores, down my throat through my opened mouth. Sweetie spoke loud and insistent to me, from the distance of time and space, *Come home, Lissa. Back where you belong.*

Layers of memory: a pack of Old Maid playing cards; a petrified Tootsie Roll; a tiny drawing of a mouth and eyes; a photo of my brother in his graduation cap and gown, a snapshot of Mother and Father two inches apart, our house in the valley, four other houses here and there, there and here; jacks (*onesies, twosies, threesies, kissies*); three marbles, including the cat's eye my big brother gave to me; a Troll doll; a dried and cracked buckeye seed; and one of Mother's food poems, and among all that were the carved bird and the diary. I blinked from my long sleep and blood rushed from head to toe, dizzying and thrumping in my ears. *Oh, North Carolina. What mysteries and secrets you hold.*

As I made my way up the mountain, the muscles of my calves tensing and releasing felt good. So long since I'd stretched my flaccid muscles, so long since I breathed in air that wasn't stale and long-breathed and re-breathed. I studied and followed the hand-drawn maps in the diary, checked the natural signs, twists, turns, switchbacks. The Great Rock should be up ahead, soon. A wind swept down and over the ridges and cooled my heated body.

There to the left was an almost hidden old log trail. Near the entrance to the trail were three rocks, as old as the time was old. The three rocks huddled together in a way that formed a small cave, a place where two young girls could squeeze in and hide away, a home to magical creatures with burning curious eyes. Sweetie's grandfather had believed in magic, had believed in a granny woman's powers to see behind the veil, had believed in mountain sprits and medicines from the fruits of the earth.

The growth was thicker on the old log trail. A creek bubbled down, tumbling over rocks. Landscapes changed with time, just as most things do if they go on with their lives unsleeping, yet the woods and mountains when undisturbed remained constant reminders of the past.

Sweetie's maps were amazingly meticulous, full of detailed drawings and instructions written in tiny letters. I could imagine Sweetie bent over the diary, taking the time to fashion the maps so I could find my way. I had a sudden thought: had she made the maps only for *young* me? Or had she known I'd need them one day in the unknown future? A bird flew by so close, its wings brushed my cheek, or perhaps it was only the air disturbed by that wing. All the same, my arms broke out with goosebumps. The hairs on the back of my head lifted.

The old trail veered off to the left, and I left it to follow the creek for a while, even as it grew narrower as I climbed. I parted a clump of overgrowth, rhododendrons and blackberry vines, and went through them. The blackberry vines grabbed me in a thorny grip, tried to keep me from going any farther, in vain. Spider webs wrapped across my face as I stumbled through the woods and I saw as through a veil until I wiped them away. I picked up a thick branch to use as a walking stick to help clear overgrowth and balance me on the incline, followed the narrowing creek runoff until it forked off, checked the map, and went to the right onto another log trail that would switchback after another half-mile or so.

After walking, climbing, swatting at webs, and pulling stickers out of my hands, I stopped at a large oblong rock that looked as if it had ancient writings on it. Maybe it was mountain fairy fossils, or maybe young Cherokee chiseled messages to each other into the rock. Maybe only wind and time had left their natural marks. I sat with my back against a giant of a poplar tree and stared at the rock. According to the map it was Tablet Rock, but I didn't need the map to know. I'd told Sweetie the rock reminded me of one-half of Moses Ten Commandments tablet. She'd studied it with one eye closed, and asked, "Which of them commands you think's on this one?"

The water flowed into the narrow creek, which flowed into the bold creek, which flowed to the river and on to the ocean; water finding water always. Like finding like. Need finding need. Never ending. Ending never.

There were wild flowers growing amongst the trees, bushes, and other growth. Overhead a red squirrel, what the old man Zemry had called Boomers, shouted down to me. I knew there could be bear, or bobcat, or big cats Zemry called painters. Or the haints come to haunt me—Zemry had told those stories, too, of the spirits of mountain men, of the Cherokee, of old and ancient times before. Of restless spirits following the living to see what they'd do next, and then trying to pull the living into their world so they wouldn't be lonely anymore.

As I looked around the long-ago-familiar woods, I thought of my friend, my blood-bound sister. Sweetie had always believed in me. She saw another person inside the timid young girl I had been. Someone much stronger, with a full-burning heart. Yet I'd become a scientific woman, a biological machine, made of fallible parts and calculating synaptic brain, peering at those microscopic worlds I pretended were more interesting than the world of real people. A woman who believed only what science showed her and not what was felt with the heart. A woman who had left behind the magic and embraced her small, tangible room of a world.

I slipped off my shoes and socks and pressed my feet into cool earth, dreaming once short and vivid that Sweetie appeared and whispered into my ear, *It's about time you got yourself back here, Miss Lissa.* I hurried to replace socks and shoes, stood, listened for whispers, then continued my journey. Sweetie had said she'd wait for me. She'd said she'd hide until everyone forgot her, hide until she was safe. I'd come back to find something in these mountains, but could it ever be Sweetie?

Around a bend stood Triplet Tree, a yellow buckeye Sweetie and I used to sit near and whisper secrets. Its gnarled trunks looked like three great trees all grown together. There were many stories of the beautiful mahogany buckeye seeds—carrying one in a pocket for good luck or to help with arthritis; rubbing the flat part of the buckeye and wishing for money, but only if one's thoughts were just right; or if the fish weren't biting, rub the buckeye and spit on the bait.

It was a mysterious tree, full of old gashes, thick vines, moss, and rough bark, and it was the place where Sweetie and I became bound together. As our palms fused, before the tearing away, we sat in its shade while she told me the secret of who she was.

The wind blew whispers. *Yes. Here. She was here. Stop here and dig.*

I quickly took my stick and dug around the tree's roots. Anything could have happened to it after all this time, but I knew it was there.

Knew it deep in my bones. After digging in an arc arou
stick hit against something hard but more giving than ;
hands and knees, dug into the rich North Carolina s
things long buried: leaves, twigs, secrets? And, there, w~~~
root. The tin box.

I lifted it from the dirt, cradled it in my hands. It was rusted and
dented, but still mostly intact. With trembling fingers, I pulled at the
lid, the latch long broken off. It wouldn't give at first, the years kept it
closed, or perhaps the wish of two young girls that it never be opened
to release girl secrets. When I at last snapped back the lid, inside there
was only dirt. No, not only dirt. A breeze pushed against my face,
moved my hair back. *Whispers. Whispers.* The spirits of our secrets blew
against me, out into the open air, a whirring whoosh, whirring whoosh,
into my ears.

I caught my breath, called, "Sweetie!"

Mountain Spirit, take our pain and blow it out in the wind.

I doubled over, cradling the tin box, pushing it into my stomach
to stop the sobs that wanted to erupt from there up to my throat and
then to my eyes, and at last, when I had control, I closed the box and
reburied it. But it was too late, our voices were already exposed.
Gathering speed and strength.

I hurried up the trail, away from Triplet Tree, calling to her as I
had many times that summer when she ran too far ahead of me.
"Sweetie! Sweetie! Where are you? I can't find you!"

As I ran, ducking branches that reached across the trail for me,
jumping over growth and scattered rock that stood in my way, I saw
the two of us so clearly—Sweetie and Miss Lissa.

There, her shining blonde hair as she disappeared behind the
trees. There, her burning eyes as she peeked at me from a tree branch.
I was twelve again, running after her, my chunky legs pumping as hard
as they'd go. I ran, and I'd never felt so alive, so strong and able, so
much a part of something bigger than I—something exciting and wild
and mysterious. Sweetie had always let me catch up to her, and gave to
me to hold all her known secrets. She trusted me with the part of
herself she'd hidden from the world, and in her way, presented back to
me the gift to see what I had hidden inside myself.

And in the end, I'd let her down. I'd pretended to forget, in such a
long sleep . . .

TWO

Then

Sweetie was on the jungle gym during recess and I knew something weird was going to happen. It always did with Sweetie because she liked to take chances, and whatever would hurt another kid only made her laugh and do something even more foolish. I stood off to the side and watched her swing from one bar to the next, slinging around like a crazy blonde monkey. I had a feeling twist in my stomach, one Mother called *intuition* but I just called *paying attention*.

Although lately, ever since we'd moved to Haywood County in the Western North Carolina Smoky Mountains, that *paying attention* feeling had become something else, something I couldn't explain. It wasn't just the big old mountains rising up all around the county or the way people talked different and acted different from other places I'd lived, but something else, something in the air that followed me into my dreams. Mostly, never had I thought to know someone like Sweetie. Never had I known someone to be so much more different and strange.

That day, Sweetie wore a cotton shirt and cut-off dungarees under her dress, but the Circle Girls still snickered behind their hands when her dress flew up as she tumbled around on the bars. Sweetie called them Circle Girls because they liked to circle around, shove some poor soul in the middle, and poke them with their mean words. She didn't have to tell me about it.

My second day in sixth grade, they'd hooked hands and walked around me, singing, "Fattie Fattie, two by four, can't get through the outhouse door. Four Eyes, Four Eyes, blind fat fool, has no trouble finding food." I was branded right then and there with the Circle Girl's hot cattle iron, right on my big fat thigh. I'd seen it on the cowboy shows. The marks stayed burned into the cow's hide for the rest of their lives, and that's how they were spotted in a crowd of other cows if they strayed to where they didn't belong.

Sweetie swung up her legs, hooked them across a bar, and then hung upside down. I held my breath as she arched over with a backwards flip and tried to catch another bar. That's where the something I figured was coming came.

The Circle Girls huffed out their air, and the boys yelled out, "Oh man! You see that? She got her finger caught."

Sweetie held onto a bar with her right hand while she worked at loosening her stuck left pinky finger from the rusted-out corner. We'd been warned about playing too rough and rowdy on the old playground equipment, but most of the kids didn't listen. (I did. I always listened.) Frannie, another of the Circle victims, said her little brother broke his arm falling off the jungle gym last year, and his arm hadn't ever healed right. Frannie always had a story about tragedy. Her cat was run over by a tractor and cut into fifty-million pieces; her dog ate a buckeye seed and vomited all over her new shoes and she never got the smell out; her father left them for a whole year and her mother went insane and cut off his head in all of their photos; how the boy who'd slipped off the ridge and never been found was her fault because they'd kissed once in second grade and he'd then been cursed to die tragical and die tragical he did. Stuff like that all the time going on with Frannie. I tried to be her best friend, but she said anybody who became her best friend met with tragical circumstances.

Sweetie's face hardened in her concentration to remove her pinky from the sharp edges of the rusted jungle gym bar. I watched; we all watched.

When he had time, Mr. Mendel the Janitor patched up the swings, jungle gym bars, slide, rocking horses, tether ball, and merry-go-round. He repainted flaky paint, sanded wood that made splinters catch in people's behinds, replaced bent chains, put on new ropes. He taped up the rusted-out places when he couldn't fix them, but the boys picked off the tape because boys just have to pick at things. Since Mr. Mendel the Janitor was out with the gout since last week, the rusted corner was open and ready, and the perfect size for a certain sized pinky finger to become jammed and stuck. And Sweetie had that certain sized pinky finger.

Frannie stood beside me and we both looked up at Sweetie while she grunted and wiggled her stuck finger back and forth. A few drops of blood dripped onto the dirt below. When I saw the blood, I knew I should help her. She was my brand new friend, and since friends didn't come easy, it was best to try to do nice thing to keep them.

When I stepped forward, Frannie told me, "Best not."

"B-b-but . . . she's hurt."

She made a 'tsk' noise, said, "I warned you about her, but you won't listen. Something tragical will come of you being her friend."

"That's silly."

Frannie shook her frizzed-haired head, then shrugged, as if to say, *Okay, but don't say I didn't warn you.*

Before I could reach her, Sweetie let go and dropped to the ground. I heard a wet, ripping sound, heard it in my head, even if it didn't really make a sound like that at all. She landed on her backside in the dirt with an *oomph* and then a laugh. The kids shoved each other as they crowded around for a better look. There was the usual, "Eeeww," from most of the girls, and "Let me see it," from most of the boys.

I pushed my way in, dropped to my knees beside her, and stared at her hand. The tip of her pinky was raw-meat bloody, mixed with dirt. I wanted to vomit up my lunch of peanut butter and jelly sandwich, banana, milk, and cookie, but I knew if I did, the next thing they'd tease would be, *Fattie Fattie big as a comet, opened her mouth and spewed out some vomit.*

"Sweetie, you really hurt your f-f-f-finger. It looks b-b-bad."

From behind me, Frannie said, "Too tragical for words."

Sweetie studied her finger as if it were a bug under a magnifying glass. It was crowded and dusty under the jungle gym and some of the kids smelled like sour milk and bologna. All I wanted to do was go back inside to the library and read a book. I used to spend all my time reading books, or watching television. It was safe. Nobody ever was hurt or teased or looked stupid while reading books or watching television. I looked up to the rusted-out part of the bar, and there was the bit of her pinky still caught like a small white worm.

Sweetie looked where I had, said, "*Huhn.*"

"We better g-g-get Mrs. P-Patterson." I had to push up on my hands and knees so I could stand up. Some of the kids snickered, and even though I tried to pretend everything was fine, I knew my face was red and sweaty.

Sweetie jumped right to her feet, pulled me up with her good hand, and whispered, "Breathe Miss-Lissa. *Breeeaaaathe.*"

I brushed off my knees, breathed in, out, in, out.

Sweetie stared at the crowd of kids with her hard face. "Move," was all she said.

The kids moved back, except T. J., who stepped in front of us. He had a bad crew cut to go with his bad breath, and that's what must have caused his bad moods. He hooked his thumbs into his belt loops. "Boy, are you in trouble, Sweetie-*Pie*."

The rest of the kids laughed, even though I didn't see what was so funny about that.

I looked at Frannie; she looked away. I knew it was the end of her being nice to me. That left me with one friend: Sweetie.

She stepped closer to T. J. and rose up to her full height. I crouched down behind her. She said, "Get out my way. I am not playing."

T. J. didn't want to back down from a girl, but Sweetie was as tall as he was, and she was tough. Besides, he'd already been in trouble for fighting at school. Mrs. Patterson had to call his father, who right in front of the class slapped T. J. across the face hard enough to knock his head back. He told his son, "I could get fired for having to come fetch you out of school, boy." The next day, T. J. came to school with a split lip and had to apologize to the class. T.J. said, "I don't got time to mess with you today," moved out of the way and let us pass.

Across the playground, away from the other kids, I said, "I'll help you fix your f-f-finger, Sweetie."

"Take them good breaths when your tongue gets tied. You can do it." Sweetie grinned at me, but her grin turned to a frown when she saw Beatrice and Deidra had come across the playground, staring at us with their lips curled.

Beatrice and Deidra were the head Circle Girls. They picked the girls to be The Circle, and the ones to be inside of it. It was never good to have their attention until you knew which one.

Deidra said, "She's weirdo schmeirdo crazy." She tossed her curls. "*Normal* people don't laugh if their fingers get ripped open."

Sweetie looked down at her finger, wiggled it. A bead of blood dripped onto the grass, sliding down a blade and into the ground. I imagined things growing from the blood fertilizer, like another pinky. "Let's g-go, Sweetie."

She stayed right where she was, let her finger drip.

Beatrice said, "Mamaw says she's a witch's daughter so that makes her a witch, too."

Deidra rolled her eyes. "You believe that stupid stuff your granny spouts off?"

"No! I was just telling you what my mamaw said about Sweetie and her mom."

"Well, my mom says they're out of their minds," Deidra said, while flipping her hair.

Sweetie's eyes went bright and hard, then a corner of her mouth lifted, just enough that I noticed even if no one else did. She scrunched her face, and let out a whimpering, "Oh, *owie*. My finger *hurrrts* something fierce!" She hopped around, holding on to her finger, her face a fist of pain.

I stared at her with my mouth hung open. One minute Sweetie was walking tall and proud without a care about her finger, and the next acted as if it hurt like the dickens.

Deidra and Beatrice backed up a step.

"Oh, poor little finger. It hurts, *hurts.*"

I dug into my satchel to find my first aid kit. Mother made me carry bandages, cotton, baby aspirin, and Mercurochrome, everywhere I went. While I sorted through the Snickers, spiral notebook, math homework, apple, chewing gum, library book, pencils with points and pencils without points, blue ballpoint pen, half a peanut butter sandwich, and wadded up tissue, the Circle Girls walked away, a hurting normal kind of Sweetie wasn't as curious to watch.

I found the kit, opened the pouch, and took out the cotton and the Mercurochrome. I said to Sweetie, "It's okay, don't cry. I'll fix you right up."

"Okay. Here." She stuck out her finger, calm as a sleepy kitten.

I unscrewed the cap and poured Mercurochrome onto the cotton. "This'll really sting, so I'm sorry." I dabbed a bit of the Mercurochrome on her finger to stop the germs. Some germs were bad; some weren't. Father showed me pictures of germs and parasites in his science books. He said germs and parasites were just like people, like friends and families, or like enemies; how they infiltrated and parasited each other, and that even though we were all made of the same stuff, we fought against each other for food and dominant space in the world. I listened to him and only understand half of what he said, but I saw in those books what bad germs could do to a body.

She said, "Give it," and grabbed the bottle. Without using the cotton ball, she poured Mercurochrome all over her finger without even a flinch. Handing me back the bottle, she said, "That orter do it." The orangey-red stained her finger, her arm, the ground, and part of my left saddle oxford.

I capped the bottle, put the Mercurochrome back into the kit, opened a Band Aid, and wrapped it around her finger while Sweetie sang, "Went to see my gal last night, thought I'd do it sneakin'; missed her mouth and hit her nose and the doggone thing was leakin' . . . "

The Band Aid didn't stick well with the Mercurochrome and blood making her finger so wet, so I tried another one.

". . . possum in a simmon tree; raccoon on the ground; raccoon said, you son of a gun; shake some simmons down . . . "

When Mrs. Patterson ran over to us, her dress flapping against her legs, Sweetie changed again. She made an unhappy face and held up her finger, calling out to the teacher in a pitiful voice, "Sure *hurrrts*, Mrs. Patterson."

Our teacher's eyes rolled back, showing a mile of white. "Oh dear Lord above, what did you do this time?" She took off her scarf and wrapped it around Sweetie's hand. "I can't take one teeninesy break from you children."

"Poor old finger," Sweetie said.

Mrs. Patterson took away the scarf and checked Sweetie's finger. The Band Aids fell into the dirt. The teacher looked ready to fall over in a faint. "Oh Lord in Heaven, part of your finger's gone missing." Two bright spots of red flamed on her cheeks. She looked over at me. "How did this happen?"

"It wasn't her f-fault, Mrs. Patterson." But I knew it was.

The teacher pressed the scarf to Sweetie's finger and led her to the school with one arm over Sweetie's shoulder and the other holding the hand she hurt. They had to walk shuffling since Mrs. Patterson was bigger than Sweetie was, and since she was holding onto her so tight. Her ankles were puffed over her thick black shoes and I felt sorry for my teacher all of a sudden, trying to corral us kids every day. She shook her head at Sweetie. "One day you'll break your fool neck with all your shenanigans."

Sweetie said again, "Poor little finger."

I was beside Sweetie as we passed the kids watching her go by. Frannie was already making friends with another Circle victim, ignoring me forever and ever.

Mrs. Patterson said, "Kids, all of you, get in the classroom and wait for me there. And no shenanigans or you'll be writing theme papers until you're ninety-two."

"C-c-can I come with you and Sweetie to the n-nurse's office?" No way did I want to be alone in the class with all those staring eyes, wondering why I was friends with the weirdo schmeirdo girl.

Sweetie had her head down when she said, "Let Lissa come, please with big rock candy mountain sugar on top?" She turned toward me and winked where Mrs. Patterson couldn't see.

"Fine. She can come. I'm too tired to care at this point. You kids will be the death of me. I can't *wait* to retire."

I glanced down at the blood and Mercurochrome spotting my oxford shoes. Mother hated dirt, blood, sweat, tears, and anything nasty that must be wiped from a kid. Mother didn't think the same way about science as Father did. He studied dirt, blood, sweat, tears under microscopes, and believed most things in life were random occurrences and things weren't really real until they were proved with science. Mother believed in God and that everything was planned for us already from birth to finish and nothing needed to be proved if one believed in it strong enough.

Sweetie and Mrs. Patterson squeezed through the school door, me on their heels. Sweetie's back was stiff, and her scarred and skinny legs looked pitiful sticking out from under her dress. I wanted to ask her how she stood it. How she stood her very own blood and pinky part stuck in the jungle gym. At the nurse's office door, Sweetie turned back to me again, this time with her eye squinched like Popeye and her lips pressed together thin and ugly—she was making fun of the nurse, I could tell.

While the nurse cleaned and bandaged Sweetie's finger, I washed off my saddle oxfords as best as I could with alcohol and tissues. Mrs. Patterson smoked a cigarette, her hands shaking, her eyeballs jittery.

Even when the nurse was rough with her, Sweetie sang as if at a campfire meeting, "Not last night but the night before, twenty-four robbers came knocking at my door . . . "

By time the nurse was done, Mrs. Patterson's cigarette was smoked all the way down to the filter and still she sucked on the tip as if her life depended on it.

I threw away the tissues. Some of the stain still spotted my shoes, just how life was sometimes. If Sweetie could sing while bleeding, then I could face Mother being mad at me for stained shoes. We then traipsed back to class. Sweetie couldn't care less; but I wished I could hide away from their staring eyes.

When the bell rang at end of class for the day, Sweetie slipped me a note, and then ran off to wherever she always ran off to. I couldn't wait to read it. My first secret note. All the way home on the bus I ran my thumb over the paper. I'd save it for when I was all alone. Then I'd see what would happen next with Sweetie. I figured with someone like Sweetie, there'd always be something happening.

THREE

I slammed into the house after an almost good day at school. No Circle Girl teasing, no T. J. calling me names, no Sweetie laughing at her hurts, and an A on my science test. Mother was in the living room with her feet propped up. She held a pencil tip to her lips and tapped it there. Her notebook rested on her lap.

"Hi, Mother." I shifted from one foot to the other. She didn't like me to go straight to my room because it was bad manners not to talk about my day with her.

"Dear, you slammed the door right as I was trying to think up a rhyme for pumpkin seeds." She pointed her pencil at me. "I want you to go back and open and close the door ten times."

"Yes M-m-ma'am." I turned away.

"Come back here once you're done. And stop that stuttering!"

I forgot to breathe right sometimes when I wasn't with Sweetie. It was as if the breaths caught up inside and then huffed out jerky. I trudged to the screen door, opened it and closed it. I knew not to do it eight times, or even nine times, but exactly ten, or she'd make me go back and do it again. *Opened it and closed it.* I imagined her sitting there mouthing off one, two, three, four, five, until ten. *Opened and closed.* I did it just as I was supposed to, nice and easy, even though I was in a hurry to go to my room and think about the latest note from Sweetie. *Opened and closed.*

The first note, the day of her pinky part gone missing, read, *this here is not a real note. i will give a real note tomorow.* Nothing but a practice note. Still, it was exciting. *Opened closed.* I'd written back for tomorrow to hurry and I couldn't hardly stand to wait for tomorrow.

I put her practice note where I kept all secret things, in a hole at the bottom of my mattress. The next note read, *can you keep secrets good and tight? i will give you a new note day after next tomorrow.* And I'd written her back telling her I could keep a secret forever.

Opened closed.

The latest note was written on thick paper, rolled into a scroll, and tied with a piece of yarn. I unrolled and read it while walking up our sidewalk; I couldn't wait until I was in my room alone: *i got a secret to show you. a secret so secret, you got to burn this here note after you got it read. i will ask if you burnt it and you best say yes or deals off.*

Opened closed.

I'd never had secrets before. *Opened closed.* I'd never burned a secret note before. *Opened closed.* I couldn't burn it until I did what Mother asked me to.

Opened closed.

I went back to the living room where Mother waited, took a deep breath and let it out slow, pretending Sweetie was there. "I'm sorry I s-slammed the door. I won't do it again."

"Thank you. Now, come over here and tell me about your day." When I stood by her, she held up her pencil. "Wait; let me write this down real quick."

I looked at her paper. She'd written pumpkin seed, and four other words under it that were scratched through: errant need, voracious greed, martyr's need, and mother's creed. When Mother cooked fancy dinners with names she made up, like *Meat Balls a la de Creamed Onion Toot Suite*, she'd write a poem about it and tape it to the refrigerator for Father to admire, though I don't think he ever did. He said food was nourishment for our bodies and to make it anything more was hullaballoo. But if Mother made something boring, he'd say, "This isn't up to your usual, is it? Where's the flair?" And Mother's eyebrows would pull together, a confused look sprouting in her eyes.

My brother said Father was two sides to a coin. Flip him and see which Father you'd get that day, or moment, or hour. He'd then laugh funny when he'd say that. Peter didn't come home much.

Mother closed the notebook, having written nothing more. "So, how was school?"

"It was good."

"What's good about it?" She eyed me over her reading glasses. Her hair was brushed in a perfect French twist. "Can you be more specific?"

"Well, I m-m-made (*breathe in and out Miss-Lissa*) an A on my science test."

She nodded, removed her glasses. "Beula said she saw you at school with that funny little blonde-haired girl." She cleaned her glasses with a cotton hankee she'd taken from her pocket.

"Her name's Sweetie."

"Sweet-tea?" The name dropped off her tongue and landed on the floor. "What kind of a name is that?"

"I don't know. It's just her name. And it's Sweetie, not Sweet-tea."

"What happened to that nice girl, that Frannie you had over once?"

"Frannie stopped being my f-friend."

"Did she now." Her lips pulled downward.

"Guess what our teacher did?"

Mother perked up. "What?"

I told her about how Mrs. Patterson came to class with a rip in her hem and her shoes scuffed and her hair messy. I knew Mother would harp on how a woman shouldn't go around in public like that, and how especially a teacher is supposed to set an example, and how tacky it was be unpresentable and *blah-blee-blah-blork-bleah-blah* she went, wound up about it so she completely forgot to ask me about Sweetie again.

At last, when I was able to escape, I stopped by Father's study for the matches, locked myself in the bathroom, and opened the window so any burn smell would go outside. I read the note again, to memorize it so I could write it in my diary. Then I lit the edge of the paper. It curled up and over, burning away Sweetie's words. I put my face close to the flames, and took into my nose the dark smoke. Part of something Sweetie wrote with her own hand was inside me and that made me shiver with danger.

I turned on the faucet, then off, put my finger into the wet ashes, and licked the ash off my finger. I washed the rest down the sink, and then went to my room to do my homework and clean my room. After that was done, I tried to read *The Call of the Wild*. It was hard to concentrate, since I couldn't stop thinking about what kind of secret Sweetie had to show me. A secret so secret I had to burn even the note that didn't even tell what it was.

At dinner that evening, my parents sipped wine in thin glasses Mother bought in Europe before I came along. Every time we moved, she packed each of those fancy glasses in newspaper and then wrapped them again in dishcloths. And every time she packed them, she'd say, "I've never broken a glass yet. No one has any like them that I've seen. They always remind me of Europe and how our surprise chunky bunny arrived." Me being the surprise "chunky bunny" that arrived uninvited nine months after my parents sent my brother away to camp so they could tour Europe for a summer.

She'd then say something like, "Oh, we were so carefree in Europe. Now we just travel all over America with our boxes bouncing around in a moving van."

I'd asked her once why we moved so much, and she'd said my father couldn't be bound down to one place; his genius was destined to be spread all across the land. She had almost the same kind of laugh as Peter had when he talked about Father.

I could still feel Sweetie's words inside me, and smell the burn in my nose and on my tongue. I chewed my potatoes, swallowed, drank my milk, tried not to show how excited and restless I was. Father sipped his wine and nodded his head as Mother told about her day: she had found the potatoes and tomatoes at a nice farmer's stand; she had written a poem and it was on the refrigerator; she had polished the silver and painted the big mirror frame; she had gone to a meeting for a charity dance and wouldn't he consider going with her to it?

I knew Father was just waiting for his chance to start talking about his class and students, or what kinds of science discoveries were in the news or in his scientific periodicals. When he wasn't being scientifical, he wrote novels that he said, with a big wink, were too brilliant to be appreciated by mere mortals. He wore his dark wavy hair combed straight back because he said it made him look like a romantic hero in a great American novel. Maybe he told me that or maybe Mother did, or maybe I thought it; I couldn't remember.

I studied my parents and just like lots of kids, I wondered if I was adopted. Except people said I took too much after Father's mother.

Grandmother Rosetta lived in California, where she planted gardens, took sick animals to adopt out, and painted pictures of barns on fire. Some showed the farm animals as they ran from the flames with whited eyes while the farmer grabbed his head between his hands, his mouth painted into a big O. And in others, the barn fire was in the distance and no one in the painting noticed the fire, not the farmer, or any of the people standing by, even though it burned brighter than anything else. Sometimes there were no people or animals, only a burning barn. Every painting she made had a burning barn somewhere in it.

I most times called my grandmother *Nonna* and she most times called me her *nipotina*.

Through my daydreaming, Mother's voice brought me to attention. "Our Melissa has a new friend." She patted her mouth with her napkin.

Father nodded. "Kids have friends. That's what they do."

She lifted her glass of wine. "Her name is Sweet-tea."

He studied a potato piece on the end of his fork. "Two beings drawn together by smell or look or some common interest, something they don't even recognize is happening but it is. Friendships and marriages don't happen by chance. Two people find some need in each other and try to fill that need. It's at times irrational, but our instincts to survive and to form community and to bond with other human beings are quite strong." Father took a bite of his potato, chewed, chewed, chewed, even though the potatoes didn't need that much chewing.

Mother sighed.

I said, "It's Sweetie, not sweet tea."

She said, "I hope we get to meet this new friend soon."

Father attacked his meat. "If you've ever been inside a slaughter house, you look at meat differently—"

"I'm trying to eat," Mother said.

"I once attended a picnic at a farm where they had a real chicken be-heading. Ka-chop! Those chickens—"

"I said I do not want to hear about it, Jack."

"May I be excused? I have lots of homework." I stood, picked up my plate and waited. She'd never know my homework was in my satchel, done neatly as I could, even though it was boring. School was too easy. My last teacher wanted to put me ahead a year, but since we moved so much, it was too complicated.

Mother sipped her wine, swallowed, stared at the glass, put it down. "Yes, but you still have to do the dishes. So I suggest doing them first so the plates won't become crusty."

"Pauline, can't you do the dishes? She said she has homework. School is more important than dishes. How will she ever succeed in this world without—"

"Why don't you do them, then, if you're so worried about her need for schooling?"

"I've got writing to do, and I've worked all day."

Mother stood up. "And what have I done? Only taken care of this house, cooked your meals. Made every place we've lived into a sparkling showcase. Tended the landscapes, raised your children—"

"—oh, come off it, Pauline—"

"—and you never—"

"P-p-please s-s-stop."

"—and that woman who called late—"

"—here we go again—"

"—just like the last time—"

"—novels don't write themselves—"

I shot air down my lungs and rushed it back up, raised my voice just above theirs. "I want to do the dishes. It helps me think." I gave Father a pleading look to let it go.

Father wiped his mouth. "I'll be in the study."

Mother smoothed her perfectly smooth hair. "I'll be in the living room."

And I cleared the table, glad to be alone with my thoughts. Just what did Sweetie want to show me? What was her secret? Nothing as exciting had ever happened to me before. Torn pinky fingers on laughing girls. Secrets. Burning notes.

I stared into the bubbled suds. Some suds had rainbows while others were clear, and beneath the suds were unseen things, some sharp enough to cut.

FOUR

I woke up with a throat so raw that when I swallowed, I had to make a scrunchy face against the pain, and I hated pain of any kind. I tried not to make any spit, so I wouldn't have to swallow it down, but the more I thought about not swallowing, the more spit I made. When I rose out of bed and went to the kitchen, my legs were wobbly and my head felt like a balloon on a string. I tried to pretend everything was normal, for if I stayed home sick, I couldn't go with Sweetie so she could show me the secret she promised.

Mother had a No School, No Fun Rule: *if a kid's too sick to go to school, it doesn't matter if the kid gets better later, no school, no going outside, no exceptions, too bad, get used to it, period, the end.* Peter was the cause of rules Mother made solid forever, even if I never did the naughty things Peter had.

Father looked up from his cup of coffee. "You don't look so good, love."

I leaned my head on his shoulder. "I have a little sore throat, but I'm okay to go to school." It hurt to talk and I sounded like an old woman who smoked ten packs a day, but I pretended I was fine.

He put his hand on my forehead and shook his head. "Fever. Your white blood cells are like an army, marching towards your infection to destroy it. That's their job, but the side effect is you have increased body temperature. Get back in bed and rest today. We'll have to see whether this is viral or bacterial. Those bacteria are—"

"I *need* to go to school."

"—What? Oh, no, sorry, Princess. Back to bed you go. The teacher will understand." He stood and turned me towards my room, followed behind me, and when I climbed back into bed, he tucked the covers around me. "I'll go make you some hot lemonade. It won't cure you, but your brain will feel my sympathetic mothering, or, I should say, fathering, and respond to it positively, and that's not a bad thing, is it?"

"I guess not." I fell asleep before he was back. When I woke up, sitting on a tray on the bedside table were the lemonade, three baby aspirin (*baby aspirin!*), and a note with squiggled drawings that must be cells or molecules or whatever, and the words, *Drink this up, take your medicine, and soon those white blood cells will calm down their marching and you'll feel better. Love, Pop.*

I'd never seen or heard him call himself Pop before, but I liked it.

Later, when I awoke again, Mother checked on me, holding a tray with chicken soup. She stood over the bed and looked down at me. "Goodness, you really *are* sick, aren't you?" She set down the tray. "I know how bad you feel, but would you mind if I didn't get too close? I have a club function and I simply can't afford to be sick—they made me president of the decoration and food committee and it's for an important cause." She smiled a glowed smile, straightened my covers. "If you really need something, of course I'll be right in the living room."

All I wanted was for her to brush back my hair. Or make me more of the hot lemonade. And even though I was twelve years old—too old—I wouldn't have minded her reading to me. Instead, I said, "Okay. Thanks for the soup." It still hurt like the dickens to talk.

She patted the covers over my feet, squeezed and wiggled my big toe, and left.

I tried to eat, but it hurt too much, so I gave up.

That evening when I again awoke, there was another weird drawing and words about germs and science and whatever from Father, along with more lemonade and aspirin. I drank the lemonade and took the aspirin, even though they burned going down, and fell back to sleep.

Later that night, when my parents and the neighborhood were quiet and sleeping, I lay burning up, sweating on my pillow and sheets, my white cells still mad and marching. I'd take off the covers, and then I'd get too cold and put them back over me. My hair plastered to my head, and my throat was as if it had razors in it. I looked at my clock and it read one a.m.

At one-thirty a.m. there was a tapping at my window: *tap tap tap tap tap . . . tap tap.* I turned my head and there, with her grinning face pressed against the pane, was Sweetie. I laughed at how comical she looked, slipped out of bed, and opened the window. The night breeze flew in and cooled the sweat. I shivered, and croaked out, "You came to see me!"

"Uh huh."

"But it's one-thirty in the morning."

"Teacher said you got a throat full of thorny-haired frogs so I brung you something."

"You could've brought it to me during the day."

"Nope."

"What if your mother wakes up and sees you gone?"

"She's sleeping good."

"But what if she does and she's so worried she calls the police and you get in trouble?"

"She will not and I will not." She leaned on the windowsill. "You sure talk a lot for somebody got a bad throat."

"But mothers all the time worry, especially at night." I coughed, shivered.

"You can't stop talking even when you hurt to do it, can you?" She shook her head, and then handed me a thermos. "Drink it all up, you hear? And stop asking about things none your business."

"What's in here?"

"Magic tea."

I opened the thermos and sniffed. "Eeeww. Nasty smelling."

"My nerves are wore up with you. Drink and get better so I can show you something inneresting."

I tipped the thermos, took a sip. It burned a little going down, but wasn't bad. "It's sweeter than I thought it'd be."

"Licorice root and sourwood honey what make it sweet."

"How can something sour be sweet?"

She rolled her eyes, then reached for a leather pouch she'd hung from a thin leather strap around her waist, opened it, and pulled out another rolled up piece of paper. "This here's a map. Follow it just how I drawed it, else you get lost forever more on the mountain." She grinned.

"A map? Why can't you just show me where to go?"

"If ever-body shows you ever little thing, then how you get learnt?" She placed the map on the windowsill and put her palm flat on it. "Now drink up so's you can get better."

I drank the rest down. When I finished, I held out the thermos, but Sweetie wasn't there. The map was left on the windowsill. I grabbed it, stuck out my head and looked around. Not one trace of her, not even a footprint on the ground. I hid the thermos in the hole in my mattress, went back to bed with my flashlight, studied the map until I was too tired, and then hid the map, too. Before I fell asleep, I wondered why Sweetie said it was none of my business when I asked about her mother.

I woke late the next morning, at ten o'clock, later than I ever had before. I tested with a swallow. My throat was still sore, but not as much. Father came in with a pill bottle and a glass of water. "Sometimes germ armies need stronger attacks. Germs have been around a long time, since before we were here. In fact they—"

"I already feel better."

He placed his palm on my forehead, nodded. "You do feel cooler this morning."

"I can go to school today."

"No, you need to rest more and let the antibiotics do their job in your body. I brought you a book to read all about how it works so you can understand it better." He put one of his science books on the bed. "Since today is Friday, that gives you the weekend to completely recover."

"But, I *want* to go."

"That's admirable, but no argument." He opened the bottle, shook out a pill, and held it out in the palm of his hand. "Here, take this and lie back down."

I took the pill into my mouth, swallowed a bit of water, even though I wanted to tell him that Sweetie's magic tea would do the trick. I knew he'd start a lecture on medicine and magic—how medicine was science and really magic was also science—he loved finding out how the magicians did their tricks, and said there was an answer for everything.

When Father left the room, I spit out the pill, hid it under my pillow, lay my head down, and waited for what would come next. I slept most of the day, and that night Father gave me another pill that I spit out and put under my pillow. Later, I flushed it away as I'd done the first one. When the moon shined on my face, and everyone was again in bed asleep, I searched the night for Sweetie, beyond my yard, out over to where the mountains made shadows on the valley. I wanted to climb out of my window and find the place on the map she'd circled, where she'd drawn a big boulder with the name Whale Back Rock. On the drawing of Whale Back Rock sat two figures. I wanted to see what she saw, see where she lived and who her mother was and why she could run around in the middle of the night without being afraid, what her secret was.

Right then, everything about my life was boring and plain, and everything in the Haywood County mountains was exciting and wonderful. Somewhere out there, Sweetie was waiting for me. I shivered with impatience, with the thought of how everything was about to change.

FIVE

I sat with my back against the sun-warmed Whale Back Rock, glad the no-see-ums weren't around to sting and itch me like crazy. I'd called them gnats until Sweetie set me straight on how since people could see gnats, and could not see no-see-ums, that's why they had their own name. I checked my watch for the fourth time. Any happy feeling I had with myself for finding the place she'd drawn on the map was chased away by worried feelings. Maybe it had been a trick all along. Maybe she and some other kids were hiding and laughing at me, at how silly I was for thinking anyone would want to let me in on their secrets and be my one true friend.

When I stood up and paced around in a circle, trying to decide if I should leave, sure enough, just as I feared, I heard laughing. I craned my head and looked around, even though I really wanted to run home like the fraidy cat I was. There was always a chance things weren't as bad as they seemed.

I heard from above me, "Haw! You sure are funny when you get antsy in the pantsy."

I looked from tree to tree, trying to spot Sweetie. "Where are you?"

"Up in this here walnut tree." She rattled branches. "See me?"

I sniffed, acted like I didn't care. "Yeah, I see you now."

"You been blowing out mad breath, ready to stomp something." Sweetie laughed.

"How long were you up there?"

"Since before you got here." She swung her legs back and forth from where she sat on a limb. "I just set and watched you."

"Well, thanks a lot. Some friend." I turned from her to walk back home.

"Lissa, wait!"

I smiled to myself and kept stomping down the trail. I heard her scrambling down the tree behind me.

"Don't go off all mad."

I waited until I heard her footsteps right behind me before I turned around to face her. "Ha! I just wanted you to have to chase after me for a change."

"Huhn." She wore a sly look. "Well, then. Guess you changed your mind about seeing something inneresting?"

I shrugged.

We stood there, each of us waiting for the other to give in. I knew I'd give in first, and so did she. When I couldn't stand it anymore, I said, "I give."

She didn't even crow about how she'd won, just said, "Come on."

We walked back to Whale Back Rock together, our arms swinging, but not touching.

"I forgot your thermos, Sweetie."

"Wasn't my thermos anyway."

"My father wanted me to take antibiotics, but I spit them out and flushed them. Your tea did the trick, all right."

"Yup."

She climbed onto the whale's back first. I sweated and grunted. Sweetie held out her hand and pulled me up the rest of the way.

When we were settled, I asked, "So, what's the secret?"

"Can't tell 'til you double dog damn swear you will not tell my secrets when I let them loose."

"Okay. I won't tell." I pulled a loose pebble from under my behind.

"Double dog damn swear, Pooter Head."

"Well . . ." I picked at the hem of my shirt, a pale yellow thing with pearl buttons, and at the edges of the hem, Battenberg lace sewn in. It was one of Mother's favorites, worn with the hideous cabin boy pants she'd also picked out in pale blue, with yellow flowers embroidered all over them. ". . . Father said swear words show a person's ignorance."

"Nothing wrong with a swear word if it got to be done."

"I don't know. I guess."

"No secrets get let loose until you swear to keep them safe in your brain."

"I don't know who I'd tell your secrets to, anyway."

"You might slip up and tell accidental. Somebody might loosen your tongue, like a secret agent does. Maybe that cat lady might pry secrets out your brain using cookies as bait."

"Why would I tell the cat lady?" The cross the street neighbor cat lady told me stories about growing up on the farm, milking cows, picking peas, and churning butter. She was nice, but she was a *grown up.*

As if I'd tell her *secrets*. I was insulted. "I wouldn't dare tell her or anybody else your secrets."

"You wear me out. Just get to it."

I held up my right hand. "Okay, I swear."

"No, you got to say it all out."

"I don't get why it makes a difference."

She rolled her eyes. "For ever-thing on earth's sake you are stubborn."

"All right; all right. I double dog damn swear."

"Now you got to swear on a head you love the most. I swear on my mama's head."

"But I just double sweared. Isn't that enough?"

"Why you got to make a fuss out of ever-thing in the wide world?"

I sighed big and loud, just to show her I thought it was stupid, but I'd do it anyway. "I swear on my mother's head." I changed my mind. "Wait; can I swear on my grandmother's head?"

"Uh huh. If that's a head you love."

"I swear on Nonna's head." I missed Grandmother Rosetta so much, I thought I couldn't stand it. She smelled like paint and paint thinner, mixed in with vanilla and honey shampoo. Whenever I visited her, we'd paint her burning barns. She showed me how to make pottery on her pottery wheel. She could cook things most people bought in the store, like her own pasta, and at Christmas, we'd bake anise cookies. After we mixed up the flour, butter, and other ingredients, we'd roll the cookie dough into long snake shapes, then we'd flatten the snakes out, and cut them into slanted pieces. While the cookies baked and we rolled and sliced the next batch, Grandmother Rosetta told me stories about Italy until I thought I'd die if I couldn't go there. She said one day she'd take me, but Mother said I had to lose ten pounds first, since, she said, I was sure to gain ten pounds once I got around my father's relatives.

"*Yoo hoo*. Lissa's talking inside her head again."

With my thighs spread across Whale Back Rock, I picked at the moss with my fingernail. "No, I'm not."

"Are, too. Eyes looking inside instead of outside. I set here and watched."

"I was thinking about my grandmother. I miss her a lot."

"Is she dead?"

"No! She lives in California. She just hasn't visited us in a long time."

"How come?"

"For one, we move a lot. For another, my mother and grandmother sometimes don't agree on things."

"Well, huh."

"But she's coming in October. I can't wait."

"My grandpaw said my grandmaw run off to Mexico, never to be seen again."

"Wow. All the way to Mexico. Nonna's taking me to Italy."

"I would go to Mexico one day and find Grandmaw, but not without Mama."

"Your mother can take you, can't she?"

"You ready for me to show you something inneresting or keep blabbing?"

"I don't see why we can't do both."

Her face pinched in. "No talking, for frog's sake."

"For what's sake?"

"Lissa, I am getting the nerves bad, dammit all."

I laughed with my hand covering my mouth.

"You are a stinker." She grinned.

I said, "How about we pinky swear?"

"Pinky what?"

"Pinky swear. We hook pinkies and that makes the promise stronger."

"Well, I'll be."

I hooked my pinky around hers, the one that wasn't still a bit scabby from the jungle gym. I said, "Now, we make the promise."

"This here day we double dog damned sweared to keep our secrets secret, so it cannot be unsweared."

"Our secrets secret, forever and a day." I shook our pinkies like shaking hands, then let go. "Okay, tell me." I leaned towards her.

"I got to do one last thing."

"What now?"

"You are bothersome as fleas biting. Just hush." She put her hands together as if she was praying, closed her eyes for two seconds, and then opened them. She looked off in the distance. "Mountain Spirit, you can see me even if I cannot see you. You got magic and your own secret ways. I am asking you to take away my pain. Fly it out to the wind and beyond." She looked at me without smiling, put the pinky she'd caught on the jungle gym bar flat on the rock, and asked,

"Ready rock steady?"

"Ready rock steady for what?"

She wiggled the finger. "Get up and stomp on it with all you got."

I stared at her. "What?"

"Stomp on my finger, Loosey Goosey. That's a inneresting thing I got to show you."

"Are you nuts?"

"Come on. Stomp hellfire out of it." She said hellfire like hell far. "It will not hurt me. I have special powers."

I pushed up my glasses, crossed my arms over my chest. "No. I'm not going to."

"Are you a scaredy cat?"

"I'm not s-scared. I just don't want to stomp your f-finger. It's m-m-mean."

"Why you bumping on your words? Means you're scared." She scrambled over the side of Whale Back, picked up a rock the size of my palm, and climbed back up. "Watch, Miss Fussy Britches." She tossed the rock and caught it, tossed and caught it. "What I got to show you is a wonderment."

I *was* scared to see what she'd do. My head spun around and I thought maybe I wanted to go lie down.

She raised the rock.

"Wait!"

She looked full into my eyes. Her cat's eye marble eyes flickered with a strange light, like the sun was in the pupils.

"What're you going to do, Sweetie?"

She whispered with a graveled voice, "Secret magic."

I looked away from her strange eyes and to the rock in her hand.

She raised the rock. "I am magical from the mountain spirit!" Down whooshed the rock. There was a nasty crunch sound and a scream tore out of my throat, hurting it all over again. She laughed, her head thrown back so far her throat showed white. She wiped her eyes, and said, "You should see your face, Lissa! You look like a scalded cat."

I climbed off the big rock and ran down the trail, with Sweetie after me calling out, "Lissa! It don't hurt a bit. Come back here."

But I didn't want to go back. Everything was weird. She was weird. Her eyes that turned fiery, her scars from who knew what kind of hurts, the pinky worm in the jungle gym then her smashing that same pinky with the rock.

At the fork in the creek, Sweetie grabbed my arm and pulled me to a stop. "Lissa! Stop!"

I jerked my arm away. "Leave me alone!" I was panting and sweating, my clothes stuck to me. "I don't understand you!"

She lowered her eyes, then looked back up at me, her eyes back to how they always were. "You are my friend. I will not try to make you scared, okay?" She sighed, then said, "But if you want to be my friend, you got to unnerstand things. You got to is all."

"But I *don't* understand."

She washed her finger in the creek, dried it on her dungarees, and held up her finger to me. "See, I didn't catch it too much. Just a little." She bent it and straightened it. "Not broken."

Her finger was swollen and the scab had scraped off, but it didn't look as bad as I'd thought it would, from the sound of that crunch. Maybe most of that sound was rock against rock instead of rock against finger. Maybe I'd over-reacted like Father said I did when I didn't think things through scientifically.

"Okay now?"

"Yeah. I guess so." Being friends with Sweetie was the most exciting thing that ever happened to me. I was invited to her secret world when no one else was. I said, "Let's go," and we walked together down the trail, following the creek.

She jumped over rocks and twigs and sang, "Cinderella, dressed in yella, went upstairs to kiss a fella, made a mistake, kissed a snake, how many doctors will it take? Onesies (jump) twosies (jump) threesies (jump) . . ."

I wondered what she would do next. Maybe I could study her, like Father did the magicians, find out how she did her tricks. Find out all the secrets to her and the whys and hows. Let her lead me wherever she went, to places I'd never been before.

SIX

The last day of school, T. J. followed me around during recess and on the way to the lunchroom, calling me names and snorting like a pig. I'd heard it all before and knew how to ignore it. I asked Sweetie to ignore it, too, and not make any trouble. She narrowed her eyes.

At the end of class, we lined up at the door while Mrs. Patterson handed out her world's best ever famous in the whole county fudge, wrapped in wax paper and tied up with bright pink ribbons for the girls and dark blue ribbons for the boys. Sweetie and I were at the end of the line and I was itching to get out of there and enjoy the first afternoon of summer vacation. I didn't even have to go home after school. Mother was at her ladies' club meeting and I had the afternoon to do whatever I wanted.

I'd made straight A's, except for one B in math. Father hated how I always made a B in math, said math was logical, whereas, he said, the non-logicals were more subjective and harder to define. One plus one was always and forever without debate two, but Shakespeare's sonnets were up for discussion. Three times two was always and forever six, but the sunset, though explainable through science, was made romantic.

And, "Math is indisputable, Princess. Love is a biological process, but Shakespeare attempted to romanticize it beyond all recognition and *blah blah boom biff bleah blah.*"

Mother would sigh, look away from Father, and later tell me love was an emotion to be felt and kept sacred, not studied like a germ under a microscope.

Sweetie didn't ever show me her report card. She only paid attention when we read certain books she liked, or when we did math. She happened to love math. When I asked her why she missed so much school, she answered, "Mama gets headaches." And that was all she'd say about that.

Mrs. Patterson had stopped me before recess one day, pointed to a chair for me to sit down, and asked, "Does Sweetie ever talk about her mother?"

"No Ma'am."

"Have you been to her house? Is it clean? Do they live alone there? Is there a man?" When she asked the last part about the man, she leaned forward and whispered it.

At first, I thought she cared about Sweetie, but then I wondered if she just wanted to gossip like Mother did with her friends. I said the truth, "I haven't seen her house."

She tapped her fingers on her desk. "How did she get all those scars? Does she talk about it?"

"N-no Ma'am."

"Is someone hurting her, Melissa?"

"No Ma'am."

"Are you sure?"

"Yes Ma'am. She'd t-tell me. We're best friends." But I wondered right then. Wondered if maybe someone *was* hurting Sweetie. Maybe her mother. Everyone said Sweetie's mother was weird. Some said she was a witch and that her own mother had weird powers to turn people into animals. And her grandfather would go up on the ridgetops, raise his hands to the sky and say things nobody could figure out the meaning to; and even after he died, some said they still saw him up there. It made my stomach hurt to think of someone hurting my friend. But I said, "I think Sweetie is just accident-prone."

"Yes. Yes. She does play rough and tumble, doesn't she?" Mrs. Patterson smiled with a load of horse teeth showing, then asked, "Well, you'll let me know if Sweetie takes you to her house, won't you? And then tell me how things are? What you see?"

"I g-g-guess, Ma'am."

"There's speech therapy for that stutter. I can arrange something?"

I looked down at my shoes.

"Well, no matter. You can go out to recess now." She'd stood from her seat and began writing the afternoon assignment on the board.

When it was my turn to take fudge from Mrs. Patterson, she patted my head. Sweetie was behind me, and Mrs. Patterson said to her, "Here, this is my phone number, in case you ever need me."

From behind me, Sweetie said, "Well, I'll be."

On the way out of the school doors for the last time until fall, I stuck my glasses in the case and put the case in my satchel. Sweetie had been brewing me tea she said would help my eyes. I'd been drinking it for five days straight and only had two more to go. Already I was seeing better.

I said, "I can't believe Mrs. Patterson gave you her phone number."

"Huhn. I done threw it away."

"But what if you ever need help from a grownup?"

She gave me one of her looks. "I can take care my own. Like always."

We ran behind the school and towards the woods. Sweetie never took the bus, and the few times I was allowed to walk home, I found out she took the longest way so she'd not have to go into the neighborhoods. She hated walking through neighborhoods and never went into town, at least as far as I knew.

At the small creek in the woods behind the school, we searched for ancient discoveries of the unknown and known universe. The water rushed over the rocks, tumbling in a song I liked to hear over and over, never growing tired of it, or of the way the sun peeked through the tree branches and touched the water with kaleidoscope sparkles. Green moss grew on rocks jutting out from the water and we carefully stepped over them from rock to rock. Sweetie told me names of the trees that grew all around, like tulip poplar, buckeye, locust, and walnut. She knew the names of flowers, and sayings that went with them, like the jack in the pulpit, *Fair is the canopy over him seen; penciled by nature's hand, black, brown and green; green is his surplice, green are his bands; in his queer little pulpit the little priest stands.* I wrote those things in my diary so I could remember them.

There were all kinds of creatures, too. Once, while wading in the creek I'd reached for a pretty white rock and a salamander jumped out at me. I let out a yelp and fell on my behind, my pants soaking, while Sweetie slapped her thighs and laughed. Another time, a snake slithered in front of me as we climbed up to the old log trail and I fell backward, rolling in a heap until I grabbed a thick vine and held on, nothing hurt but my pride. Sweetie laughed that time, too.

On our treasure hunts, we found things I knew Mother wouldn't let me keep, but Sweetie could. There was the turtle shell with the bones still inside. The turtle must have died and decayed away in that very spot. Sweetie wrapped it in her leather pouch so as not to disturb the bones. She was always picking up special rocks, bird feathers, interesting-shaped bark, nests blown out of trees, a deserted hornet's nest. I imagined her room over-filled with her treasures. I wanted to see where she lived, but she hadn't invited me yet. I hadn't invited her

34

to my house, so I couldn't say a thing about that.

We crossed to the other side of the creek. Sweetie plucked a sparkly rock, turned it over in her hands. Her pinky finger was healed, but the nail didn't grow right, and with the swelling gone, the first knuckle looked a bit crooked to me. She held out the rock. "You can keep a little rock in your room, right?"

I smiled, stuck the rock in my satchel, next to the fudge. I couldn't wait to eat my treat. Sweetie was teaching me to be patient about things. Before Sweetie, I would have gobbled down that fudge soon as I left the classroom. But with Sweetie, I'd eat it with my back against a tree, enjoying every little nibble.

Sweetie stopped so suddenly, I bumped into her. She put her finger to her lips. "*Shhh*. Listen."

I stood still, but didn't hear a thing. "What?"

"We best get going." Sweetie pulled my arm. "Come on."

"What is it? Sweetie?"

"Just hurry."

"Sweetie?" I was slipping and tripping, trying to keep up with Sweetie.

"I am not in the mood for no boys."

"Boys?"

Then I heard it. T. J.'s big mouth. When he stepped out from behind a clump of weeds and bushes, he stopped and stared at us. Three other boys from his Posse spilled out, laughing like a pack of hyenas. Beatrice and Deidra pranced out next, swinging their satchels back and forth, and giggling, of course.

"Well, well, if it isn't Ugly Fat Fart Face and her weirdo friend."

"You best get on away, T.J." Sweetie turned her back on him.

I couldn't stop looking at T. J., as if he'd cast a spell on me and I was in a trance, a trance that caused my stomach to slosh around.

T. J. spit, and then looked at me. "What're you looking at, Fat Ass?"

Sweetie swung back around. "Boys, get on somewhere's else and leave us be." She said to Beatrice and Deidre, "Miss Prissies, go on with them."

Behind T. J. and his Posse, Beatrice and Deidra giggled again.

T. J. came to the edge of the creek. It was only a few feet to the other side, where Sweetie and I were. He put the toe of his shoe in the water and splashed. "We're thinking we'd like to have your fudge, Fat Ass. Less'n you gobbled it up already." He made piggy sounds, pretended to stuff food in his face.

My face turned hot.

"I am warning you," Sweetie said.

"You are? Well, gee whiz. Let me think on this development. See if I care." T.J. put his finger on his chin, then shook his head. "Nope, don't care."

Deidra struck a pose, fluffed her curly black hair. "I'd like to have weirdo schmeirdo's fudge and Beatrice could have that other girl's." When Deidra said, "that other girl's" she'd pointed to me and made a disgusted face.

Beatrice said, "I don't care about fudge. I have to watch my figure."

"Oh shut up, Beatrice," Deidra said.

T. J. said, "I'll get that fudge. If I got to beat it outta them."

Sweetie held her hands together as she had the day she smashed her finger on Whale Back. Maybe just like the day she'd smashed her pinky, she was praying to Mountain Spirit to take away her pain. I didn't have a mountain spirit to take away my pain and I didn't want to think about what kinds of pain T. J. could dish out in his beating.

T. J. splashed more water. "You can make this easy or you can make this hard."

"It's not w-w-worth it, Sweetie. Let's give him the f-f-fudge." I reached into my satchel, but Sweetie grabbed my arm. She looked at me with her eyes flickering bright, fire leaping up, blazing. She shook her head *No.*

"Yeah, guh guh guh give it." T. J. turned to his friends and laughed a big fake laugh. He then stepped onto the first rock to cross over to us.

With pleading eyes, I searched out Jeremy to send him a secret message to make T. J. go away. I held a secret love for Jeremy, with his brown eyes and shiny brown hair. He told me hello once, or he was about to when the bell rang and he had to run to class, and he kind of sort of smiled at me one day. In my diary on page fifty-three, I wrote how I would kiss him one day under a willow tree. I'd also drawn a picture of Jeremy's eyes and mouth, put it next to the candy bars and bubble gum I hid from Mother in the secret hole in my mattress. Jeremy was staring at Beatrice, not me.

T. J. had stepped onto the biggest rock jutting out from the water and was pin-wheeling his arms, pretending he couldn't get his balance and was about to fall into the water, making his Posse and the girls laugh and giggle.

Sweetie shook my shoulder. "Pay attention, Lissa."

I turned my eyes to her.

"You let a boy like that get over on you, he won't ever leave you be." She looked at me deep and deeper, dove way down into my eyes, so far down I wondered what she saw there. Something strong and alive from her shot inside me and I grew taller and stronger and my breaths felt even, filling up my lungs and leaving my lungs, in and out, full and fuller, empty and emptier, then full again. It was as if she gave me her own breath; I took it right out of her body and into my own.

T. J. stepped onto the last rock and balanced on one leg. "Look at me, *whoop whoop!*" He jumped onto the grass and stood three feet from us.

Sweetie put down the paper sack she carried her school things in. "You better get on back where you come from. This is your last chance."

T. J. wiggled his hips. "Yew better git o-wen ba-ick where yew come from. This is yer last chaince." He put his hands on either side of his cheeks and widened his eyes. "Ohh, I'm sooo scared."

The Posse hooted at T. J., but hadn't followed him, so far.

I said, "There's more of them than us."

"Just got to take out T. J. here, the others will run off with tails between they legs."

T. J. took three steps, puffed out his cheeks and made more grunts. Then he jumped to me, grabbed my satchel, pulled, and the satchel flipped and fell onto the ground. *Where the Wild Things Are*, Peter's book with his name scribbled in it, the one he'd given me when he outgrew it, the one I carried with me most all the time because I missed my big brother, tumbled down into the water. I ran to pick it up before the pages soaked. My rolls rolled as I bent over; I heard the snickering.

Heat built up from the bottoms of my feet and made its way to the roots of my hair as though my head was going to blow right off my shoulders. My breath rushed in and out, fast and hard. I wiped my book on my shirt, and looked up at T. J. as if I could pierce him with my stare. He was in a red haze, the blood behind my eyes made the whole world take on red. The red rushed in front of my eyes back and forth, in and out, with every beat of my beating heart. Sweetie's breath in me was hot as dragon's breath.

T. J. laughed and pointed at me, then snorted again.

Through the pounding in my ears, I heard Sweetie say, "Lissa, show him your fire inside."

I screamed, "*You idiot!*" Spit flew from my mouth and I wiped at it.

"Oh no! Look at the dog slobbering fat ass!" He looked back at his gang. "Be careful, she might sit on us."

It all happened fast, before I had time to think, even though it seemed as if it was in a dreamy slow motion. The pounding in my ears, Sweetie's scorching breath, my brother's book, my fat, my stutters, all the teasing from all the kids everywhere I'd ever been, T. J.'s torments that never stopped, all of it whirled around in a tornado of blazing red fury and heat—I was one of Nonna's burning barns that people didn't see but was there, big and bright.

I bull-charged T. J., hit him with all my might. He stumbled back and fell into the creek. The boys laughed, even though it was against the Boy Posse Rules: *Boys Stick Together Always.* His eyes were widened in surprise, his clothes, hair, and face soaking with creek water. He sputtered, cursing and thrashing.

"Hot diggity dog!" Sweetie jumped up and down, clapping her hands. I looked over at her, a grin pulling at my lips, puffed up with my bravery and strength. I was about to say, *That'll teach him, won't it, Sweetie?* when she shouted, "Look out, Lissa!"

T. J. blindsided me, hitting me with an open palm and knocking me on the ground. He stood over me. "You fat piece of crap."

All my brave and strong left me then and I was just a fat girl sprawled on the ground.

Sweetie ran up to him, pushing him away from me. "Leave her be."

His face purpled, the veins sticking out in his neck. "I'll beat the fat off your friend, *Sweetie-Pie*, and then I'll beat your crazy ass into the ground."

"I am *not* crazy!" Sweetie swung, hit him on the side of his head with a solid *thwunk.*

T. J. turned and punched Sweetie right in the mouth and there were "Oh's!" that came from the Head Circle Girls or the Posse or maybe me, or all of us. Sweetie didn't even flinch, only crossed her arms over her chest and laughed. When he hit her again, her head bounced back, she lost her footing a bit, straightened, and when she grinned, her lip split open.

"Sweetie!" I was still sprawled, a slug in the grass. The side of my head throbbed from his open slap—what was Sweetie feeling with his punches? I tried to think what to do. Get up and start swinging, that's what I would do. I would then grab Sweetie and run to hide us away inside the old three-rock cave, where they'd never find us. I stood, feeling dizzy and scared. I wanted to be like Sweetie, tough and unafraid.

Sweetie said, "That all you got? You big sugar tit."

T. J. raised his fist to her again, but he didn't look so sure of himself anymore.

"Don't hurt my friend!" I heard the sound of my own trembling voice—a baby sound, a fraidy cat sound. It made me mad with shame.

T. J. cut his eyes to me. "Soon as I'm finished with her, it's your turn, Fat Ass."

From across the creek, one of the Posse said, "It ain't right to beat up on girls. Just 'cause your dad does it to your mom, don't mean you got a call to."

Jeremy called out, "That's right, *Sugar Tit*," and the boys whooshed out all their air laughing.

Sweetie said, "You losing all your power, T. J. Even your posse's laughing at you."

T. J.'s eyes bulged.

Deidra hollered, "*Get her, T. J.!* She isn't a lady, so it doesn't count if you beat her up!" She flipped her hair over her shoulder and glared at the other boys. "If he gets that fudge, I'll let him kiss me."

The Posse went, "Ohhhh. It's loooooove." They made kissing noises.

Through clenched teeth, T. J. said to Sweetie, "I'm kicking your ass, you goddamned *freak*!"

There was a blur, and Sweetie was on him like a wild cat, clawing and scratching and hitting and hissing. T. J. held up his hands to protect his face, then his stomach, his face again. Sweetie spat out cuss words like dirty pearls on a dirty necklace. T. J. backed up, backed up, and again fell into the creek. He looked as if he didn't know where he was or who he was or why he'd just been beaten up by some wild creature of the woods.

Sweetie stood at the edge of the creek, her hands in fists, her chest heaving in and out.

Just as Sweetie said, the boys ran off. Jeremy grabbed Beatrice's hand and pulled her away with him. Deidra stood with her hands over her mouth and her eyes widened. She called, "T. J.? T. J.?" and ran into the creek to him, soaking up her shiny shoes and her neat white socks.

Sweetie walked over to my satchel, picked it up, put my things back inside.

I picked up her sack, keeping an eye on T. J., who pushed away Deidra and stood. Deidra handed him her white hankee and he wiped bloody snot from his nose. It was quiet, and weird, as if the whole world hushed over Sweetie beating the dog spit out of T. J.. He dunked the hankee into the water, washed a scratch on his face. Deidra looked at Sweetie and said, "You're nothing but a heathen. Look what you've done to my boyfriend," and T. J. told Deidra to shut the hell up. She burst out crying and called him a meanie.

It was a moment sweeter than fudge.

Sweetie handed me my satchel; I handed over her sack. She said, "Let's go, Warrior of the Creek."

"I'm coming, Fists of Fire."

We ran off, holding on to our satchel and sack, the fudge still nestled inside for us to eat with our backs against the poplar tree.

Later, as we slowed to a walk, I touched my face and wondered if I'd have a bruise. I almost wished I would. I wanted a sign of my bravery. I turned to look at Sweetie, at her split and swollen lip, a big red angry bump under her left eye. She sashayed along, her arms swinging, licked the blood off her lips, not a care in the world.

I was beginning to think there was something to that Mountain Spirit magic she was always talking about. I wondered if I could get some of it for myself.

SEVEN

I woke and felt all the good days of summer vacation stretch out far and wide as the earth looked when standing on a mountaintop. Sweetie and I were meeting at Turtlehead Rock at eight. I pointed and flexed my toes, raised my arms to the ceiling and let them float there, rose, made my bed, stretched my arms up, bent to touch my knees, flopped my arms to the right and left, and did two jumping jacks.

From the chest of drawers, I grabbed a pair of orange pedal pushers and a paisley top. Mother picked out all my clothes, and I hated them. She took me to Sears and Penney's. The fancy stores she liked didn't have my size, and it wouldn't have been any better anyway.

She'd sigh and say, "Oh Melissa, think of the cute frocks you could wear if you'd lose some of that weight. Your chubbiness keeps you in bondage." The sales girls would overhear her comments and snicker with their hands over their mouths. I'd pretend I was on Saturn, my favorite planet.

With my orange pants glowing on my hips, I looked at myself in the mirror, frowned, imagined Mother behind me frowning more. I wanted to wear cut off shorts, but my thighs pulled up the inner seam and the material bunched up between my legs, while the outer seams stayed down as they were supposed to.

After pulling on my white Keds, I tiptoed to the kitchen and looked in the cupboard. I'd sell my favorite charm bracelet for a bowl of Lucky Charms, or better yet, a strawberry Pop Tart. I toasted a piece of Mother's homemade wheat bread and spread orange marmalade on it. I heard Father already at his typewriter, so I peeked in on him.

"Hello there, Princess, you're up early." Whiskers shaded his face, and his voice was husky.

"Did you even go to bed, Father?"

"Oh, no. I couldn't. The thoughts are coming out too fast. I must capture them before they head off to Manitoba and are lost forever." He scrubbed his face and his palm scratched against the stubble. Looking at me with a half-smile, he said, "Hey, call me Pop when it's just us."

"Okay, Pop."

"I was just writing a scene about a man who locked himself in his basement just to get away from his demanding wife. I'm still working out the details. But, eventually, she becomes ill, and he has to leave his basement to help care for the child." He fumbled through the pages. "Let's see. There was something else here I wanted to remember. Some detail. I had a note. Wait, hold on."

"I got to go. See you later. Bye." I backed out of the room before he found his notes and began telling me the whole plot of his story, and then I'd never meet Sweetie on time, even though she was usually late.

After I brushed my teeth, I did my chores. Mother had taped to the refrigerator my chore list: 1) dust the living room; 2) sweep the porch. Every day my chores were different, and I always did them without fuss. But since Sweetie, I'd been rushing through them with a swipe-flop of cloths or broom and mop, and galloping out the door before Mother could tell me to do something else.

After dusting, while I was sweeping, the cat lady waved to me, shouting across the street, "I've made cookies. Come get some when you're done."

After I put up the broom and grabbed my satchel, I crossed to her house. She went inside, and soon returned holding out a paper bag. "There's chocolate chip and sugar."

I opened the bag and smelled goodness. The cookies were wrapped in paper napkins and looked to be as big as one of her cat's heads. I closed the bag. "Thank you very much."

"Why, it's nothing at all. Run along and have fun." She smiled at me, four cats swirling around her legs meowing and groveling.

At Turtlehead, I sat and ate one of the sugar cookies. At eight thirty, and still no Sweetie, I ate one of the chocolate chips and made up stories in my head about how I would suddenly go into a mysterious coma, and since I couldn't eat, I'd lose weight. When I woke up from my long deep sleep, everyone would say, "Look at Melissa. Where has she been? What has she done? She's changed so much we wouldn't recognize her." For not only had I lost weight while in my coma, but my hair grew long and shiny to my waist, and I didn't need my glasses even at school since some miracle of the coma had left me with perfect vision. I smiled at the image of a beautiful mysterious me.

"You look like a cat what's lapped up a whole bowl of sweet milk to go with them cookies."

I jumped up—more like a start with a slide and a flop and a heave-ho up. "You scared the ever-loving snot out of me, Sweetie!"

Sweetie haw-haw'd.

"You're late." I had my lip poked out just a little bit.

"Nuh uh."

I shoved the Timex in front of her face.

She didn't even look at it. "I got busy."

"If you wore a watch, you'd be on time. I have an extra one in my jewelry box you can have."

"I am not wearing no watch. Gets in my way." She rose up on her toes and swung her arms in a circle. "If I got to get somewhere on time, I'll do it."

"But you're hardly ever on time."

"Huh. Well, you want to come with me or you want to stand round fussing?" She began walking and I followed. Sweetie knew many secrets on the mountain. Like the giant tree that was hollowed out in the middle. Sweetie said we disappeared when we were inside it so that no one could see us even if they were looking right at us. It was far off into the woods, so we didn't go there often, besides Sweetie said she didn't want anyone following us and finding that tree. Once she'd climbed in it and she did disappear; I swore by it and wouldn't have believed it. When I went in, she said she saw me disappear, too. Father would laugh, but I saw what I saw.

There were the three rocks that made a small cave that I could barely squeeze into with Sweetie. Sweetie said it was a magical creature's home, so we could only stay a little while in the case it came back and kicked us out by blowing its breath hot and sour at us. There were nooks and crannies and secret clearings with mossed ground. There were trees that were older than the oldest tree I'd ever seen, and they let us sit on their branches—I always had to sit on the lowest branch as long as it was heavy and thick. There were weird bugs I'd never seen with orange bodies and thousands of legs.

My head tingled. "Where're we going?"

"If I tell you things ahead, it stops being mysterical."

I danced around Sweetie. "Give me a hint."

"You drunk silly juice this morning."

I pirouetted, sort of. "One little hint."

"Silly Brains."

"I'll keep bugging you until you do." I poked at her arm.

"Promise you won't wear them orange britches again and I'll spill a few beans."

I laughed at my pants, suddenly they were funny. "Okay, I promise."

"And do I get any of them cookies before you smash them to kingdom comes."

I handed the bag to her. "They're from the cat lady."

She took out a chocolate chip cookie and bit into it. As she chewed she said, "ummmmmmmm." Cookie crumbs were sprinkled across her mouth and chocolate was in her teeth as she grinned with one corner of her mouth higher than the other. Her lip was all healed and it made the day with T. J. seem as if it didn't happen. "I got a fella I want to show you, and he wants to meet you, too."

My stomach curled. "You have a boyfriend?" If Sweetie had a boyfriend, what did that mean for me? To us? I wanted to feel happy for her, but I felt something else, something darker than happy could ever be.

She curled her lip as if she just ate bug guts. "A *boyfriend*? You sure are full of it. He's a old man, for frog's sake."

My stomach uncurled from itself.

She crammed the rest of the cookie into her mouth, and hurried up the trail. Over her shoulder, with her mouth spewing crumbs, she said, "Let's go. I do not got all the live-long day." She turned a corner and disappeared.

I ran to catch up. "Sweetie? Where'd you go?" I parted rhododendrons. I looked up in trees. "*Sweeeeetie....*"

When I passed a thicket, she jumped out from behind it and said, "Hah! Here I am." After that, she stayed beside me. She grabbed the sugar cookie from the bag, crumpled up the bag and gave it to me to put in my satchel, and ate the sugar cookie in big greedy bites.

"You won't give me any more hints about the old man?"

"Why you got to know ever littlest thing, Miss Prisspot."

"I like to know stuff."

We swung our arms and if we touched, we jerked away, so the other one wouldn't think we were trying to be gross and hold hands.

"You don't know the ending to them books of yours, right?"

"This isn't a book, this is real life. Come on, one more hint and I'll leave you alone."

"Uh huh, I bet." She grabbed a low-hanging limb. "His name's Zemry." She swung on the limb, leaped into the air, and landed in front of me with her arms spread out like, *Ta-Da*! "He's Cherokee blood and white blood mixed."

"Wow. I never met an Indian before." I waited for her to tell me more. When she didn't, I asked, "Well, what else?"

"You said you'd leave it be if I told you some."

"I can't help it. I have to let out my questions or my head'll get too full of them and explode in a million gazillion pieces."

"That's the silliest thing I ever heard." But she smiled.

"I'm serious. If you don't want to be covered in exploded brains and skull bone then let me ask questions."

She shook her head back and forth. "Silly is all it is."

"I'm getting a headache. *Unggh, ugh.*" I squeezed my head. "I think it's going to blow."

She laughed, pushed escaped wild hair strands out of her face, thought a minute, then said, "Okay. Zemry's Cherokee great grandpaw hid in the mountains so's not to go down that Trail of Tears. That's how Zemry ended up here instead of Okle-homa."

"Trails of tears? What's that?"

She looked at me with her eyebrows raised in surprise. "You don't know? That's when they made the Cherokee move away from they's home here. And it's *Trail* not trails. They had to walk a long long long long long way, and the Cherokee were so sad and so many died." She snapped a small twig from a branch and scratched her arm with it. "All those tears on that long long trail."

"That *is* sad."

She did a cartwheel, bounced up, pin-wheeled her arms in away that showed me she was being silly and not really going to fall off the edge and down the decline.

"I wish you'd stop scaring me like that."

She tee hee'd, and walked along like usual.

"What else?"

"Well, since his great grandpaw hid out, Zemry's grandpaw was borned here, and he married a white woman. Zemry tells all kinds of inneresting stories."

I tried to grab a low hanging branch to swing on as she had, but I missed and fell on my behind, once again. My backside sure took a lot of beating. Seemed it'd be smaller for all the falling on it I did. Getting up and wiping off my pants, I tried to pretend nothing happened. "Like what kind of stories?"

When she quit laughing at me, she said. "Like how they was named another name, something like anaa-yun-weeja. No, let's see; was it anee-yan-weeya? I don't recall just how Zemry said it. But, ever-body called them Cherokee, so they kept it."

"Like how I'm called Fat Four Eyes and it stuck? But my real name is Melissa?"

She stopped me on the trail and stood facing me. "Nobody got a mirror tells the truth like a friend, and this here friend says you *are not* that way." She began walking again.

I smiled, swinging my arms by my side with a sudden happy joy to be with Sweetie. "What else?"

"I am tired of talking."

"It makes the time go faster."

She shrugged. "Time's nothing but what it is."

"What if I go in a coma before we get there and never get to hear more about Zemry?"

"Good gawd-a-mighty, you are not getting in no coma." She scratched her leg.

"You never know."

"I do so know."

"Nuh uh."

She picked up a rock from the trail, examined it, then dropped it. "Sometimes I want to be a Indian. But I don't reckon I am."

"My father's family is Italian."

"Maybe my daddy's people is Indian, so I'm sorter like Zemry."

"Hey, you never talk about your father. How come?"

She shrugged.

"Where is he? What's he look like?"

She shrugged again.

"You don't know your own father?"

"I know some." She kicked at a mushroom.

"Like what?"

"Like, Grandpaw said Daddy had a wandering soul and sailed round the world to find treasures for me and Mama."

A sticker grabbed my orange pants and when I pulled, the sticker ripped a hole.

Sweetie looked at the hole and grinned. "You could rip them up the rest of the way and I'd be fine with that."

"I told you I wouldn't wear them again." I sniffed. "So what else about your father?"

"Well, like I said, my daddy liked to wander."

"My father likes to wander, too, but it's not wonderful sounding like yours."

"I reckon." She undid her ponytail tied with a piece of leather, gathered up hair that had come out of it into the thick tail, and tied the leather back on. "But your daddy's with you."

"I wish my father sailed the world for treasures. It's so mysterious and wonderful."

"Sounds that way, don't it?" She reached up and pulled leaves from a tree, crushed them in her hand, held them to her nose.

"So, where is he now?"

"After his boat was full of wondrous things, he tried to get back to the mountains so we could all live together, but a big storm come and tossed him all over the sea so's he got lost."

"Like a shipwreck?"

"Uh huh. Grandpaw said he was on a island all alone, living off coconuts and monkey brains."

"Eeeww. That's nasty."

"Not nasty if you got to fill your belly."

"Oh. Yeah. So, what next?"

"Daddy got sick and didn't know where he was. A island native took him in."

"Sick from monkey brains, I bet."

She huffed out her air, then, "*Like I was telling*, they kept him until he got well. After that, he remembered about us."

"But, how did your grandfather know the stories? I mean, if your father was lost at sea and couldn't get home and couldn't remember anything, how?"

"Well, Smarty-Prissy-Pants, Daddy sent a letter to Mama soon as he got well." She walked with her arms stiff.

"Did she show the letter to you? It might have a return address to know where he was."

She shrugged.

"Well, what then?"

She didn't answer.

"Sweetie? What then?"

"He had to go to the war to save America."

"He went to war?"

"He got in the jungle and his friend was about to get kilt. When he went to help his friend, he got kilt himself." Sweetie stopped walking; put her hand over her heart. "He loved my mama and me so much, when he died he had a locket with our pictures in his fist." She

---

held up her fist. "They buried him right there in the jungle with the locket still held in his hand. A fella brung Mama his army jacket, and that's all we got of him." She smiled, and walked again, her arms loose as she swung them.

"Wow. It's so romantic how he held the locket at the end."

"Nothing romantic about getting blowed the hell up." She jumped over a log in the middle of the trail.

I stepped over the log so I wouldn't bust my backside for the millionth time. "Tell me more about Zemry and the Indians."

"Do we got to talk the whole way? I never talked this much in my whole life." She stooped and picked up a rock. "This here rock's shaped like a owl. I'll give it to Zemry." She stuffed it into her pocket, jumped high into the air, grabbed a handful of leaves from a bush, and just as she had before, crushed them in her right hand. She held out the crushed leaves to me. "Smell that."

I put my nose to the crushed leaves, said, "It smells like summer after the sun's dried the rain."

"You got a way of saying things." She tossed the leaves. "You orter be telling *me* stories."

We turned a curve in the trail and came upon a tiny shack with an old mule grazing in front. She said, "That there's Miss Annie."

"Miss Annie the mule?"

"Uh huh."

"A mule right in front of us."

"She don't like to be called a mule. Just call her Miss Annie."

"Oh. Okay." I looked at the shack. It was made of old wood and had a tin roof. "Does Zemry mind us coming?"

Sweetie stopped to pet Miss Annie. "Nuh uh, he don't mind."

Miss Annie stood in front of me. "Hey. The mule won't let me by."

"You got to pet her or she won't get out your way. And you got to quit calling her a mule."

I gave Sweetie a *you're kidding* look.

"For spit's sake, just give her a pat."

When I touched her soft and satiny muzzle, she didn't bite. "I've never petted a mule before, I mean, a Miss Annie."

Sweetie pranced up to the door and knocked once. "You in there, old man?"

A voice boomed from the other side. "That you, Sweetie?"

"Yup." She turned to me and winked.

The door swung open and I out-right stared, even though it was rude. A real mountain man mixed with Cherokee. Right in front of me.

Sweetie said, "Miss-Lissa here thought you was my *boyfriend*."

They both burst out laughing, slapping their thighs.

My face heated up, but mostly I was excited. I stepped up to meet my first real Mountain-Cherokee man. Being friends with Sweetie formed my whole world into other shapes. Those shapes were more interesting than the ones Father showed me under his microscopes any old day.

EIGHT

Zemry had wispy gray hair, but his beard was darker, grown all the way to his stomach. He had the beard braided from the middle to almost the end, and the braid was thread with rawhide. Shaggy eyebrows shaded his deep brown eyes. His dungarees were faded from many washings, as was his gray shirt. He stuck a corn-cob pipe in his mouth.

Sweetie said, "What're you doing with that there pipe?"

Zemry winked big and slow at Sweetie.

Sweetie turned to me. "He likes to tease tourists, right Zemry?"

He grinned big and wide, his teeth still clenched on the pipe stem.

She put her hands on her hips. "Miss Lissa is a *friend*, old man, so get that silly pipe out your mouth."

Zemry took out the pipe, gave a chuckle while he stuck it in his pocket. "Them tourists like thinking we all're hillbillies smoking corn cobs and laying around drinking moonshine. I give them what they think they want."

"Huh," Sweetie said, "Like I said, this is my friend."

Zemry nodded, his face turned serious, but his eyes still twinkling.

Sweetie handed him the owl-shaped rock. "I found this for you since you like owls."

"Wah-doh." He stood aside from the opened door. "Oh-see-yoh."

Sweetie walked inside.

Zemry turned to me. "*Osiyo* means hello there and come on in. And when Sweetie gave me the owl I said thank you." He bowed and motioned for me to come in.

Inside the shack there was only one room that I could tell, but it was scrubbed clean enough that even Mother would be impressed. What caught my attention first was lined on a wall to the left side of the fireplace. Masks, some made of wood, but others I wasn't sure what they were made of. Zemry led me over to them.

"These was made by my great grandpapa, my grandpapa, and me." He pointed to a mask with slitted eyes and feathers in the forehead and at the eyebrows. "That one's made with a gourd, and very very old." He reached to take down a wood one with a long nose and carved lines in the face. It had a piece of fur on the top of its head. "I made this one out of buckeye. A beaut, huh? I colored it with blood root, just like my grandpapa showed me." He looked at me. "Like it?"

I nodded.

He asked Sweetie. "Can she speak? Is she deef or dumbed?"

Sweetie laughed, a big bark sound, then said, "For sure she can talk up a storm and she hears you just fine."

I cleared my throat but I felt shy.

He put the mask back on the wall, and pointed to another one. "That one there's made from a hornet's nest."

Sweetie pointed to one with a bulging nose, bald head, tiny little teeth, and comical face. "Tell her about that one."

He said, "That's a booger mask."

I backed away, finally finding my voice, "Eeeww. It's made of b-b-boogers?"

Zemry let out a guffaw.

Sweetie put her hand to her mouth and snickered.

"Child, that's what it's called, not what it's made up of. The Cherokee made booger masks to poke fun at the Your-peans or some other enemy." Zemry put on the mask and did a funny dance while Sweetie and I laughed. He took off the mask, grinning as if he had a sudden shy feeling upon him, too, and pulled on his beard. "Them real nice ones over there are called effigy masks. Here's a effigy mask I made." He took down another of the wood masks that looked like a bear, put it on, and struck a fierce pose. Through the mask he said, "Now I got the spirit of the bear."

I pointed to one. "And that one?"

Zemry said, "Wolf clan. *Ah-ni-wa-ya.*"

I knew right then why Sweetie loved to come to Zemry's place. Other than Sweetie, he was the most interesting person I'd ever met. I looked around the rest of the room. There was a bed with a furry blanket across it, and another colorful cotton blanket folded at the end. Propped against his pillow was a porcelain-faced doll, out of place in all the rough man-stuff. In the fireplace, a big iron pot had something bubbling inside. It smelled good and my stomach growled.

Zemry pointed to my stomach. "I hear a rumbly go rumble in the belly there."

I shook my head, embarrassed.

He smiled, and I felt stupid for shaking my head.

Sweetie nudged me with her elbow and mouthed, *Breathe in and out.*

"I was just ready to have some that stew, and I'd be lucky if y'uns would have some with me. I got it full of ramps, rabbit, taters, and carrots, and some corn cakes there to sop it with."

"I sure am hungry," Sweetie said.

"I guess I am hungry, after all," I said.

Zemry filled three wooden bowls almost to the top. "I carved these bowls m'self." He placed what looked like a grainy pancake on top and handed us our bowls. We went outside, sat on a couple of logs set around a big tub of steamy water with glowing ashes underneath.

Sweetie pointed to the tub. "That there's the tub we used to have to put the hogs in to get their hair off. I helped Zemry with hog killing before."

I wrinkled my nose. "That's horrid. I never could kill an animal."

"A hungry belly makes a person do things they'd rather not but got to." She bent to her bowl again. Then, "And what you think you eat at your house? Them animals kill theyselves to get on your plate?"

I was ashamed of knowing I had choices. Mother went to the store and bought groceries and I could eat them or I could turn up my nose and decide I'd have something else. Not everybody could do that. I ate my stew and thought on that.

The stew was hot and good, and so were the pancakes, which weren't sweet, had bits of corn inside, and were thicker than Mother's pancakes. To drink we had jars of honey-sweetened tea. For a while, the only sounds were birds singing and squirrels chattering and Zemry slurping from his spoon.

When we finished, we rinsed our dishes in a bucket of water, and put the bowls aside to be washed later. Zemry took the dirty water and put out the glowing ashes under the tub of water. He said, "Got some warsh to soak, and I surely do hate that job."

"You need a woman to do that, Zemry," Sweetie said. "But not this girl. I'll do a man's job any old time. Woman's jobs are boring."

"I do a woman's and a man's work. Me and my woman used to share the load. God rest her."

I liked Zemry even more.

From a pail, the old man lifted out apples and handed Sweetie and me one each. While we munched, Zemry and Sweetie talked about animals they'd seen, and what kind of herbs or roots they needed for different sicknesses or arthritis or whatever, how Zemry's tobacco growing was coming along, and when the berries would be the sweetest. I listened to them, feeling sleepy, and thought it the best place on earth, and how if I were to take a nap on Zemry's bed, it'd be the softest bed ever there was in the whole world.

Miss Annie nodded her head up and down whenever Zemry spoke. He handed her an apple and she loudly crunched it. He said, "The day after my wife passed on, this old mule showed up and never left." He whispered when he said, *this old mule.* "I think it's my wife come back, so I named her the same name." He looked over at Miss Annie. "My wife was *special.*" He patted her side. "My wife could find water when nobody else could. She always got the weather right. Saw visions, too. Dreamed what would happen to people. Dreamed of her own death so she made me take her to town and buy her a pretty dress to be buried in."

I said, "I had a cat once came around the day after my great uncle died. I was little and thought it was Uncle Stewart come back to life."

Zemry leaned towards me. "Was it a black cat with yallar eyes?"

"How'd you know?"

"They're most always black with yallar eyes when it's a loved one come back. When my Annie passed, I kept awaiting for the black cat to come, and it never did. So, when *she* showed up," he threw his thumb towards Miss Annie, "I figured my wife put her spirit into a critter that could do me some good 'stead of a critter don't do nobody good." He slapped his knee and laughed.

"I named my cat Stewart."

"I see now," Zemry said.

"Yeah, he slept under my window, but he'd never come into the house. My great uncle didn't like my mother, either." I took a bite of apple to shut up, but both Zemry and Sweetie looked interested, so I swallowed my chewed apple and went on. "Before he died, Uncle Stewart told me she was wound up tighter than an old broken watch. He said her underwear was on too tight, too."

Sweetie and Zemry laughed.

Up until then, I hadn't known I was such a grand storyteller. "One day, Stewart ran over and slashed up Mother's brand new stockings. She wanted me to catch him and get rid of him, but I never did. Then, Stewart was suddenly gone and never came back, just like my great uncle Stewart. I sure miss him."

"Well, I bet he misses his girl bad, too." Zemry yawned, scratched his stomach. "Sometimes they do that, them cats do. Run off to go see the world. Now a dawg won't leave. He'll pine on his master's grave until someone pries him off. I miss my old dawg." His face fell into folds of wrinkles. "Good old dawg."

"What was your dog's name, Zemry?" I asked.

"Dawg." He laughed, and I didn't know if he was teasing or not, but he didn't say anything else.

"I had me a cat once." Sweetie ran, jumped up and swung on a tree limb, and then flung herself onto a stump. From the stump, she jumped back to the limb, and then flopped onto the ground.

"Best be careful there, Bitty One."

Sweetie did three cartwheels, then she said, "I named my cat Mr. Shitters 'cause he shit all the time. And it was smellier than a skunk fart."

We all laughed and I thought how I'd never heard so much laughing, and how I'd never seen Sweetie laugh so much. I decided Zemry had Indian magic in him.

Zemry had a little knife he used to cut his apple. He carved out a slice, poked it into his mouth, and around the apple said, "Did I tell you girls about the stickball my great grandpapa played?"

I put my elbows on my knees and leaned forward. Sweetie stopped cartwheeling and sat cross-legged on the ground.

"Well, it weren't for the faint of heart." He wiped the knife on his pant leg and stuck the point into the log. "Afore the games started, the medicine man would scratch up my great grandpapa's back with a turkey bone. Then grandpapa went to the river and warshed the blood off with the rest of the ones who'd be playing the stickball with him. Then, after they warshed the blood off in the river, they'd rub bear grease all over them."

"Bear grease?" I wrinkled my nose.

"That's right. They had ways they had to follow and they stayed strict about it. They couldn't eat no rabbit meat like we just did, or no frogs, and they couldn't kiss their wives even." He handed his apple core to Miss Annie. He took from his dungarees' pocket a pouch and a packet of small, thin pieces of paper. He pulled out a piece of paper, and from the pouch, poured a bit of tobacco near the edge of the paper, rolled it tight, and then slid the homemade cigarette once in and out of his mouth. He fished a match out of his pocket, struck it with his thumb, and after it flared and steadied, he lit the cigarette, drew in, and blew out a stream of smoke. He then said, "Ah, now. I done good on this 'baccy." He put everything back into his pocket and happily smoked.

I was about to bust with wanting to know more. "How come they did all that, Zemry?"

"Them was their *ways*, Poot Butt." Sweetie pushed my leg. "Let him tell the story how he likes."

Zemry let out another stream of smoke, plucked tobacco from his lip, and went on. "The night afore they played the game, they had a secret dance. They went in a circle with their sticks and the women sang and clapped hands. And Great Grandpapa got to be the woodpecker one time." He looked at me, as if expecting me to ask.

"What's the woodpecker do?"

He winked. "He calls out sounds like the woodpecker, and then he turns to look out towards where the other team is. Then they'd say how's they were going to stomp the fire out of them!" He looked at us with a fierce-eyed look, then continued on, "My grandpapa loved to tell the stories about that. He showed me how to do the stickball, but I weren't allowed to get scratched by no bone, or get bear grease rubbed on me. My mama said no, a thousand times no." He shook his head. "But I got knocked upside the head with the stick plenty times."

"I could do that," Sweetie said. "I could beat the hell fire out of the other team, I could." She stood up, grabbed a stick and waved it around, making growling sounds, danced around, jumped up and swung around.

"That water's still mighty hot. Be mindful of it." When Sweetie didn't listen, but kept on acting up, Zemry warned, "Girl . . . "

It was just like on television shows where a person's no sooner warned about something than it happened.

Sweetie said, "Hiya-*Pow*," jumped backward and stumbled over and into the tub of water, calling out, "Whoa!" as she struggled to right herself.

Zemry and I let out a cry at the same time as we jumped up. He ran over to Sweetie, helped her out of the tub, while I stood with my hands over my mouth and my eyes popping out.

But Sweetie was laughing. I couldn't believe it. She was laughing and laughing. She let herself flop on the grass, a red-skinned blonde fish.

Zemry looked her over. "Are you scalded? Jiminy Christ! I best get the ointment." He picked her up, gently sat her on the log, and ran inside.

Sweetie called to Miss Annie and petted her nose as if nothing had happened.

"Sweetie, you okay?" I touched her arm. "Does it hurt real bad?"

"Nuh uh." Sweetie shrugged her shoulders. "Don't know what the fuss is about, just some water."

"That was *hot* water, Sweetie."

"Leave it be, Lissa. I am not hurt." She stood up and twirled like a wild ballerina.

I wanted to smack her one.

Zemry came back with two more wooden bowls and a white cloth. "I got something here to clean you and something to put on your skin."

"Is it bear grease?" I asked.

Zemry said, "Got some boiled slippery elm bark in this bowl and—"

"I said I am not hurt, Old Man."

"Maybe it don't hurt, but your skin's red. Respect the ways give you. Now take this bowl."

She shrugged, took the first bowl and set it by me.

"This one here's got onion paste, wild ginger, grease, and some lavender."

"That stinks," Sweetie said.

"You can't smell that good lavender?" Zemry handed me the other bowl and the cloth. "Fix her up while I catches my breath. She'll give me heart death one day." Zemry sat and put his head in his hands. He mumbled, "Jiminy Christ."

I dipped the cloth into the thin stuff first and cleaned the dirt from her skin, then patted on the stinky lotion while Sweetie sang, "I asked my mama for fifty cents to see the elephant jump the fence; he jumped so high, he reached the sky, and didn't come back 'til the 4th of July . . . "

I said, "This stuff is pee-eww."

"Skunk grease, Lissa. From out a skunk's butt."

"Eeeww." I put down the bowl and wiped my hands on the grass.

"It is not. Stop teasing your little friend." Zemry pulled on his beard. "Tell your mama I'm surely sorry about this."

"I am not telling Mama." Sweetie stood up.

He stood and faced her. "I'll tell her m'self next time I see her."

"Nuh uh. You will not." She stared down Zemry until I saw him give up.

"Aw now, shoot." He patted her head. "I promised your grandpapa I'd watch over his girls."

"Mama and me take care of each other, now don't we? And you, too, right?"

"That we do. Take care of each other." Zemry rocked back on his heels. "Now, afore y'uns go, I got something to give." He went inside.

"What's he got, Sweetie?"

"You ever get tired of asking questions?"

Before I could answer her, Zemry was back with a cotton sack. He thrust it out to Sweetie.

Sweetie took it from him. "Wah-doh."

He reached into his pocket. "You put it by your bed and it'll sing to you in the morning, thanking you for saving its life that day." He opened his palm and there was a little carved wooden bird. Each feather shone and its beak was slightly opened; it looked as real as any that flew in the sky.

Sweetie petted it with her finger, then took it and cupped it in her palm. "It's the most beautiful thing ever, Zemry." She looked over at me. "I told Zemry about the day you and me started up being friends. This here bird's about that day."

Zemry turned to me. "Now, I didn't leave out the other pretty girl." He pulled from his pocket a carving of a dark wolf, its legs in a full run, eyes searching. "You got spirit. I can see it in you."

I felt like crying. He called me pretty, said I had spirit, and made me a present before he even met me. "Wah-doh, Zemry."

He patted my head, too. "That's okay. That's okay now."

Sweetie told Zemry, "I'll bake you a pie and some cornbread. And I'll cook up some beans."

"Now, no need. I like the comp'ny."

"But we come without," Sweetie said.

"You gave me that owl rock."

Sweetie smiled, and we turned away to head back down the trail away from Zemry.

When I glanced back at him, he stood there still, waving at us with Miss Annie at his side nodding her head.

We were quiet for a time; we didn't want to break up the magic of the day. When I was tired of the quiet, I asked Sweetie what was in the bag.

"I don't ever look until I get home. But I bet he put some flour and sugar, and maybe some eggs from his chickens he got in the back. He used to put some his tobacco in there for Grandpaw."

"I didn't see any chickens."

"They's there somewhere."

"I really like Zemry."

"He's good people. He and Grandpaw were bestest friends, like you and me."

I felt warm and happy all the way to my toes. I pictured his home again, how it smelled, the masks on the wall, the comfortable bed, the doll. "Why'd he have a doll on his bed?"

"It was his little girl's what died when she was a bitty thing."

"Oh, that's sad," I said. "I guess that's why he wants to help you and your mother, since he lost his family."

"I told you we help each other. I take no charity."

"Yeah, I know. It's Even Steven."

"Huh?"

"When you trade something off that makes it even. Like, if I did a favor for you and you didn't do it back, it would be lopsided. But, if you did a favor back, it'd be Even Steven."

"Huhn. Even Steven." She swung the bag along without a care in the world.

"Sweetie?"

"What you gonna ask this time, Nosy Rosy."

"I just wonder what makes you so tough?"

"I'm not so tough."

"You laughed when you got scalded."

She stopped, looked down at her legs. "Well, my skin's still on me." She walked on, singing, "Jack of Diamonds, Jack of Diamonds; I've known you from old; you've robbed my poor pockets; of my silver and my gold . . . "

"Yeah, but still—"

"My horses ain't hungry; they won't eat your hay; I'll drive on little further; I'll feed 'em on the way . . . " She swung the bag around a few times, then stopped. "Dang it, I forgot all about there might be eggs in there. Hope they's not busted. Sometimes I don't think about busting them eggs up, I just think about how fun it is to swing the bag around." She said, "You know what I mean? Them eggs in there don't know they's been busted up either, so ever-thing seems like usual?"

"Hey Sweetie, look! A two-headed hummingbird." While she titled up her head to where I pointed, I ran off laughing.

I didn't get far before she was past me, off into the woods, laughing at me as she disappeared out of my view. She was always disappearing out of my view and I was always running to catch up with her. Some nights I dreamed I ran and ran, calling her name. I would hear her voice, but she stayed hidden away from me until I was able to get past some thing, like a rock or tree or ridge or heavy mists, that stood between us. So far, in those dreams, I'd not been able to get past those things to find her.

NINE

In spring, everywhere sprung with flowers. I looked up their names in books from Father's library: lady slippers, trillium, daffodil, violets, Dutchman's breeches, wild cherry, crabapple, Bradford pear. Then summer brought rhododendron and fire pinks and lilies and turkeybeard and daisies. There were so many plants, trees, and flowers, I'd never learn them all.

Sweetie tried to teach me about how things taken from the earth could heal sicknesses, but it was hard to remember which roots, stems, and leaves were poisonous and which were good. Sometimes a part of the plant would be helpful, while the other part would be poisonous. I liked to look at them and smell them, I told her, not eat them or drink them unless they came from a store. She reminded me about the teas she made me that I drank. But I kept trying to explain how medicines came from lots of the plants, how Father said they were perfected in laboratories by scientists who knew how to make them all safe for us where we didn't have to worry about which were poisonous and which were good—the scientists figured that out and the pharmacists filled the prescriptions for sick people. She'd just snorted.

For our explorations and discoveries, Sweetie said we'd meet at a different place on the mountain every morning to make sure we weren't followed by T. J. and his Posse. So far, we'd not seen any of them again, but she said we shouldn't take chances, since T. J. was sneaky. Our main station was Whale Back Rock. At the end of the day before we went back to our houses, we met there to decide where to go the next day, each taking a turn to decide. We had a special stick sharpened at one end to write down our meeting place in the dirt so no one could hear us say it if they were spying on us.

If we had to, and only if we had to, we'd leave a note hidden in the thick bushes, under a rock. Sweetie called it moccasin mail, something she'd read about in a book where the trappers left notes in the toe of an old moccasin and then put the moccasin where it would be found and read by another trapper.

I was on my way out to meet Sweetie where Jabbering Creek forked off, when Mother held out her hand to stop me.

"All this running in the mountains is good exercise, but I worry about you becoming too wild."

"Aw, Mother. Come *on*."

"Don't talk to me that way. You're only proving my point."

I let my sigh stay inside. "It's summer vacation. I'm not any different from other kids." I loved saying that. A lot.

"I suppose you're right."

I started to turn away; she stopped me again. "Nevertheless, it's time you bring this Sweet-tea here for me to meet properly." She tapped her foot and folded her arms across her chest. When Mother had that look, she meant business.

"Yes Ma'am, okay." That should stall her a bit by agreeing, then waiting until she forgot it. Sometimes that worked. It was in the How to Get Away with Stuff Rules: *Pretend to agree to something, but secretly hope not to have to do it once the parent's old person bad memory kicked in.* Peter had relied on that one a lot.

"Ask your friend to brunch tomorrow."

"Brunch? T-tomorrow?" I tried to imagine Sweetie sitting at the table with the good china, shiny silver, and gleaming white napkins and tablecloths. "That's so soon, Mother."

"And why not? Seems like the perfect time to bring your friend. Show her some sophistication."

"What d-d-does that mean?"

"Dear, your friend lives in some old shack on a mountain with no father, and who knows about her mother. It sounds so . . . so . . . *rustic*." She wrinkled her nose, then continued, "However, we are well-traveled. Your father and I have eaten with senators and governors. I know how to set a beautiful table. You see?"

"But she knows all k-k-kinds of things. She's been teaching *me*. About herbs and roots for medicine and stuff, and when it's going to rain (*them cows lay down*). She reads books and is g-g-good at math (*breathe Miss Lissa!*)." I took in a deep breath, let it out, and added, "But she doesn't show off about the things she knows."

"Don't get sassy with me, Missy."

"I'm not, Mother. I'm just saying she's smart, even if she d-doesn't like school." I almost slapped my hands over my mouth. I shouldn't have said anything about Sweetie and school.

"Whether a child likes school or not is no matter to the child. It is up to the parents to make their children do things they'd rather not. Where is her mother in all this?"

Breathe in, out. "She's better at math than I am. She can do numbers in her head like nothing I've ever seen. Her mother *makes* her go to school (*oops*)."

"Makes her? She doesn't see the need to go to school?"

I was tired and ready to give in so I could leave. "I'll invite Sweetie to brunch tomorrow so you can see how g-good she is."

"I'll tell your father we're expecting company." She started to turn away, then said, "Oh, and invite her mother, too, of course."

Fat chance, I thought. I'd never even met her mother, but I wasn't going to admit that.

When I at last escaped and hurried to Sweetie, I dug around in my brain for ways to talk Sweetie into coming to my house. She hated town. Hated it worse than raw bloody cow's liver with a side of bloody chicken livers. Sweetie could find any spot on her mountain with her eyes shut tight, but ask her about town, and she only shrugged and said, "Why I got to know how to get around town? Got nothing there I need, except for the church and the school, and those are for Mama."

I'd reminded her how she came to my house with the sore throat tea.

"Good thing I did, right? But, if I don't got to go to town, then why do it?"

She had her way of thinking and her way of doing and I had to respect them, even if they drove me crazy. But having her over for brunch was different. If I didn't do it, Mother could mess up my whole summer with her wondering what I was hiding about Sweetie.

She was already there waiting at the creek. She looked at her wrist as if checking the time, even though there was no watch there. "Huh. Miss-Lissa is late late late!" She laughed with her head thrown back, then said, "I been waiting *forever* to say that."

"Oh you're very clever."

"That I am." She made her face look cleverer than the most clever girl of all.

I took off my Keds and socks, put them by Sweetie's boots, sat by Sweetie, and put my feet beside hers in the water. We watched a red-tailed hawk circle and disappear behind a mountain ridge. I liked how the mountains looked like layers and layers, and how they could seem purple or blue sometimes, and how the mists curled around and about them and over the valley making them a secret dream. I never wanted to leave. But we always left. Always. I hoped the moving would stop. I hoped as hard as I could until my brain hurt with hoping.

Sweetie said, "That there hawk coulda been my Grandpaw. He said when he passed on, he'd turn into different critters so he could watch over me forever."

"Would he be that squirrel up there?" I pointed to a chattering red squirrel. Then I pointed to a centipede. "Or that ugly bug?"

She shoved me. "Hush up, Priss-mouth."

I then told her a story about how Nonna's cat Mittens ate a whole cherry pie and vomited it all over her living room and I had to help clean it up.

"I never heard of no cat eating cherry pie."

"Cross my heart and hope to die stick a needle in my eye, it's true."

"Well, I'll be. Shoulda give it ginger root, if you had any setting about."

"I haven't eaten cherry pie since that day. Every time I see cherry pie, I think of cat vomit."

"You got to get over that. Any kind a pie's too good to never eat again."

"I can't help it. It looked nasty and smelled nasty, too."

"Well, no wonder since it sloshed around in a cat's gut." She stood up, slipped on her boots. "Want me to show you something inneresting?"

"Yeah!" I hurried to put on my socks and shoes.

"They's usually down in a little holler about now."

"Who?"

"Not a who, a what. And I am not telling, so come on and hush up for once."

Sweetie wove through thick brambles, while I kept my eyes on the ground watching out for snakes. Sweetie said they were more afraid of us than we were of them, but I bet I was more scared of the snakes any day.

As if she read my mind, she said, "Don't be turning over any rocks or logs. Them's where the copperheads and spiders might be."

I'd forgotten about spiders. The webs liked to wrap around my face as we walked and I'd start yelling and slapping while Sweetie doubled over laughing. She once said something about how spider's webs were good for cuts, but that didn't sound right to me.

"Them snakes will not hurt you lessen you go to fooling with them."

I carefully picked my way over stumps, logs, and rocks. When I caught up with Sweetie, she was on her hands and knees, and had her finger over her mouth in a *shhhh*. I crept up beside her on my hands and knees. She pointed down into a little hollow.

I whispered, "I don't see anything."

She pointed down again, and mouthed, *Look*.

Into the hollow walked two deer. They looked our way and became still. I'd never seen deer that close. The only time I'd ever seen one was at the zoo, a dead one on the side of the road, and once in Louisiana I saw one tied to the top of a car with blood on it and its tongue hanging out—that made me so upset, Father had to stop for ice cream.

The deer were beautiful. Their soft and delicate noses were raised in the air as they sniffed. After a while of standing still, they lowered their heads and began eating. We stayed there for six minutes. I checked my watch, so I knew. I finally had to move my legs around, and when I did, the deer jerked up their heads and ran away on their long pretty legs. Even their fright was perfect and beautiful.

"I'm sorry I scared them away."

"Well, we couldn't set here forever, right?"

She jumped up and ran off into the woods. "Bet you can't catch me."

And I couldn't.

***

That afternoon at Whale Back, I wrote in the dirt, *My house, eat with Parents*.

Sweetie stared at the words.

I underlined them. And when she still didn't answer, I underlined it twice more, digging deep into the mountain dirt.

"You don't got to holler at me."

I erased the words. "It's important, Sweetie. *Please*. You know I don't ask for stuff that isn't important." I tried not to sound too beggy. "Mother wants to meet you and she won't let it go."

She leaned against the rock and blew through a blade of grass to make it screech.

When I tried it, she took it from me and said, "Nope, this here's how you do it." She made the screech louder than ever, as if showing off to me since I couldn't do it right.

"She invited your mother, too."

Sweetie shook her head. "Mama's sick."

"What's she sick from?"

She didn't answer me, screeched the grass blade again.

"Well, if she's sick, I guess she has a good reason not to come."

Sweetie screeched it again.

"Come at ten-thirty tomorrow morning. Please don't be late. Mother is funny about that kind of stuff."

"Uh huh." Sweetie stood. "I best get on home now." She turned to go down the path towards her house.

"Wait!" I jumped up and ran to her. "You *could* come by now instead, if you want to."

"Can't. Got to go somewheres."

"Where?"

"Get Mama's medicine."

"A mushroom or root or something?"

"Curiosity kilt the cat."

"I could help you find it."

She eyed me as she did when she was trying to figure out whether to tell me something. "Mama said she got to have them pills she takes and the preacher is where I get them from. Stupid pills."

"Pills?"

"She thinks she got to have them." Sweetie blew out her breath.

"And you get them from a preacher? That's weird."

"It just is what it is."

"Well, Doctor Timothy could give them. Father said he's a good doctor."

"I got to get them where Mama said to."

"Sounds complicated. I don't get it."

"You got to pick apart ever littlest thing, don't you?"

"But when Mother needs medicine, she calls Dr. Timothy, then she goes to the drugstore and buys it."

"Why can't you let things be?"

"I get curious."

She stamped her foot. "The preacher said them pills get paid by somebody secret and they give it to the church for Mama, since she believes in the church and not in no doctor." She lifted her chin.

"Oh! I wonder who it is. A secret admirer?"

She stared up at the top of the trees.

"Nobody would think bad of you. If your mother's sick."

"I tried to cook up cornbread and pie for them what paid for them pills, but one time I saw that preacher stick it all in the trash." She frowned, then said, "I don't cook for that church no more. I just

65

get them stupid pills and be on my way."

"What kind of pills are they?"

"Let it be, Miss Mouth. I got to go." She turned, ran off into the woods.

"Sweetie! Wait! Are you coming tomorrow?"

She was already gone. I sure hoped she was going to show up. And on time. And cleaned up. And on her best manners. I walked back home, wondering about the mystery of her mother. What kind of pills she took and who paid for them and why at the church and not at the drugstore and . . . nothing made sense to me, but then, nothing about my friend ever did.

TEN

That evening, during my parents' cocktail time, I told them Sweetie would be coming over for brunch. I prattled away. "She has a friend Zemry and he made us stew. And he's part Cherokee, and has all these masks that mean different things. He carved me a wolf, and Sweetie a bird." I swallowed Coca-Cola fast to feel the burn on my tongue, but that didn't stop the babbling. "We saw deer today, and Sweetie visits the preacher for her mother's medicine, but he threw away her food . . ." I pressed my lips together so I'd quit telling Mother about Sweetie's business, especially when her eyebrow raised at the last part. Sometimes it was hard not to talk when things backed up and bubbled over.

"Isn't that nice." Father didn't look up as he shook his head back and forth over the newspaper story he read. "This war. It worries me."

"Jack, I don't want to hear anything about that nasty war stuff. Talk to your students about it, not here while I'm having a cocktail." Mother took a sip of whisky sour, swallowed and said, "War war war. You'd think that was the most important thing in the world."

"It is important, Pauline. Our boys are dying and—"

"Oh rot! The war isn't happening here. What's happening here is I'm having a drink on a glorious Saturday evening. I simply don't want to hear about bad things right now."

"What do you think, Melissa?" Father folded his paper and faced me.

"What?" I wasn't used to my father asking me important questions during cocktail time, or really any other time.

"What do you think about the war?"

Mother stood up. "I'll refresh my drink." When she huffed off, I noticed that her stocking had a big run in the back.

"Well, Sweetie's father got killed in a war and that makes her sad. I bet there're lots of sad people because of it."

"Yes. But don't you think sometimes it's necessary to have wars?"

"I don't know. I can't figure it out. Every time I think about war, all I can see is Sweetie's father blown up so he can't be with her."

"I suppose that's as good an answer as any." He went back to reading his newspaper.

When Mother came back into the room, I thought to tell her about the run in her stocking, but I decided not to. I let it be my secret that she wasn't perfect for once. She sat in her easy chair, crossed her right leg over her left, and asked, "Will Sweet-tea's mother be joining us, Melissa?" She eyed me over her glass.

"No Ma'am. She's not feeling well."

"The ladies at my club said she's too ashamed to come to town."

"We don't need to hear gossip from your ladies' club."

"No, we'll just talk about war war war." Mother smoothed her skirt. "My friends say her father isn't dead at all. That he lives in town married to someone else and takes care of Sweetie's mother through the church. What you said confirms that."

"That's n-not true. He died in the war holding onto a l-locket with their picture."

"Now, don't start it up," Father said. "All you two are doing is proving how societies clash and how war begins. Two people can't agree, push their opinions on the other, they argue, they push, they shove, next you know, rocks are thrown, guns are drawn. You are just proving how war happens." He sipped his drink and raised his perfectly manicured pinky.

Mother stared at Father, then said, "Dinner is almost ready. I've prepared roast pork with a cherry cream sauce. I'm calling our dinner *Pig in a Berry Patch*. That's the name of a poem I wrote today." She watched Father, to see if he'd ask her to recite it. When he didn't, she lowered her eyes. "Anyway, it inspired me to cook pork in a berry sauce and all I had were these cherries." She ate the cherry out of her drink, then said, "Not that you'd notice. Not that anyone notices at all. Not that I'm appreciated."

"I think we've heard enough, Pauline."

"Except for war war war."

Father rose from his chair. "I think I'll have another scotch."

Mother waited for him to walk into the kitchen before she turned to me. "If it was up to me, children wouldn't be allowed in the cocktail hour. Sometimes parents need to discuss things children shouldn't hear."

"Yes Ma'am."

"Now, run-along."

I went to my room to make sure it was all set for Sweetie's visit. I hid my stuffed animals in the closet; she might think them babyish. In my chest of drawers, underneath my underwear, was my diary. I had to keep hiding it in different places ever since Mother found the hole in my mattress and had gone through my things. She'd thrown away the candy and gum, questioned me about the picture of Jeremy's eyes and lips, and asked me was there anything in my diary that she should know about (I couldn't believe she hadn't picked the lock to read it), until I thought I'd die of embarrassment. I planned to lend the diary to Sweetie so she could write things in it, too.

Later at dinner, my parents drank their wine in the fancy glasses, and ate their dinner saying boring things like, "Pass the salt," and "This cream sauce is quite good; cooking is both an exact and inexact science . . . ," and "Keep your elbows off the table, Melissa," and "Scientific blah blah and biological bleah bleah and ladies' club blah blah bloing bloink and my poetry blah bleah and yes dear oh dear dear ding dong doodle blah bleah blah."

I wanted to be sitting on a log eating stew with Zemry and Sweetie. There was a hunk of pork on my plate, and the cherry sauce looked like blood. I ate the potatoes and asparagus around it, and tried not to think about the cute little pink piglets I saw at a fair once.

After dinner, while I was washing the dishes, Mother wrote the brunch menu into a poem and stuck it to the refrigerator with a magnet shaped like a bouquet of flowers. When she left the room, I read:

Ode to the Brunch! Crepes filled fatly with golden cheese—oh here's to you cow!—and delicately fragile eggs—oh thank you chicken!—scones with blueberries nestled like baby boys in the womb, and finally, exactly, perfectly, beautifully cut to a paper-thin parchment, the lowly potato—oh bless you farmer! To drink! The mimosa—orange and fizzy with champagne, guggle guggling down the throat with glee (except for the girls who shall imbibe orange juice and ginger ale to mimic our delightful mimosas.) Oh! What joy to sip and eat what has been made with perfection by earth's bounty and a woman's touch.

She came into the kitchen while I was reading it, and her mouth straightened out, as if she knew I was laughing inside, which I was. She said, "Go brush your teeth and get ready for bed. I'll finish up the kitchen."

***

The next morning, I woke at five. I read Charlie Brown and the Peanuts gang comic books for thirty minutes. I slipped out of bed, stretched my arms to the ceiling, bent over and touched almost to my ankles, swung my arms back and forth back and forth, did six jumping jacks. Tiptoeing down the hall to the bathroom, I eased shut the door, scrubbed my face with Ivory soap, and then went back to my room.

It was still early, so I spread out an old sheet, took out my paints, and began painting, trying to get the flames on the burning barn just right—Grandmother Rosetta could do it the best. When my parents stirred around at nine, I put away the paints, went to the bathroom to wash up, and once back in my room I dressed in a plaid skirt and white shirt, for Mother made us dress nice for Sunday Brunch.

When I poked my head out of my room, I listened to see where my parents were. Mother was in the kitchen; Father was in his study, probably to work on his latest story about a veterinarian whose marriage was a mess, called, *Love Became Too Heavy, So He Put It Down.*

I eased out the front door and sat on the front steps to wait for Sweetie. When my Timex read ten thirty-one, I began sweating.

At ten thirty-two, I heard, "You hot in that there get-up?"

"Sweetie! You came and you're on time." Two minutes late wasn't late at all. I almost hugged her.

She stood in her battered boots and a blue dress with tiny white polka dots that was similar to the yellow dress with the roses she wore to school. The dress was clean and unwrinkled and looked as if it hadn't ever been worn. Her hair wasn't brushed very well but it was tamed, pulled back with a piece of wire wrapped with a red cloth, like a headband. Her face was scrubbed clean, shiny and cheeks pinked. She smelled like warm sugar.

Stiff-armed, she held out a bunch of wild flowers in one hand and a bag in the other. "Mama said never come with empty hands to someone else's table. The flowers are for your mama, and the bag's got some cornbread I made myself."

I took the bag from her. "Wah-doh." I didn't take the flowers. "You can give Mother the flowers yourself."

Her eyes widened. "Oh. Huh. Okay."

I held the door open for her. "Come on in . . . um, o-see-ya?"

She smiled at that. She then looked down at her feet, then back to me with an unsure face. "My boots got mud on the bottoms. I don't want to take mud in your nice house."

"We can both take off our shoes."

She looked hopeful and it made me feel bad.

I put down the bag, took off my shoes and socks, and left them by the door.

She'd taken off her boots, without socks, and put them by my shoes. Her toes were like little niblets of pink corn.

Grabbing the cornbread bag with one hand (and it was still warm), I held the screen open for her with the other.

She put her skinny shoulders back and walked in.

It was strange seeing her in my house. She was like an animal trapped inside where it didn't belong and any minute would thrash around to get back to the woods. Like the bird I saw in a house they were building on the next street over. After the workers closed it up and left, the little thing kept peering out of the window. I watched it for twenty-two minutes, wishing I knew how to set it free. It flew up to the sill, looked out at me with little begging eyes, and then flew off, over and over. I was too sad to watch it anymore. When I went by the next day, the door was open. The bird found its way out and sang sweetly in the sky as it flew to freedom. I hadn't *seen* it happen, but I knew it *could* have happened, and that's how I decided it was.

I led Sweetie into the study first. "Father, this is Sweetie. My best friend." It felt good saying best friend.

He put on the mask I knew was the one where he noticed Sweetie's scars and hurts and was curious about them but it wasn't the time to ask. I thought maybe he would want to later ask me, and if he could ever think of a way to ask Sweetie he would, but he'd be careful about it, like he always was about things he was curious about. He stood, straightened to his full length, and held out his hand. "Nice to meet you, Sweetie. I've heard so much about you."

Sweetie took his hand with the one that wasn't clutching the flowers and pumped it up and down. "I never heard too much about you, but you seem nice enough from what Lissa did say."

My father laughed, sat back down, put his fingers on the typewriter keys, and said, "Go on and see your mother. She's in a good mood." He began typing again.

When we stepped into the kitchen, Mother's back was to us. She turned a crepe with a flip of her wrist.

I sucked in air, blew it out slow and easy, then said, "Mother, this is Sweetie. My best friend. She made this cornbread for you. It's still nice and warm." I set the bag on the table.

When Mother turned around, her eyes widened. She caught herself and smiled. It reminded me of the plastic smile one of my dolls wore. She said, "Why, now, there you are. How nice to meet you at last."

"Here in my flesh." Sweetie stiffly held out the flowers to her.

Mother took the flowers, and nodded to the cornbread. "Thank you for the gifts. You needn't have." She set the flowers in the sink. "I'll put them in a vase for our table this morning." She said vase like vaahhzz. Turning back around, she put her hands together in a silent clap. "Well. Let's see here now . . ." then, " . . . what's your *real* name, dear?"

"Sweetie's my name."

"No, I mean the name your parents gave you, not your nickname." Mother spoke through her Barbie Doll smile.

"Just Sweetie." She threw back her shoulders even more.

Mother patted her hair, let down to her shoulders (I thought she looked pretty with it down like that instead of pulled up tight). "What about the one your father gave to you when you were born."

"Nope, just Sweetie."

"Well, then, everyone has a birth last name," Mother said. "Ours is Russo, the next door neighbor's is Tanner."

"Mother, when's your d-d-delectable food g-going to be ready?"

She tore her attention from Sweetie. "Brunch will be ready in fifteen minutes. Go wash up."

I swallowed, breathed in and out. "Yes, Ma'am."

I was almost out of the kitchen when she said, "And where are your shoes, young lady? Is this some kind of statement?"

"They're on the back steps."

"Since when do we sit at the table without shoes?"

Sweetie rolled up on her toes. "My boots was muddy from walking here. Lissa said I could leave them off so's not to track dirt in your nice house. She done the same to be polite, like you been teaching her to be."

Mother's cheeks turned pink. "Well, I suppose it won't hurt this once."

"That's what my mama always says." Sweetie showed her teeth, like a dog baring its fangs in first warning.

"I hope to meet your mother one day soon."

"Mama's got bad headaches most days here lately."

"Oh, well, perhaps another time?"

Sweetie turned to me. "Show me that room you're always carrying on over." And she led the way out of the kitchen.

I shouldn't have made her come. Sweetie's face was wound so tight, I was afraid she'd run away before brunch was served. We went into my room and she stood like a rooted tree in the middle, moving nothing but her eyeballs from one side to the next.

I said, with more hope than I wanted her to think I felt, "Do you like it?"

She relaxed her shoulders, smiled, nodded her head, and walked around my room, touching things as gently as a butterfly lighting on them. She stood in front of the two pictures I'd painted while at Grandmother Rosetta's, and touched each of them with only the pad of her finger. She next studied the one I had been working on that morning. She asked in an almost whisper, "You done these?"

"Yeah, my grandmother showed me how. They're oils, painted with real boar brushes," I said. "They're not so good. Mother says I should take piano or violin or something."

She turned to me with wide eyes full of what looked like wonder. "Well, I say you done them *real* good. *My* mama would say you got a calling that don't touch many folks." She turned back to the painting, and with the fingers of her right hand, without touching, she pretended to pet the dark horse running away from a burning barn.

"I like to copy my grandmother. She paints scenes like that, those burning barns." I wanted more than anything for Sweetie to be proud of me. "She's real good at it and I want to be as good as her."

"I never seen nothing like that, Lissa. They's the most beautiful things I ever ever seen."

I turned before she could see tears building. I blinked fast and looked up to the ceiling. When the tears sucked back in, I went to my chest of drawers, took out the diary, and turned to her. "When we leave after brunch, I want you to take this home with you."

"What do I do with it?"

"You write stuff in it, like secrets, or stories, or whatever you like."

She took it, placed her open palm across the cover.

"I want it to be both of ours. You can write in it and I'll write in it."

"What about?"

"About our adventures, that's what I've been writing about. Open it and see."

She opened it to a page. "Says right here how we found the turtle bones in the shell that day."

"Yeah. It helps you to remember things a long time from now."

"I remember ever-thing all the time. I never ever forget a thing. Mama said she's never seen anything like it. I remember being borned."

I decided to let that one go, about remembering being born. "It isn't just to remember, it also helps to sort yourself out, I guess. You know, get things out of your brain to make room for other things."

"Huh. Well I'll be."

"If you don't want to, you don't have to."

She opened it to another page, and read, "'Today, Sweetie gave me a hawk feather and I will keep it forever and ever.'" She looked up at me, grinned.

"Let's put it outside so we can get it later." I took it from her, put it in a paper lunch bag, folded a tight square around the diary, then tossed it on the ground under the window. "There, now, let's don't forget it."

"I told you, I don't forget *nothing*. Grandpaw said I got a calling for that," she paused, then, "and other things."

Mother called us to eat before I could ask what other things, and we left my room. Mother had already changed into her long, silky morning dress and piled her hair on top of her head. Father was at his place waiting. Just as I knew it would be, the table was set with the good china and the silverware shone so I could see my nervous face in it. The food looked good and normal for a change.

Mother said, "Have a seat, you two." She sat close to Father.

Sweetie and I sat next to each other across from Mother.

I put two crepes on my plate, a big pile of potatoes, and extra butter on my scone. The butter was whipped together with cream, so I had to dip it out with a spoon.

I was about to dig in when Mother asked, "Don't you think that's too much food, Melissa? Look at how your thin friend there eats, like a bird."

The food on my plate grew bigger and bigger. My thighs and stomach exploded right there on the spot. My hips and behind spilled over my chair and puddled on the floor.

Father said, "Leave her alone. It's genetics. She'll get over it, like I did. Look at me now—fit as a fiddle, handsome and strong and virile."

Mother sighed as she put a few bites of food on her plate. "It's different for a woman, a girl. I was a chubby child and I'm always fighting my weight. I just don't want her to have to go through what I did."

I'd never heard her say something like that about herself, but it didn't help; it made it worse. I thought I'd go ahead and let myself slip under the table and stay there in a big fat lump while my parents said things to embarrass me.

Then Sweetie began piling more food on her plate, as if she meant to do it all along. She put two more heaping spoonfuls of potatoes on top of the small pile already there, along with another crepe, and an extra scone that she floated in the liquidy butter. She asked my mother, "Got any kat-chup?"

Mother sniffed, stood up, and took the bottle from the refrigerator. "Here is your condiment. I would have put it here earlier, but we usually do not eat Ket-sup with our brunch."

Sweetie smiled, said, "Well, that *is* inneresting." When she finished pouring ketchup over her potatoes, she leaned over and snuffled the food like a dog, stuck out her tongue, licked, then made a growling noise and bit into the ketchup-covered potatoes.

I watched her with my mouth slung open. I heard Father clear his throat in that way he does when he wants to laugh but isn't sure about things or what was really going on. Mother breathed as she does when she's flabbergasted. I couldn't look at her or else I knew I'd laugh and then there'd really be trouble.

Sweetie lifted her head, ketchup and potato hanging from her chin. "This here food's so good, I'd feed it to my dog even. That's why I pretended I was Freckles. Just got away from myself." She then leaned back in her seat and said to Mother, "Thought I'd just be silly for a spell to ease things up." She wiped her face with her napkin as dainty as a Queen, put the napkin in her lap, then began to eat with such perfect manners that even Mother would be proud to show her off at her ladies' club.

I chanced a look at Mother across the table. She had her fork halfway between her mouth and her plate, staring at Sweetie. When she saw me looking at her, she gave me a *look*, and then brought the fork to her mouth.

Father shoveled food into his mouth as if it was the last he'd get. He swallowed a mouthful, said, "Did you know the white squiggle in the egg is called chalazae. It supports the yolk, in the center of the albumen . . . "

"I've told you. I don't want to hear those kinds of things about my food while I'm trying to eat it," Mother said.

He kept on talking about chickens and eggs that didn't have words like *fry or butter or scramble or yum this is good thank you for preparing it* and instead words that had roosters and fertilizing and experimental injections and other disgusting things about chickens and roosters and eggs, on he went, *blah blah diddly doo scientific boodily blah and—*

"I never heard such talk at the table ever in my whole life." Sweetie looked at Father, innocent surprise all over her face.

Not only had Father stopped talking in the middle of his sentence but his face turned red as the Ket-Sup. He cleared his throat, said, "Pardon me; I was carried away, too." Then he went back to eating.

Mother actually had a tiny smile lift the corner of her mouth before she caught herself and stopped the smile from coming.

I grabbed the ketchup and poured it over my potatoes. With Sweetie there, it was as if no one could do or say anything to make me feel awful. I ate every bite of my food and had seconds when Sweetie herself asked, "Please can I have some more of them fine tasty taters?" And Mother said "Of course," and gave us both more potatoes without even asking if I wanted any, or worse, telling me I shouldn't have any more.

After we finished eating, Sweetie and I escaped outside. I didn't even say, "May I be excused?" or offer to clean up. It was heaven.

We ran to get the diary, and took off for the mountain, laughing all the way.

I asked Sweetie, "Hey, what happened to Freckles?"

"I made that dog up out the air. Never been no Freckles."

"I'm writing all about today in the diary." I skipped along, feeling free and happy.

Sweetie cut between two houses, and pointed to the woods. "Let's go that way."

"But it's longer."

Sweetie acted as if she didn't hear and ran towards the woods.

When we were on an old log trail, I said, "I'm sorry my mother asked all those questions about your name and all."

She shrugged. "Ever year at school I get questions from the teacher and the principal."

"Can't I ask questions since I'm your best friend?"

"Huh. You asking if you can for a change?"

"Well, yeah."

"And up to me if I give you a answer?"

"Yeah, I guess so."

A bluejay shrieked at us, and Sweetie mimicked it.

"And if I had anything to tell, I'd tell you." As if I had anything good to tell.

"Okay. Even Steven, right?"

"Yeah."

We walked along, then she said, "You can ask me some questions now if you want."

I acted casual. "Let's see." Pretended to think it over. "Okay. I got one. How come your mother never leaves the house?"

"Maybe she's too tired since she gets sick a lot.

"How come she doesn't like people coming over?"

"One time way back, a fella come to the house and Mama got so upset, she set the shotgun in his face. Then she cried for a week, saying how that man disgraced her. I do recall he was a handsome man, with pretty eyes, but I was sorter little."

"You have pretty eyes."

"That so?" She kicked at the dirt.

"Did you ever find out who he was?"

"Don't reckon I ever did." She reached down, picked up a rock and threw it hard as she could into the woods.

"Your mother wasn't always sick, was she? I mean, she used to go to town and be around people?"

"I guess so."

"I wish I could meet her."

"You will." She ran into the woods, and as always, I ran to catch up with her.

***

That night, Mother started in about Sweetie. How she wasn't so sure about *that girl*, and how *that girl* seemed a little strange, and how *that girl* this and *that girl* that.

Father surprised us both. "You wanted her to get out and play instead of staying cooped up in her room or watching television. Well, that's what she's doing. Aren't you ever satisfied?" He rattled his scientific periodical. "Besides, I found the girl intriguing. At least *something* interesting happened around here while she visited." Father crossed his legs. "Leave them alone, why don't you?"

Mother stared at him. She stomped off to her bedroom and slammed the door.

Father looked at me. "So, tell me about this Sweetie. Where does she live? What's all those scars about?" He leaned towards me.

"I have a stomachache and need to excuse myself to the bathroom."

"Now?"

77

"Yes, sir."
"Then go on about it. We'll talk later."
I didn't want to talk to Father about Sweetie.

***

A week later, Sweetie wrote in the dirt, *mama wants to see you.*
I nodded, hiding the excitement bubbling up.
I ran back to the house that night filled with special feelings that out of everybody in Haywood County and anywhere else and beyond, I was the only one invited to see Sweetie's mother.

ELEVEN

I woke early while the light was still pink over the mountains and the early birds just beginning to twitter. I wiggled my toes, pointed and flexed them, then shot out of bed. I made my bed, stretched up to the ceiling on my tip tippy toes, bent forward to touch my ankles, straightened and turned right and left with my arms straight out, and then did ten jumping jacks. I hurried through my chores and sneaked out of the house quiet as a cat burglar, except I wasn't stealing anything, I was escaping it.

I was at Triplet Tree by six forty-five. I reached my hand into my satchel and touched the presents wrapped in the newspaper comic section. I'd had those presents made since right after Sweetie had said, "You will," to my meeting her mother. I'd just been waiting for her to say when. I worked for hours on two leather and bead bracelets for them.

The idea came when Mother had to go to the grocery in another town. She was preparing *Cluck in the Grass*, which meant chicken on top of lettuce. She wanted to have with it the dressing she'd had at a restaurant when we lived in Arizona. She couldn't remember what the seasonings were, she kept trying to perfect it, and that meant looking for special ingredients in different stores. Father said she just liked to get in the car and go places because she was a bored housewife. Mother sighed when he said that.

She first dropped me off at the five and dime. I couldn't wait to be where she couldn't see me so I could buy a treat to enjoy in peace. While I read the menu at the lunch counter, three old men were sitting on stools talking about a time when some students sat in a five and dime, and how they'd changed history just by sitting at a counter and being brave and strong. One of the men smiled and wiped his eyes with a napkin, and the other two smiled back at him and said something about an anniversary and they all smiled again, then took big happy bites of their sandwiches.

I didn't want a sandwich or fries, or even a malted. Those things would take too long to make and eat. As I walked through the five and dime, I passed two teenaged girls giggling as they picked up lipsticks and tried them out, smacking their lips and making kisses in the air. I passed a very old woman trying to reach a tube of toothpaste and I reached it, handed it to her, and she said, "Thank you kindly, sweetheart," and tried to give me a quarter. I said, "No, thank you," and she said, "Oh! Bless your parent's heart for teaching you good manners," and tootled on her way.

I passed a row of Fli-Back paddleballs, jacks, yo-yos, pick up sticks, and Old Maid cards, and wondered if I had enough money from my allowance to buy Sweetie and me a game. We couldn't play Monopoly with just two of us. Peter and I had tried that, and it was nothing but boring for two people to play by themselves. Chinese checkers or regular checkers would be fun, but I had those already in my closet along with the Monopoly game.

I headed to the candy aisle to buy my treat, and there they were, right where all the sewing stuff was: a bin full of pretty glass beads. I forgot all about the people in the five and dime, the candy bar, the toys and games, and began sorting through the bin.

When Mother came in to get me, I was still picking through gajillions of beads. She said, "I've a few things to get. I'll meet you up front."

I searched until I had all the perfect ones I'd need, and then found two strips of leather to thread the beads on. When I went to the front to pay, Mother was tapping her foot, but she didn't make a fuss about it and I was surprised. She even admired the beads I bought. She was always doing things to confuse me.

That night, after I ate dinner and did the dishes, I ran to my room, poured out the beads and admired them again, held them up to the light and watched how they sparked. The leather was a bit stiff, so I pulled and stretched and rolled it until it was soft. Then I sorted the beads into two piles, so each bracelet would be different. Next, I threaded the beads onto the strips of leather, knotted behind the first and last so the beads would stay on, and left enough at the ends to tie the bracelets to their wrists.

When done, I admired my work, and at the same time, was nervous with hope that they would like my gifts. I wouldn't go to their table empty handed, if she had a table, and if we were going to eat. Sweetie never said.

When Sweetie showed up I checked my watch even though I just had three minutes before. "Late again. It's twenty-two after seven."

She dropped an old cracked leather bag on the ground, and

flopped beside it. "If I start getting on time, people might start expecting other stuff out of me, too." She smirked her lips. "Seems you been late before, too, Miss Lissa."

"I was late *once*. And only because Mother wouldn't let me leave."

She shrugged, put her hand on her bag, hummed.

I tried to act as if I didn't care about anything she had to say or do. I picked up a rock and threw it into the woods, and then looked up at a squirrel jumping from one tree to the next. I whistled. I knew she hated whistling more than she hated history lessons with a side of boiled goat liver. When she opened the leather bag and took out a man's white cotton handkerchief and then some twigs bound up with a piece of yarn, I couldn't stand it anymore. "What's that for? What're you going to do?"

She sang, "A sailor went to sea, sea, sea; to see what he could see, see, see; but all that he could see, see, see; was the bottom of the deep blue sea, sea, sea . . . "

"Sweetie!"

She looked inside her leather bag.

"Stop fooling around."

She pretend yawned.

I leaned forward and tried to look into the bag, but she closed it up tight.

I poked her skinny arm. "Come *on*."

She grinned at me, opened the bag.

I scooted forward.

Sweetie pulled out of the bag: a box of matches, a tin box with a latch to keep it closed, our diary, a tiny pinecone, some green stuff that looked like parsley, a vial filled with yellowish liquid, and a shiny curved knife.

I stared at the knife. "I bet that's pretty sharp, isn't it?"

She untied the twigs and placed one on top of the other, crisscrossed, leaving a few to the side. On top of the criss-crossed twigs, she put the green parsley stuff, and on top of that went the tiny pinecone. She poured most of the yellow liquid onto the twig mound.

"What's that do?"

Sweetie lit the pile, and the flames jumped up high, then settled down to a small, crackling fire that smelled bittersweet. She laid the handkerchief on the grass, smoothed it out until it didn't have any wrinkles, and then put the knife on top of it.

"What's that knife for?"

Situating herself cross-legged, she picked up the tin box and held it with her right hand on top and her left on the bottom.

"What're you doing?"

She finally spoke. "We will bury our secrets deep in the earth under guard of Triplet Tree."

"What're you talking about? How can we bury secrets?"

"You able to stop waggle-womping that tongue for a second?"

"You don't have to be rude." I put my lips together and pressed them.

She then sang, low and sweet, about rivers, cold creeks, and old mountains, about Whale Back, Turtlehead, Bear Claw, Tablet Rock, Jabbering Creek. She sang of the bear we saw running up on the high ridge one early morning, and about other animals that lived in the woods, and of the hiding wolf we were sure we both heard howl as we played—and Sweetie'd howled back.

It was as if I'd laid my head right down on the soft grass and fell into a dream.

When she stopped singing, she added a couple more twigs and a little more liquid, and up jumped the flames again, reflected right into her eyes. She picked up the knife and waved it over the flames. "The mountain spirit is happy we will be bound-sisters." She pointed the knife towards me. "Tell your secret first." She put the knife back on the handkerchief and waited with her hands on her knees.

"What kind of secrets?"

"Whatever secret you got to let loose. What's been itching at your insides." She opened the box, "Tell it so it goes in the box."

"Tell the box?"

"Just do it for frog's sake."

I leaned forward towards the tin box. "Well. Um. Let's see." I felt foolish, just a little.

"Tell what you wouldn't tell another soul."

Then I knew. "Sometimes I hate my mother. Sometimes I wish she wasn't my mother. Sometimes I wish she'd go away and I'd never ever see her again."

She closed the tin box, rubbed the top, said, "Keep the secret forever and ever." She then re-opened the box.

"Won't the secrets escape when you open it?"

"Hush." She spoke into the box, "One night I snuck to T. J.'s house and peeped in his winder. He was sleeping like a ugly baby. I had a stinky dead coon in a sack. I put it nice and easy through his winder and on his floor. The next day at school, T. J. come to class with a swolled up eye. I felt sorry I did it. His daddy must a tore into him for it."

"He deserved it."

She closed the tin box. "Nobody deserves to be treated like a dirty worm under a dirty foot by they's own kin. T. J.'s mean but his daddy's a long-sight meaner. Guess his daddy teaches him how to be." She rubbed the tin box, told it to keep the secret forever and ever. "Your turn again." She opened the box.

"I have a hole in my mattress where I hid things from Mother, like . . . like candy and stuff. She found it and took the candy bars and told me I'd never get married as long as I was chubby and acted stubborn." I lowered my head. "But I had candy hidden in my sock drawer and in the pocket of my winter coat. I locked myself in my room and ate all five candy bars." I looked up at Sweetie to see if she had a disgusted face. She didn't. "I don't want to get married anyway. But still . . . that's why I'm fat."

"Huh. If I was you, I'da eat all them candy bars, too. Just for spite." She closed the box, rubbed it, and kept it closed. "We got to let the secrets get to know each other and get settled in." She rubbed it faster, said, "Secrets, stay in."

I picked up the diary. "Are we going to write stuff in here today?"

She snatched the diary from me and set it back down.

"Sorry! I just asked."

Her face softened. "I wrote up some stuff in it last yesterday we can read later, okay?"

"You did?"

"About how we went to Zemry's and all. You was right, it made things fun all over again." She said, "I made some maps in it, too."

"Maps?"

"So you won't ever get lost up round here." She leaned into me, her face serious. "The next secret I got to tell is so secret, I cannot tell it unless we are bound." She picked up the knife, held it between her palms, and looked to the sky. "Grandpaw, me and Lissa are telling our secrets. You told me not to tell a soul mine. But I just got to, it's itching at me something fierce."

A cool breeze whooshed by and goosebumps marched on my arms. Father would shake his head at my foolishness, but I felt as if we weren't alone. Behind Sweetie, the air seemed to bend, move in and out, wavering like heat waves, but it was cool not hot.

Sweetie added the last of the twigs, the rest of the yellow liquid, and when the fire jumped up once more, she stuck the knife into the flames and held her left hand over her heart. "Mountain Spirit, I am calling to you. I got my friend to be a bound-sister. If you could take off her pain, too, I would be truly thankful."

My stomach turned. "What pain?"

She stood, raised the knife high into the air. "Mountain Spirit, take our pain and blow it out in the wind!" With her bare left foot, she stamped onto the flames, grinding down into the dirt.

I rose up on my knees. "Sweetie! Stop it!"

Without changing her wise-face, without looking at me, she brought the hot knife down, and sliced into her left hand. Blood dripped onto her foot where she'd just stomped out the flames.

I jumped up, my eyes bugging as if they would fall on the ground at Sweetie's feet, my hands held to my mouth to hold in any vomit or fat baby crying.

She stared at me, holding tight to the knife. Her eyes turned burning bright.

And even though I didn't want to and tried not to, I did cry. All the times Sweetie did weird things welled up and gushed out as sobs. Her scars and puckers, cuts and bruises, her wild ways, all of it was too much to take anymore. I thought about what she said about T. J.'s father being mean because of his father, and I wondered what had happened to Sweetie to make her the way *she* was.

"Lissa, stop crying." She said it so quiet and so low.

"Why do you do these things? *Why?*"

She blinked slowly. "I been trying to show you."

I swiped at my snotty nose with my arm. "I don't *understand*. Show me what?"

She picked up the handkerchief, and handed it to me. "Wipe your nose."

I blew and wiped. "I can't stand your hurts. Please *stop* it."

"I do not hurt."

I glared at her. "*Stop saying that.*"

She held out the knife with her right hand, her left hand bleeding. "Come here, Lissa."

"No!" I backed away. "I don't want you to cut me. I'm not like you. I don't like being hurt."

"I ever hurt you?"

"No, but everybody thinks you're crazy. People in town talk about you and your mother all the time."

She lowered the knife, a hurt in her eyes that shamed me. She kept them locked on mine and asked, "That how you think?"

"I don't think you're crazy. But Sweetie—"

"Then come here and hold out your hand."

I took a breath, let it out, walked to her, and stuck out my hand. I needed to trust her. She was my only friend. The best friend I'd ever had.

She took the tip of the knife and laid it against my palm.

I waited for her to slash me as she had done to herself. She was brave and took it, so why couldn't I? When she pressed the knife into my skin, there was only a sharp sting and then a line of blood beaded up.

"We got to put our hands together now to mix up our bloods. My blood will go in your body, and your blood will go in mine and that makes us be bound."

"I'm ready, Sweetie."

Sweetie pressed her hand to mine and squeezed. Her blood was hot against my hand. She squeezed harder and her hot blood heated my hand. She said, "We are bound forever. Nothing can stop our bond. Not no bad winds, not no wrongful hearts, not no time before or after, nothing in this world or beyond will change our bond. Forever." She pressed harder still. "Now you say it."

"We're bound forever. Nothing will stop our bond. No bad winds, or bad hearts, or time before or after, nothing in this world or beyond will stop or change our bond. Forever." I squeezed back hard as I could.

"Our bloods is mixed now and running up around inside us. I got your blood, and you got mine. Bound forever and ever."

"The blood's running all the way to our hearts, huh, Sweetie?"

"That's right. Just like you said." She released the pressure of her hand and at first, it was as if our hands were sewn together. As our hands parted, there was a tearing feeling. I wondered how we could be bound but still have that tearing away feeling. I wanted to take her hand again and not let go. I didn't like the tearing feeling.

"We got to put our blood print in our diary." She reached for the diary with the uncut hand, handed it to me. "Find a clean page."

I opened it. Past my writing and Sweetie's scrawls, and the maps Sweetie drew, I found the next blank page.

"Now, stick your clean finger in your blood and spot the page."

I did what she told me and then held the book out to her. She put her print beside mine.

I stared at our bloody fingerprints, and then blew on them so they'd dry. Sweetie leaned over and helped by blowing, too. When the blood was dry enough to close the diary, she said, "Now. It is done."

The diary had smudges of blood on the leather. There were dribbles of blood in the dirt. Blood on our hands and on Sweetie's feet. Sweetie took two pieces of cloth from the leather bag, handed me one, and held the other to her cut hand. "Press to stop the bleeding."

I pressed to my cut. "Sweetie? You didn't tell me your secret."

"But I am *showing* you."

"I still don't understand."

She sat on the ground, pulled a canteen of water and leaves from the bag, poured water to clean her hands, and then pressed the leaves into her cut, tied the piece of cloth around it. She handed me the canteen and two leaves.

I sat and did as she'd done. Where the leaves were, my palm tingled, then felt a bit numb.

She opened the tin box and spoke to it. "I was borned magical under the moon with the mountain spirit's breath. I will never hurt. I will never die until the day of my choosing if I so choose." She looked up and over to the ridgetops. "Grandpaw said when he called for the old granny woman come birth me from my mama, the granny woman knew what I was when she saw the moon in my eyes. She whispered me a name that cannot ever be said and nobody knows it except the granny woman. Grandpaw called me Sweetie and that is my name." She removed the cloth and leaves from her hand and squeezed drops of blood into the box, closed it, rubbed the top. "Keep our secrets safe."

I stared at her, for once nothing rushing out of my mouth.

Sweetie looked at me with what I thought was hope. "Maybe some my blood will help your hurts and maybe some your blood will help . . . help me be more like you. I get tiresome having to keep the secret. I get tiresome thinking on how long forever is if I can't choose." Sweetie looked as if she really *was* tired all of a sudden, as if she'd walked a thousand miles. She pressed the leaves into the cut again.

I found my voice. "But, everyone feels pain. Everyone dies. It's biology; it's science. Everything is made of stuff that dies and decays when it's time to, not when we choose to."

"No, not me." She sighed.

"Our bodies aren't made to last forever. I could show you stuff in Father's books so you'd see."

She shook her head back and forth, slowly.

"You can't feel *any* pain when you hurt yourself? *Nothing?*"

She shook her head again, just as slowly.

"But you can get infections. Germs are like colonies that—"

"Grandpaw showed me what to do to make sure." She put down the box, and straightened her feet out in front of her. "I brung me some stuff to fix me up. Mama would have a hissy if I didn't. She worries I don't do proper things. She thinks I got a curse from God because of something she did, but Grandpaw says I am not cursed by no god." She firmed her mouth.

"What kinds of proper things?"

"My magic powers aren't perfect."

"Huh?"

"I got to remember to drink the bearberry tea to help my pee-pee-parts. I got to remember to check myself for things out a whackity on my body, and check my eyeballs to make sure nothing flung in them, and when it's cold I got to remember to dress warm."

"None of this makes any scientific sense at all. It doesn't make *any* kind of sense."

"Why're you all'a time talking that way, about science and germs and all? Like it's the onliest thing that makes the world turn round?"

"I'm just trying to figure things out. There's always an answer to everything. My father says so."

"Well, the mountain spirit and my grandpaw know the other answers."

"If you're magical, how come you have to check yourself? How come you bleed and could maybe get infections?"

Her shoulders dropped. "Maybe when I grow up things will be more perfect. Maybe I done something to make the mountain spirit mad. I do not know."

I gave her a bug under a microscope stare, instead of a best friend bound sister look.

From the leather bag, she pulled out a jar with a cork in it, and clean white strips of cloth. She uncorked the jar and from it poured something green-tinged over the cut, wiped at it with a piece of the cloth, then wrapped strips around her hand. She wouldn't look at me. She then worked on her foot, where she stomped the flames out.

I knew cuts and burns needed to be taken care of before they were dirtied. If a tiny, microscopic bit of dirt ever settled into a hurt, it would make a nice home in there. And it didn't matter how tiny it was, that tiny bit of dirt would cause an infection to begin. Then, before the person knew it, the little dirt turned into a big nasty pus-filled sore that had to be lanced and drained. If it wasn't lanced and drained, if it was allowed to stay filled with pus and nasty, the infection traveled all over the body. All that trouble from a tiny bit of dirt.

She finished wrapping her foot and as before, handed me the jar and clean cloth strips.

"We have to make sure we keep these clean so they don't get pus and the pus goes all the way to our hearts and we go into a coma where we sleep our life away," I paused, "or it kills us."

"Sweetie; that is me," she pointed to herself, "will not die." She sang as she worked on her hurts, "My old hen's a good old hen; she lays eggs for the railroad men; sometimes one, sometimes two; sometimes enough for the whole damn crew—"

"Everybody dies." I poured some of the liquid over my cut. The green stuff stung like the dickens. "All it takes is a tiny piece of dirt. Just one little bit of dirt turns into a nasty infection. Bam! Just like that, you could die or go into a coma."

"Silly Brains. You and your comas."

I wrapped my hand. My palm was throbbing just from that little prick of the knife and the sting of her medicine.

She watched me fix my hand.

"Sweetie?"

"Huh?"

"How do you stand it?"

"I am what I am." She poured the rest of the water in the canteen over the fire to make sure it was out, and then put everything back into her bag.

I tried to figure how it could all be real. How a person couldn't feel things in her body that everyone else felt. And how could a kid remember to do what she said she had to do? I wondered if there really was a mountain spirit. I'd always thought it was just a silly game she played, something to sound mysterious, and that she was only a really tough girl who could take things other kids couldn't take. Or she liked to keep people away from her by acting strange.

But after everything she'd shown me, everything she'd said, and after the way our hands felt pressed together, and the weird air where I knew we weren't alone, there had to be something magical or mysterious about it. Maybe Father was wrong. Maybe some things couldn't ever be explained by science and scientists. I knew no normal person was like Sweetie.

No matter how weird it all sounded, I'd keep following her because it was more fun to be with her than without her. And it made me even more curious to see where she lived, how she lived. I couldn't wait to meet her mother. I hoped she hadn't changed her mind about that.

TWELVE

We dug a hole for the box with good strong sticks. Rock and root and old earth crumbled away.

"Sweetie? What happened when you were born? You said you were born magical."

She leaned her stick on the tree. "Grandpaw said the mountain spirit noticed me when I was in my mama's womb." She made a large circle, touching her fingers, circling, then coming around to touch them again. "He said the moon was big and full and orange the night I was borned, and that the big wolf he'd been seeing stood out by a ash tree and howled all night. Mama was in the worsest pain." She grabbed her stomach, as if in bad pain. "Grandpaw said Mama screamed and screamed, and when I finally come out, I did not cry." She raised her hand and swatted down. "He said the old woman slapped my butt hard, and I still did not cry. I looked out the winder at the moon with my big ole eyes holding the moon in them and it was like I knew all the moon's secrets." She held her arms as if cradling a baby. "Then Mama held me and rocked me and Grandpaw said she prayed over me, crying and praying over what the granny woman and Grandpaw were saying. She said she didn't want that for me and Grandpaw said, 'It's too late.'"

I shivered.

She picked up her stick. "Soon as we bury this here box we'll put leaves and rocks on top, so as nobody never ever finds our secrets." She picked up the tin box and held it out. "You and me got to put it in the ground together."

I took one side and she the other and we slipped the box in the hole, under a root, then began to fill in the hole with dirt.

"I guess we can't write it in the diary."

She picked up a rock and set it aside. "We can't chance it. Grandpaw said if people find out they'll put me in a circus act or do things experimental on me. That's why I don't go to no town lessen I have to. That's why I pretended my pinky hurt that day, so's they'd not start up they's gossiping. I forget to pretend sometimes."

We next packed down the dirt and then gathered leaves, twigs, and rocks. I wondered what other kids were doing. Going to parties, to the movies, to the pancake place to eat the best-ever-in-the-world pancakes then down the road and up top of the mountain to ride rides with the pancakes sloshing around and then watch the Wild West shows, swimming and then ice cream or hot salty fries and malteds. I wonder what other kids would think if they knew what I knew. And I couldn't even tell anyone, and even if I did, which I would not, they'd think we both were crazy and weird.

Sweetie picked up the rock and set it just so over the packed dirt. "Mama says God got some purpose for me, but why'd he give her all the pain and give me none? I don't know about no god and his mysterious ways."

"That's why you hurt yourself? You're trying to feel something? Or make it Even Steven with your mother?"

She stared at me. "That is not how it is."

I arranged my own twigs and leaves over our hidden secrets.

When we finished, it looked like a grave.

She pointed up. "Up there, top that ridge. That's where that boy got kilt and never found again. He used to hold a Bible ever-day."

"That's the kid Frannie said she'd kissed and it brought him to his tragical end."

"Grandpaw used to go up there to smoke kinnikinnick and talk to the mountain spirit."

"Kinniki-what?"

"Mama said Grandpaw went up there too many a time and denied God and made him mad, so God sends death angels to toss people off the ridge when they don't listen to his ways. That kid fell away and then forever and ever he goes *woooooo woooooo I'm a lost and lonely haint woooooo.*" She laughed, stepped away from the tree, picked up her leather bag.

"Mother says God's not vengeful like some preachers say. And Father says he doesn't exist."

"Kinnikinnick is what Zemry mixed for Grandpaw for his special prayers." She turned and walked away from Triplet Tree and our buried secrets.

I grabbed my satchel, and hurried to walk alongside her, our arms touching without our jerking them away as we usually did. As much as I wanted to, I didn't ask if we were still going to her house.

Father said we were biological machines. But maybe there was more to the world than I ever was told. Maybe there was more to the world than even Father knew.

As we headed up an incline, Sweetie's hair blew wild around her face, hiding her eyes from me. My hair couldn't hide my eyes anymore. I'd chopped it off as short as a boy two days after Sweetie came to our house for brunch. I went into the bathroom with Mother's pinking shears. As I cut away the brown strings, it became shiny and softer looking. The shorter my hair was, the bigger my eyes looked and the smaller my cheeks seemed. I cut it until the sink was full of hair. When I walked out of the bathroom and into the kitchen where Mother was making shrimp with creamed onions and pears, she threw a conniption fit. I stood and listened to her fuss until she pointed and told me to go to my room until dinner. As I walked away, she'd said, "I'll make an appointment with Cheryl to fix that mess. I don't know where your mind is lately, Melissa."

At dinner, Father looked at my hair and said, "A pixie has joined us for dinner."

Mother ignored him and kept her mouth in a straight line.

After she had Cheryl fix the straggled ends, Mother quit bothering me about it so much. The next day, I went through my brother's old clothes she'd put away into boxes and left in the extra bedroom. When I opened the first box, it held some of Peter's treasures and the inside smelled like Old Spice and glue from the model airplanes he used to put together (a finished airplane was at the top of the box and I took it out). I opened another box, and that one held the clothes he'd outgrown but didn't want to give away. The next one had belts, shoes, and other things that meant something to my big brother.

I slid two of the boxes down the hall to my room. From them, I took out two pairs of his jeans, his football jersey, three t-shirts, a button-down shirt, his boots, and a belt. I put the airplane on my dresser, and the clothes and the belt in the bottom of my chest of drawers. I hid the boxes in the back of my closet, with his leather boots placed on top.

When I put on Peter's jeans, I couldn't believe they fit. I studied myself in the mirror, but it was hard to see myself any different from before, other than the short hair and the boy's clothes. Yet I had to be different. When I walked into the living room, Mother was reading a recipe book. Without looking up at me, she asked, "Did you eat the pastries I baked for my bridge club?"

"No Ma'am."

"Well, I suppose your father took them to his office. They aren't in the kitchen where I put them." She licked her finger and turned a page. "I suppose that's what happened to them. Since they're gone."

"I don't know. But I didn't eat them."

"Perhaps ginger scones will do." She licked another finger and turned another page." Do you want something?"

"No Ma'am."

She looked up, dropped the book on her lap. "What in the world? What are you doing in boy's clothes? You look ridiculous. Go change immediately."

"This is more comfortable, and fits better than my other clothes."

"I'm not in the mood for an argument, Melissa."

"I'm not arguing with you. I'm asking you to let me go out in clothes where I don't have to worry about getting them dirty or torn like I do the nice ones you buy." I smoothed down Peter's blue t-shirt. "I won't let your friends see me dressed like this."

"Why don't your other clothes fit? I just bought you clothes a few months ago. It's just an excuse not to wear the nice things I pick out."

I couldn't believe she didn't notice I'd lost weight. After all the fussing she did about it. "If I'm excused, I'd like to go now."

"Don't be late for dinner." She went back to her recipes.

When I'd showed up at Bear Claw Rock that day, I'd modeled for Sweetie my new old clothes.

"You're falling away. Leaving pieces of you all over the mountain." Then she'd added, "And you stopped bumping on your words when you get nervous."

"Oh, yeah, I f-f-forg-g-got all a-a-a-b-b-bout it." We both laughed, and then we'd looked for blackberries to make Zemry a pie.

Sweetie poked my arm. "Where you at?"

"I was thinking about the day we picked blackberries to make Zemry a pie." I danced around the trail, pretending to be the lightweight boxing champion of the world, *punch punch*. "That was the day Mother almost choked on her spit when she saw me in Peter's clothes." Then I was a chunky ballerina, did a chunky pirouette, and sang, "The mountains are aliiiive, with the sounds of their muuusic!"

Sweetie shook her head. "Just one like you, that is a sure thing. You are sillier than anything I ever seen."

When I tripped over a rock in the trail and fell to my knees, I decided to quit dancing. Sweetie turned her head. I knew she was laughing. "Well, that hurt, so I must not have enough of your blood in me." Brushing off my jeans, I asked, "Do you think when you grow up you'll feel pain?"

"Don't know."

"If you grow up and you still don't feel pain, will you still try to hurt yourself so much?"

She stopped on the trail. "I don't try to . . . " and then sighed and said, "It is all strange and mysterious like the moon."

We walked on.

I pinched her arm. "How'd that feel? Any different for you?"

"Nuh uh." She put her arms out and lifted up her face to the sky. "I feel the wind on my face, and I feel the ground while I walk."

"I think it would be great never to feel pain."

"I reckon that's what most would think." She bent, rooted in some old leaves, and picked up a buckeye that had been hidden from the squirrels. "Look, this here buckeye has a holler spot it in." She handed it to me. "Rub your thumb on it when you get to feeling worrisome." She pointed ahead. "We're almost there."

My heart thumped hard. What would her mother be like? Would she be weird? Would she yell at Sweetie and tell her she was cursed. Did she hurt Sweetie like T. J.'s Father hurt him? I rubbed the buckeye as we walked. I also let myself worry about Sweetie's hand, the same one with the hurt pinky, and the deep cut. I wondered if she'd cut off her whole hand a bit at a time. I worried that Sweetie's mother wouldn't like me and would get the shotgun out. The buckeye got a good rubbing of my thumb as we walked the rest of the way to Sweetie's house.

We'd crossed a forked creek, two huge fallen trees, a boulder that looked like a shark fin that we stopped and named Shark Fin Rock, and lots of brambles, vines, rhododendrons, wildflowers and trees. When I thought I'd drop dead from hunger and achy feet, she said, "Right up there it is."

I gulped some spit, and followed Sweetie. At last, I was going to meet the mother who had a daughter like Sweetie.

THIRTEEN

The cabin was a part of the mountain, just as Sweetie was, with the wild all around, except for a tamed pretty garden with plants and flowers growing.

"Grandpaw built it."

I liked how it was far away from everyone, and how the logs were old but sturdy, and how a creek flowed right beside it. The wind blew through the leaves and it was so peaceful, I wanted to fall upon the grass and never move again. The front door we came to was a solid wood turned gray from the rain and sun, and hung on a rusted nail was the skull of an animal.

Sweetie said, "That's Mr. Shitter's head."

"*Eeeww.* That's gross."

"Nuh uh." She reached up and petted the skull. "I made him special potions and he lived and lived and lived until he up and died a very old kitty. I buried him under that there sweetgum tree where he used to lay down and watch over me." She pointed to the tree to show me where. "Then one day he poked his head out so he could keep watching me, so I put his skull up here." She opened the door and we stepped inside.

We stepped into a room that was a kitchen, dining, and living room all in one. There was a closed door to the right of the kitchen, and on the other side of the room were log steps that led to what may be a loft like we had in an apartment in California. The kitchen held an old woodstove that looked heavier than a car and had *Home Comfort* written on the front door. To eat on there was a polished wood table and chairs. In the living room part, a rocking chair, a fat stuffed chair, and a ladder-backed straw-seated chair were in a semi-circle in front of a big old stone fireplace that had an iron pot with legs sitting inside it.

Sweetie said, "Put your satchel here by mine."

I set it down next to hers by the front door, and turned back to Sweetie, who was at the closed door.

She stopped with her hand on the knob and listened. Knocking softly, she asked, "Mama? You wake?"

A voice answered, "I am."

Sweetie motioned for me to come with her, and I held my breath, let it out slow. She opened the door; we stepped in. On an iron bed, under a pretty quilt, lay Sweetie's mother. I'd pictured a sickly bird woman, but the mother on the bed was much more than that. Her pale hair spread across the pillow and down the covers. It was long enough to reach below her waist. As we drew near the bed, she tried to sit up, so Sweetie gently helped her prop up against three pillows that had embroidered flowers sewn on. When she smiled at me, I had a catch in my heart. Sweetie's mother was beautiful. Not in the way movie stars were, but in the way I imagined Christmas angels were.

"You gone to make our acquaintances, daughter?" Her voice was strong and breathless at the same time.

"Yes'm. This here's Miss-Lissa, the girl I been telling you all about."

I hid the thrill that Sweetie had been telling her mother all about me, and stepped closer. "Nice to meet you, Missus, um . . . " I looked at Sweetie.

"Call me Mae, like the month with a E instead of a Y." She laughed and it sounded sweet like the creek bubbling. She then said, "Well, you was right. She's a humdinger of a friend."

My face warmed with pleasure.

Sweetie pushed a strand of hair from her mother's face. "Mama, you hungry?"

"No. I ate me something a hour ago. And, you can get that hand out from behind you. I seen it." Her mother sighed, shook her head. "What am I to do with you? You'll be the death of me yet."

Sweetie lowered her head. "I'm sorry, Mama. It was accidental."

"You got to be more careful, baby girl." She looked at my hand. "You, too?" She shook her head.

Sweetie leaned over and kissed her mother on the cheek, then said, "We cleaned and wrapped our accidents real good. Got some dirt on but we'll change the wrappings."

"What about praying? You been praying to God to watch over you?"

"Yes Ma'am." Sweetie winked at me.

"I saw that wink, you little stinker." She picked at the covers. "I get worrisome over you."

"I'll use the liniment before I go to bed tonight."

"Please do. Now, I'm gone take me a bit a rest now." Mae closed her eyes. We turned away and tiptoed out; Sweetie closed the door behind us.

She moved to the kitchen and lit the stove. "You hungry? I sure am. I got cornbread and greasy beans." She stroked the stove. "Grandpaw was so proud of this stove. Likened to never got it up here. Best one he could find, he said. I forget what he sold to get it."

"It's a really nice stove."

She smiled.

"Can I help?" I asked.

She shook her head no, pointed to the table.

While she prepared our meal, I listened to the birds outside. My mouth watered as the beans heated, though I worried about the greasy part. Sweetie went outside and came back with a little porcelain pot that she set on the counter. From a clean dishcloth, Sweetie took a cake of cornbread, broke thick pieces from it, set the pieces on tin plates, and sliced into them. From the porcelain pot, she dipped a knife and spread what had to be creamy butter inside the sliced cornbread. There was a basket of tomatoes and she took one from it, lightly pressed into its skin, and nodded her head when it gave just a little. She sliced it, the meat of the tomato dark red and juicy, and put the slices on a small plate. When the beans were bubbly, she ladled them out into two thick pottery bowls. One had a chip on the side, and Sweetie put that one at her place on the table.

On another plate, she put a few spoonfuls of beans, and a tiny piece of cornbread without butter but with a drizzle of honey. She set the plate on a wood tray, along with a glass of water and two white pills. She looked at me, "This for Mama in case she changes her mind. She'll be needing them headache pills. You can start on that there food."

"I'll wait for you."

She picked up the tray and turned to go to her mother's room.

I looked around the room again while Sweetie was giving her mother lunch and her medicine—the pills must be what Sweetie said the preacher gave her. When we'd walked in, the cabin smelled as she did—mint and earth smells, but with a medicine and sick smell I imagined became caught in the corners like spider webs. There were no pictures or mirrors around, but on the walls were small quilts, tapestries, and needlepoint pictures. Beside the rocking chair was a basket of yarn and knitting needles. There wasn't a television or radio, and it was quiet and peaceful, with only the creek, the wind, and the birds making noise. I leaned over and sniffed the beans, my stomach rumbling.

When Sweetie came back and sat down at the table, she nodded to my food, then dug into her bowl.

We ate without talking. The greasy beans, which weren't greasy at all, reminded me of green beans, and I could have eaten more, but wouldn't have asked Sweetie for more food I didn't figure they had much of.

When I was done, I said, "Thank you for lunch, Sweetie." I took our bowls to the old sink.

"You set right back down."

"But, Sweetie—"

"I won't hear of it."

I put the dishes into the sink and sat down.

She said, "I hope you left room for pie?"

I nodded.

She went to a pie safe and took from it a pie covered with a clean dishcloth. "Yep, nothing like pie to make a smile. Uh huh. A good pie's what's hiding under this here dishrag." She grinned at me, then let out a giggling laugh like I'd never heard from her.

"What's so funny?"

When she uncovered the pie, I laughed and clapped my hands. A cherry pie. She remembered the story about Mittens and the pie. I wondered how much it cost to make a pie like that.

"This here pie will taste so good that from here on out to beyond, you will not think about upchucking when you see a cherry pie." She cut slices and put them on two pretty little china plates with tiny roses around the rim.

I dug in and ate every bite. Then we both cleaned up, even though she fussed at me for wanting to help. We used heated water from the stove to do the dishes and I thought how easy I had it at home with our electric stove and modern kitchen.

Sweetie dried her hands, went back to the door and peeked in on her mother. Over her shoulder, she said, "She's sleeping good, but I orter give them pills earlier." She closed the door and came back beside me.

"Your mother looks like an angel on top of a Christmas tree."

"Want to see her picture before she got so sick?" She grabbed her leather bag and headed up the stairs with it.

I followed her up the stairs, until I remembered the bracelets. In all the wonder of Sweetie and her mother, I'd almost forgotten. "Wait!

I made you and your mother a present." I ran to get my satchel, pulled out the packages, ran back to Sweetie who'd come back down the stairs, and handed them to her.

Her eyes were wide. "It's like *Christmas*." She stroked the comic paper the gifts were wrapped in. "Can I tear off the paper now?"

"Yes, tear it off."

As she opened the gift, I watched her face open up like a sunflower. When she held up the bracelet, she said, "Oh Lissa! I never had a present so fine."

"The other one is for your mother. They were made especially by me."

She surprised me by hugging me, quick and hard. I was the most special person in the whole world. She said, "I'll give Mama hers when she wakes up. It'll make her happy like nothing in a long time."

I was glad I'd spent so much time picking out the right beads. I helped Sweetie tie on her bracelet, and she put her mother's on the counter for later. She said, "Come on," and we climbed the stairs.

Her room was tiny, but as I'd imagined, it was full of her treasures: the rocks, feathers, bones, pieces of bark shaped like animals and fish, buckeyes, the skeleton-turtle and shell, dried leaves, and other mountain things she picked up along the way. Her bed was iron just as her mother's was, and on the mattress was a colorful quilt almost like her mother's, except her mother's was white, green, and pink, and Sweetie's was red, blue, and yellow. I sat on the bed; the mattress was thin but soft.

She crouched down to an old wooden chest with carvings of animals, birds, and trees. "Grandpaw's chest. He told me to take care of it the night he passed. Said to put all my special things in it." She turned the key to open it, and from inside pulled out a silver-framed picture. "This here's Mama before I was borned. She's something else, isn't she?" She handed over the photo as if it were a fragile egg.

I stared at the photograph of a young, pretty woman who looked like a softer kind of Sweetie. "Yes, she sure is something else." Like you, I thought inside my heart. She put the picture back, locked the chest. From her leather bag, she took out the diary and handed it to me.

"Your time to take. I've had it a long while."

I thumbed through it. Her handwriting was messy, scrawled across the page, but I knew how she described everything in more detail that I'd ever have thought to. She remembered the tiniest of things, like how the dirt felt under her feet, and which way the wind was blowing, and what clothes I had on that day, what animals we saw, the smells in the air. Her maps were much neater, even more detailed, and showed all the places we went. The bloody thumbprints were last. I couldn't wait to add to it, but I knew I couldn't write about our secrets. Maybe if I did it in code.

It was past three, and I needed to go home. Sweetie looked in on her mother. I listened to Sweetie's soft voice that sounded almost like a mother cooing to her baby. She stepped out of the room, closed the door, and said, "Mama will sleep for a long while."

We set out for Whale Back. The way back didn't seem as long as the way there, funny how that happened when coming and going. I asked Sweetie, "Did you draw a map to your house?"

"Naw."

"Why not?"

"You can follow me there."

"But what if you need me and I can't find you and you go into a coma?"

"What is with you and that coma?"

I huffed out my air.

"What you huffing over?"

"You know how to get to *my* house, but I'm not supposed to know how to get to yours?"

"I just showed you." She turned to me with her eyebrows pulled up.

"You know I can't find it by myself." I crossed my arms over my chest.

"You sure are acting ornery."

"What if I need you real fast and you aren't at Whale Back, and there's no moccasin note, and I'm searching and searching until I get lost in the woods forever and ever?"

She put her hands on her hips. "Well, huhn."

"I mean, *think* about it." I sounded prissy, even to my own ears.

"You act like a gnat that won't get slapped away."

"I do not."

"I will draw you up a map later, okay?"

"Hey! It would help if you'd mark the way to some of our places until I learned them better. Like, oh what's that book? Where they mark their way in the woods?"

"I do not know."

"Like Hansel and Gretel, or something like that. Except something where the birds won't eat it."

She shrugged.

"I know! You could use some of your mother's yarn and tie a bit on the tree branches. You could do that to your house and let me see if I could follow it. I mean, the maps are good, but it'd just be something different, you know?"

"I guess so."

"It'll be adventurous and fun."

"I reckon it might."

That night I lay in my frilly girl's bed with my nice things all around me, the television going in the next room. I lay there with my stomach full from Mother's steak medallions with mushroom sauce. I lay there and listened to Father's typewriter clackity clack away. I wanted to be back at Sweetie's place. I wanted to stay there forever. I wanted her mother, and I wanted to be like Sweetie and never feel any pain. I wanted her life instead of mine. That was my foolish-biological-sciences-that-wished-anyway heart.

FOURTEEN

I was at Dead Owl Trail at first light, even though I went the wrong way and had to double back, which would prove my point to Sweetie about how I sometimes still had trouble finding my way on the mountain, even with her maps. I didn't want to admit to her how I was being a little lazy and following yarn stuck to branches would be easier than reading maps. To me, the mountain could look the same, until Sweetie showed me the little things that made them different, then I'd understand better.

Mother was going to throw a fit over the chores I'd left undone. For once, I wanted to leave the house and go have fun without worrying about sweeping, mopping, dusting, cleaning the bathroom, scrubbing the bottoms of pots, or washing my clothes. There wasn't a reason in the world I could see to have to do chores before I left every day.

Dead Owl Trail had an opening in the trees that faced east and Sweetie said to sit with my back against the maple tree and wait for all the colors, reds and oranges and yellows, to cross the mountains and sky. Sometimes the mists would cover the mountains and glow as if they had a light inside.

It was so beautiful and peaceful, I didn't care if Sweetie showed up on time or not. I liked the feeling that I was the only person in the world. Sometimes I felt the weight of Sweetie's secret. There were times I had shameful thoughts against Sweetie's ways and friendship. Thoughts like what if I did the stuff my brother used to do with his friends, the things other kids did with their friends. But then Sweetie would say, "I got something inneresting to show you," and I'd be trapped in the spell of her mysterious, beautiful mountain world.

After the magic of the sunrise colors drifted away, I didn't feel so brave when I thought about Mother lecturing me, taking away my allowance, and the punishment to my room. I stood up and ran almost all the way home.

Opening the door without a sound, I crept in. All was as quiet and still as I had left it. I checked my watch; I'd been gone an hour and thirty-five minutes. I peeked into the study, but Father wasn't there.

He must have left for work early. The door to Mother's room was closed, and when I pressed my cheek to the door, there weren't any sounds. Sometimes Mother slept late if she was extra tired.

I swept and mopped the kitchen, and for good measure, did the same to the living room floor. I washed Father's dishes left in the sink, and then toasted a piece of wheat bread, spread peanut butter on it and toasted it again in the oven until the peanut butter was gooey and a bit browned on the top. I ate it with a tall cold glass of milk, and cleaned up my crumbs. I heard Mother stirring around in her bedroom, so I ran to brush my teeth and gargle, and wipe down my bathroom.

I was walking down the hall with my satchel when she stepped out of her bedroom. She had her hair brushed back into a low ponytail. Her eyes were a little red.

"Good Morning, Mother." I gave her a big smile.

"Good Morning, Melissa. I see you're headed out. Did you do your chores?"

"Would I leave the house without doing my chores?" I smiled bigger.

She raised an eyebrow. "We sure are happy this morning, aren't we?"

"Yes Ma'am. It looks like a beautiful day."

"I suppose it is."

I shouldered my satchel and walked past her. I was almost at the end of the hall when she called out to me.

"Melissa?"

I stiffened and turned around. Maybe she knew. Maybe she had been up earlier and knew I was lying. I kicked myself in my behind with an imaginary big fat boot.

"I have to go on a trip for a little while. Do you think you and your father can manage to keep from burning the house down?"

It was hard, but I kept myself from jumping up and down and yelling yippee. "Um, we sure will miss you." And just to be sure, "We'll miss your cooking, too."

She pulled her housecoat tight around her throat. "Well, I suppose you both will eat horrid things while I'm gone. Come with me to the kitchen."

I followed her, and hoped she wouldn't tell me I had to go with her. I prayed to the mountain spirit as hard as I could pray. I asked it to forgive me for saying I believed in science and only what could be proved right in front of me.

In the kitchen, Mother looked around. "How nice everything looks."

"I swept and mopped the living room, too."

"This is unexpected." She put her hand on my head. "You're growing up . . . so fast." As she took away her hand, her fingers brushed my cheek. "Melissa . . . I . . . I have something to tell you."

"Yes Ma'am?" My spine kinked up. I didn't like how she looked.

She didn't say anything at first, then her face changed. "You be good, okay?"

"Oh. Okay."

"Well, I was worried about leaving you here to run wild, but now I'm feeling much better about it."

"Where're you going?"

"I . . . " She had that funny look again, then, "Some things aren't a child's worry. Now run along where ever it is you were going before I interrupted you."

"Yes Ma'am." I opened the door.

"Wait!"

I kept the sigh inside. There was The Sigh Rule: *never sigh (or roll eyes) near mothers because sighs (and especially rolled eyes) make mothers go crazy.* I turned back to her. "Yes Ma'am?"

"Mrs. Tanner next door will keep an eye on things. In fact, I have eyes all over town, so don't think you can get by with any foolishness." She plugged in the percolator, then muttered, "That goes for your father, too."

When I finally escaped, it was past the time I said I'd meet Sweetie. I ran on a cloud of happiness. I skipped on the parts of the trails that were even, feeling as if I could laugh aloud every step of the way.

Back at Dead Owl Trail, I'd been there twelve minutes when I heard a crashing through the woods. At first I worried it was a bear and hid behind the rhododendron bushes. Around the corner trotted Miss Annie, with Sweetie sitting on her back. I stepped out from behind the bushes and waved to her. She waved back, and when they were next to me, she jumped off the mule, her face split with the biggest grin I'd ever seen on her. She had a slim rifle or shotgun slung over her shoulder, which she took off and stuck in a holster fashioned across Miss Annie.

"What's with the gun?" I'd never seen a gun in real life, only on television. I sure hoped she wasn't going to shoot herself in the hand just to prove a point.

"That there was my Grandpaw's twenty-two from when he was a boy. I take good care of it. I brung it in case I see a rabbit or maybe a big ole frog I can give to Zemry to make a stew. When I was little I tried to shoot him a tiny frog for his supper, but it blowed to bits and sent frog guts ever-where." She laughed and laughed.

I started to say *oh, that's gross,* or *poor little animals,* but then I thought of how Sweetie lived, how things were different for her than for me. How I'd never in my life been hungry, but the opposite—I ate too much food. But I secretly hoped she'd not find anything to shoot while I was with her.

Sweetie was twirling around with her arms in the air, sing-songing, "Guess what? Guess what?"

"What? What?" I had my own news I could dance about.

"Zemry and me caught a mess a trout." She did a funny little dance. "And Mama is hungry for them fish. She got up!" She pushed her face in Miss Annie's neck, as if to stop herself from showing so much happiness.

"I got good news, too."

She turned to me, her face still open and happy. "What you got that's good?"

"Mother's going on a trip and I don't even know how long!" We both danced around, holding onto each other hands and hopping about, turning in a circle. Sweetie did three cartwheels, and I did a half-way, not so good cartwheel that sent me sprawling.

She said, "Get on Miss Annie. We got to help Zemry clean them fish."

"Get on? Clean fish?"

"That's what I said. Let's go."

I'd never been on a mule before, but I'd ridden a horse at Grandmother Rosetta's. Sweetie hopped up and held down her hand for me to grab and climb up behind her. I struggled just a little, but it wasn't bad. I had on my brother's jeans I'd rolled up, and a t-shirt with a hole in the bottom. I liked my good mule—Miss Annie, that is— riding clothes.

Sweetie grabbed Miss Annie's rope and turned her back down the trail. We rode along and I thought about how nice it would be to go home to a house without Mother waiting to lecture me on being a lady or where did I go and what did I do or was that what I was wearing or don't slam the door or *ding dong flamalama ping pong.*

When Miss Annie trotted up to Sweetie's house, Zemry was sitting on a log with a basket beside him. He had a fish on a plank of wood and three knives beside it. "Y'uns ready to help me clean fish?"

We jumped off Miss Annie.

Sweetie went right to it. She hunkered down, picked up a fish from the basket, slapped it on the wood, and grabbed one of the knives. She cut off the fish's head and held it up in front of my face.

"*Eeeww.*" I stepped back.

She laughed, pointed with the knife. "Three a them fish's not gutted yet. The others we done right after we caught them, right Zemry?"

"Yep."

"You . . . you cleaned them alive?"

"Nuh uh," Sweetie said. "We took care of that before we cleaned them."

I felt a little sick.

"Yep. If we don't poke them fish right away, they suffer something fierce," Zemry said. "Can't breathe. Be like you being underwater and drowning. Well, them fish drown out of the water, slow and long. We poke them and it's quick. We do it where they don't know a thing, I promise."

"Okay." I tried to smile, and hunkered down like Sweetie.

Sweetie said, "Watch me, this here's how you clean a fish." She slit it from the tail to the head, and then drew out its innards. "See?"

"Oh. Okay, I guess."

Zemry took out his tobacco pouch and made a cigarette, letting Sweetie show me what to do.

Sweetie poked out an eyeball and shoved it at me. "I seeeee you." She and Zemry laughed and slapped their knees.

"Stop it, that's *gross.*" But I laughed, too.

"Now, watch." She sliced right below the gills and around until the head was off. "Now you follow along with yours." She took two more fish and handed me one. "Follow me. See, now, slit up it."

"Like this?" I slit the fish as she did.

"Yeah, that's it." Sweetie nodded. "Now, reach your finger up in there, and pull out the guts." She pulled out guts and slapped them on the ground. "I think I will ground up these guts and make a fish-gut pie."

I stared at her, until she laughed and I knew she was making it up. It took me a few tries to get them all, but I slapped the guts on the ground like it was something I did every day.

She took the knife and sliced behind a fin, working her way up and around as she had before. "Now you do it like I just done."

I cut off my fish's head, almost as clean as she had.

"You done a good job, Lissa. Huh, Zemry?"

"She's earned her plate, that's for sure." He blew out smoke as he talked, pinched off the lit end of his cigarette, and put the butt in his pocket. "A fine job."

I almost puffed out my chest.

When the fish were ready, Zemry washed them. "Sometimes I keep the head on and do it whole, but Sweetie's mama likes the head off. She says she don't like them staring at her while she's eating." Zemry wiped the knife on his goo-splattered dungarees. "These are going over the fire."

"Mama likes them without all the bones, but they's too small to filet."

"Yep, trout's a tasty fish, but y'uns got to work to eat them, with all the bones in there."

"I'll get the bones out for Mama," Sweetie said.

"Where *is* your mother?" I asked.

"She'll be out, directly. She's making taters!"

"Oh-wee! Miss Mae's fried taters. Now that's a treat I haven't tasted in the longest time." Zemry rubbed his stomach.

"Uh huh. We're having fried taters, these here trout, biscuits, and a blackberry cobbler."

We washed the fish again in the pan re-filled with clean water. Zemry took long skinny sticks that he had soaking in a bucket, and with a length of string, tied the fish nice and snug onto the sticks. He rubbed the fish with butter, salt and pepper, laid them on a clean piece of wood, picked up the plank of wood and took the planked fish over to a fire he'd built earlier in a hollowed out place in the dirt. Waving his hand over it, he turned to us and nodded. "This fire's good and ready. This fish'll go over it, and I'll cover it up with these wet leaves. It'll get the fish so tender you won't ever eat another kind again without thinking of this fish."

Sweetie and I sat on the log and watched him. I bit my tongue every time I wanted to ask her if I could go inside and say hello to Miss Mae. Wonderful smells floated out of the opened door. I leaned back, pretending to stretch out my legs, and caught a glimpse of her at the stove. Her hair fell long down her back, past her hips, and she had on a blue cotton dress. Miss Mae was taller than I thought, and thinner.

Sweetie knew what I was up to. She pulled me up. "Nobody ever was as curious as you. Come on."

We went into the cabin and I inhaled all the way to my bones. It smelled like a happy home should smell. Sweetie said, "Mama, look who's here."

Miss Mae turned around. Her blue eyes glittered like when the sun strikes the creek, and her cheeks were reddened from the heat of the stove. "Well, hello there, Lissa. I'm glad you come back."

I was shy all of a sudden. "Thank you for having me."

"Our pleasure, it's for sure." She smiled at me, said, "I woke up this morning and I had to have some fish and taters. I told my daughter she best get Zemry and catch a mess before things changed." She checked inside the oven. "Oh, that cobbler is bubbling so fine."

Sweetie stood beside her mother. "Mama, I can finish, if you want to go outside where it's cool."

"Let me have some fun, okay?" She smoothed Sweetie's hair and they looked at each other in a way that showed their love.

I didn't want to feel envious, but I did.

"Pour the tea, baby girl, and get the plates ready. These taters are about done. I already got cat-head biscuits waiting under that dishrag." She lifted the dishcloth and under it were the biggest biscuits I'd ever seen, the tops golden brown and dusted with flour.

"Those biscuits look real good, Miss Mae."

"My own mama taught me. Before she left." Miss Mae frowned, her hand resting on her hip; then she said in a lower voice, "Before she just run off without a word. Not one word. I never seen her again." Her shoulders slumped in.

Sweetie took her hand. "Mama? Zemry's got that fish on the fire and it won't be long. What a feast we'll have, right? Right, Mama? Mama?"

Miss Mae shook her head, as if she had cobwebs clinging. "We sure will. These taters is done. Let's eat, girls."

She put the potatoes into a bowl, while I put the biscuits onto a platter. Sweetie went outside with a pan for the fish. When she was out of sight, Miss Mae touched me on the shoulder. "I got to ask you something important."

"Yes Ma'am?"

"I know you to be a sensible one. I listen to my girl talk about you all the time. Sometimes my little gal is too wild. Full of . . . of ideas and wonderment. When you can, just watch for her, will you?"

I became lost in her sparkling eyes. They were so shiny I couldn't tell how blue the blue was. I'd never seen eyes that shiny before.

"I can't put anything on your shoulders that God won't help you with. I know you're just a child."

I blinked, then said, "I can do it and I will."

She put her hand on my head. I closed my eyes and pretended she was my mother. When I heard Sweetie coming back, she lifted away her hand. Away the warm feelings flew from me, and right back to her own daughter. I opened my eyes to the real world. ·

We took everything outside where it was breezy and ate until we couldn't stuff any more down our throats, barely leaving room for cobbler. Zemry gave Sweetie and me whimmy diddles he'd carved from rhododendron twigs, and showed us how to play with them. The whimmy diddle had two parts. One was a long stick with notches cut into it and a propeller at the top, and the other stick was used to rub along the notches to get the propeller to turn. After I tried and failed, he showed me how to place my finger to get it to work. He said the gee haw part had something to do with mules or horses, but I was half listening as I tried to get the propeller to turn faster than Sweetie could. Zemry said there were contests to see who could whimmy diddle better than the next person.

Zemry made himself a cigarette and in between puffs, told stories about his great grandfather. Miss Mae sat on a blanket with her back against a poplar tree and listened. She didn't talk, but she had a small smile the whole time.

Later, after things were cleaned up, Zemry said, "I need a good long nap under a shady tree." He bid his goodbyes, and he and Miss Annie ambled on down the trail.

Miss Mae closed her eyes, and leaned back her head. The breeze blew strands of her hair across her face. She still had a small smile on her lips, but her forehead wrinkled.

"Mama, you ready to get back in bed?"

"Bring me my yarn basket, please."

Sweetie ran inside.

I waited for Miss Mae to tell me something else, but she stayed quiet, kept her eyes closed.

When Sweetie came back and handed the basket to her, Miss Mae took a pile of yarn from the top. But it wasn't a pile of yarn, it was a beautiful shawl. "I made this for your mama." Miss Mae held it out to me.

I took it from her. The shawl was dark blue, with touches of light blue threaded in. It was beautiful. "Thank you. It's so pretty." It smelled like mint, earth, the potatoes and biscuits and cobbler. I wanted to bury my face in it.

"I made something for you, too." She picked up a red knitted cap and held it out. "Seeing as you cut your hair within a inch of its life, I thought this would keep your head warm."

I took the hat from her. "It's beautiful, too. I can't wait until it's cold enough to wear it."

"You tell your mama I'm sorry I been too sick to meet her. If she reared up as fine a daughter as you, she must be real special."

Sweetie opened her mouth to say something, but Miss Mae held up her hand. She looked from Sweetie to me. "We all do what we can with how we know." She rubbed her forehead. "Now, daughter, help me back to bed. I'm give out."

We both helped her back to her bed. Sweetie gave her a pill, and Miss Mae lay back on the pillows and fell asleep.

Back outside, Sweetie said, "She'll sleep for a long long spell."

We ran to the creek and hunted for smoothed stones until it was time for me to go home.

***

Father brought home food most nights and we'd eat leftovers for breakfast, and for lunch if I was home. When he didn't do that, we ate sandwiches or soup or eggs. When Mother had been gone four days, I asked Father where she was, but he changed the subject. After a week, I asked again, and again he didn't say. After eight days, and still no mother, I began to run out to the mountain with Sweetie without doing my chores, and I quit asking where she was, but it was strange and weird. Father would talk on the phone, but always where I couldn't hear.

After two weeks, Father took me to an Italian restaurant in Asheville. I wore the shawl and he complimented me on it. I told him Sweetie's mother made it and it was really for mother, and not for me. He said, "Well, she'll never know if you wear it this once."

Father ate only half of his dinner. He told me about his book and the characters, and then talked about how things go wrong in our bodies because of our infallibility, how the innocent and good are stricken the same as the bad and guilty. That things were decided by mere chance. How since time began people had sicknesses and to blame anything but our ancestors and possibly what we eat or didn't eat or just by a fluke in the genes was silly. Science and biology and chance. Nothing was by any hand of some god. Nothing by magic. Everything had an explanation even if it seemed there wasn't one, even if one could not be found, there were scientific answers to everything . . . *blab blab blab blabbity blork.*

I thought different things in my head than I usually did when Father talked. I thought about Sweetie and how maybe I could believe in magic and things that couldn't be explained. I could. I could believe in *some*thing, Father.

He winked at the waitress when she poured his wine, and she giggled with her hand over her mouth.

I knew something wasn't right with him, but I couldn't figure it out. He'd be smiling and telling stories, and winking, and then the next minute, he'd stare down at his plate, forgetting I was there until I asked him a question and he'd start in again about science and sickness. I thought he was missing Mother, even though that made no sense to me.

I ate my lasagna, and even though it wasn't as good as Nonna's was, it tasted wonderful compared to the lasagna Mother made with goat cheese and poor baby lambs. I always pretended I had a stomachache and couldn't eat when she cooked lambs.

Father had let me have a tiny glass of red wine, as long as I didn't tell Mother, and I felt like a grown up. It was so much fun, other than his funny moods, that I couldn't help but think that Mother might never come back. I hated wicked thoughts, but sometimes they stomped around in my head anyway. I wanted Father and I to live by ourselves. I could have Sweetie over to spend the night, and I could go to her house and spend the night. Father and I could go fishing and I would show him how to clean and cook the fish outside like Zemry did. He'd buy me the microscope he'd promised me a year ago and show me the tiny mysterious worlds magnified. I'd discover something new and strange that no other scientist ever had and it would be named after me. Father would be so proud. Maybe I'd discover how people went in comas and where they were when they went there. Maybe when people went in comas they lived whole other lives, lives just as we lived where they didn't even know they were in a coma at all, they were just living their lives not even aware they were lying in bed for weeks, months, years.

When we were home, Father said, "Thank you for a wonderful

evening. Now, if you will excuse me, I have to make a private phone call, and then I will write for a bit."

"I'll go read awhile before bed."

"That sounds splendid, love." He leaned down and kissed my forehead. I watched him walk off, and noticed how stooped in the shoulders he looked. I went to bed and read *To Kill a Mockingbird* until I fell asleep.

When I woke up the next morning, I didn't remember any of my dreams. I jumped out of bed, stretched and bent down to touch my toes, did twenty-two jumping jacks, washed my face, then dressed and went to the kitchen. I wanted to make Father breakfast. Eggs, toast with marmalade, coffee, and orange juice. I set to work. It was harder than it looked when Mother did it. The eggs were a bit overdone, but the toast popped up fine. I sipped a bit of Father's coffee, and it was too strong.

Father trudged into the kitchen, still wearing the same clothes, his eyes shadowed dark and heavy. "Ah, my princess has made a feast."

I brought everything to the table.

"It looks great." He sat and stared at his food.

I took a sip of my coffee with three spoons of sugar and some cream, sat up straight in my chair and attacked my breakfast, pretending my feelings weren't hurt that he wasn't eating his.

When I was almost done, he'd taken only a few bites, drank the first cup of coffee and was pouring another one when the phone rang. He leapt up to answer it before it barely finished with its first ring. With his back to me, he listened, then mumbled into the phone, listened again, and I heard him moan-cry, "How will I tell her?" He hung up the phone and turned to me, tears spilling over his eyes, his chin trembling as if he was five years old.

I stood up. "What's wrong?"

He went into the living room, sat on the couch, and put his head in his hands.

"What is it? Is Mother okay?" I thought of my horrid secret wishes. I wanted to run fast as I could, dig up the box, shake out that secret wish, and let it blow out to the winds. "Father?"

He mumbled into his hands. "It . . . it's your Grandmother Rosetta. My ma."

"Nonna?"

He looked at me through his fingers, not bothering to take away his hands and face me full on. "That's where your mother went. I couldn't go. I couldn't go. She went to help her. I couldn't go." He scrubbed at his face and dropped his hands to his lap. "I couldn't watch it. I'm a coward."

"What? What are you saying?"

"I didn't want to upset you. We thought there was more time." He stared right through me, whispered, "It was a woman's cancer."

"Nonna has cancer? We have to go to her now." I grabbed his hands with mine and pulled. "Get *up*. We have to go *now*. She needs me. Get up! Hurry!" I pulled harder, but he didn't budge.

He squeezed my hands. "*Listen*. Listen to me, Melissa."

I became still. That still where I knew he was going to tell me something bad. I wanted to put my hands over my ears so I'd never have to hear it. All my insides turned to squishy Jell-O, but my outsides turned to stone.

"She died this morning. She's gone." He released my hands.

I stepped back.

"Our bodies are infallible. Biological machines that break down . . ."

"Stop it!"

"Biological death follows clinical death . . ."

"Stop!"

"Brain cells die from lack of oxygen, *hypoxia*, death of tissue and . . ."

"*No!*"

"Clinical death occurs when biological machine stops breathing and tissues begin their immediate journey to decay, and—"

"*Shut up shut up shut up shut up shut up!*" I slammed my fist into the side of his head. I felt it all the way through my body—the hardness of his skull, the softness of his face, the electricity of how angry I was pass between us.

He put his face back in his hands, and sobbed with his shoulders shaking.

My tongue shaped into a point and flicked out at Father. "You lied! You both *lied*. I should have been the one to help her! You should have sent *me*. I hate you! I hate both of you! All you do is talk about your stupid scientific stuff and your stupid books and your stupid everything is *stupid stupid stupid!*" I stomped my foot until the whole house trembled. "And Nonna's not a biological machine! She's my grandmother and I love her—you *liar liar liar!*" I stomped my foot again. The house shook around the rafters, the floor trembled underneath me. I turned, ran to my room, locked the door, and flung myself on my bed. All the squishy water inside me squirted out of my eyes and nose and soaked the bed covers.

Later, when Father knocked and called out to me, I ignored him. He said, "I've made flight arrangements. We leave at eleven o'clock tomorrow morning." I listened to his breathing, then to his footsteps as he walked away.

Grandmother Rosetta, my nonna, was gone, and they hadn't let me say goodbye. She'd been sick, and no one had told me. Father sent my mother, instead of me. I should have been there. I could have made her better. I hated both my parents. I hated everyone. I hated the whole biological world.

FIFTEEN

Early in the morning, I threw on Peter's clothes and ran to Whale Back to leave a moccasin mail note. The air was chilly, and from above, the mist settled thick and heavy over the valley, as if trying to protect everyone and everything, or to hide things. I didn't understand how everything looked so normal when everything was so wrong.

Inside a sandwich baggie, tucked in Peter's jacket, was the letter to Sweetie I'd hide in the brambles under the rock. In the letter, I told her how I hated my parents, and how nothing would ever feel the same again. How it wasn't fair that her father and grandfather were gone, and my grandparents were gone, even though we loved them. And that she was right, if God did exist, he was mean and cruel. I spewed out all my hurt so hard in places on the page that the paper tore.

At Whale Back, when I placed the letter under the rock, the world fell silent. It was as if all the creatures knew how sad and angry I was and looked at me in pity. The animals began chattering and twittering again as soon as I sat with my back against Whale Back. I turned my thoughts to what Father talked about on the phone last night as I sneaked near to listen.

Father said that against tradition, and to a lot of arguing from some of the family over her immortal soul, Grandmother Rosetta wanted to be cremated, and her ashes thrown into the Pacific Ocean, except for a bit that must be buried in her garden. She wanted those garden ashes poured right into a hole in the ground and then covered up. Father, and his brothers and sisters, agreed to do everything Grandmother Rosetta had asked, even if the rest of the family was against it. I heard him say, "All this religious tradition hullabaloo isn't helping matters. Religion has been the cause of more wars, more—yes, yes, okay, I know."

I couldn't imagine my nonna as a dead body, like I'd seen in Father's books where they did scientific stuff to them, the people who donated their bodies. It was too horrible to think about.

When twenty minutes slugged by, I knew it was time to get ready for the worst days of my life. I went home, bathed and changed, and with my suitcase in my hand, I waited on the steps for the taxi to take

Father and me to the airport. The cat lady worked in her garden, and she turned to me to wave. I pretended I didn't see her. She soon went back to her work, four cats winding around her legs.

During our flight, Father tried to talk to me about what we were passing over, but I stared out of the window as the earth first flew away from me and then later rushed back to me. Once we were in California, we took a cab to Grandmother Rosetta's, and I ran to the room where I always stayed when I visited her, the room she let me decorate the way I wanted to. There were paintings hung about, mine and Nonna's. The walls were a soft purple and trimmed in bright white. Scattered on the floor were lavender throw rugs, on the white painted bed was a lavender bedspread with lots of pillows in different shapes and colors, and white curtains trimmed in lavender that were so light they blew in the wind like angel wings. I lay under the nubby bedspread, and wouldn't talk to anyone. Mother looked in on me, and I was surprised, but glad, when she said not one word, and only smoothed back my hair and then left me alone.

Later that night, Peter came to my room. "Hey, sis," he said as he pressed my shoulder, "I'm sorry." He sat in the rocker and read Grandmother Rosetta's *Reader's Digest Condensed Books*. I didn't speak, and he didn't care, but I felt better having him there and soon drifted away towards sleep. When I woke later, he still sat reading by a tiny light. I wanted to thank him, to jump up and hug him, but I fell asleep again under the eye of my big brother. When I woke again, he was gone, but the book lay on the chair, a reminder he'd stayed and watched over me.

***

It was time for Nonna's memorial. I just couldn't stand it. Grandmother Rosetta's family and her friends spilled in and out of the house. I barely noticed any of them. The world around me was as if in a dream. I floated above the ground, feeling more a ghost than my nonna would be. I'd floated out of my room, floated down the stairs, then floated through her front door, floated to the long black car, floated to the beach, floated on the sand.

As Grandmother Rosetta wanted us to, the memorial service was by the ocean, where she loved to paint. Mother, Father, Peter, and I stood together during the services. After, I walked away to be alone.

Father came to me, held out a vial filled with ashes.

I stared at it.

"Take these ashes and toss them out into the ocean."

I shook my head.

"If you don't, you'll always regret it."

I looked away.

"Princess, this is what she wanted." He took my hand, placed the vial in my palm, and closed my fingers around it. Walking away from me, I saw that his pant legs were wet and sandy, seaweed stuck to his good shoes.

Peter took Father's place by me. After a time, he said, "It hurts and it always will, but don't let it stop you from doing what you need to do to say goodbye."

"I don't want to say goodbye."

"Who does?" He sighed, then said, "It's what Nonna wants, okay?"

I shrugged, but I knew he was right and he knew I knew. He punched me in the arm. "You look smaller, and almost sort of kind of pretty even, for a sister, I guess," then he turned and walked away toward Father and Mother. I tried to imagine him in a white coat, looking at x-rays of people's bones, how he'd heal their hurts one day, make them stronger. That's why he stayed away from us, so he could study and do well in school and become the orthopedic surgeon he wanted to be. That's why he stayed away.

I sat upon the sand and watched the waves reach out to me and then go away, reach out and go away, reach out and go away. Nothing ever stayed still. Nothing ever stayed in one place. I thought of Sweetie on her mountain and pushed her away, too.

I took off my sandals, stood, and walked to the edge where the water foamed up on the sand. I threw the vial out to sea, without opening it, and watched it bob and float, bob and float. I liked that some of Nonna's ashes would float like that, in their own little boat. They would have a journey to who knows where. Maybe someone would find it washed up on the beach, open it, and then pour her out in a strange land, or she'd be swallowed by a whale and taken down to the deep and then up again in a big spray, or a dolphin would nudge it to its friends and they'd play with it. I almost smiled.

Father came to get me and we climbed back into the black car to head back to Grandmother Rosetta's house, though it was within walking distance. There were more cars parked alongside her street, more people standing inside and out. Inside her bungalow, there was food and noise and some people were laughing. I didn't want to hear people laughing, and couldn't understand how anyone could smile, eat, or laugh at all.

I wandered into her garden and called her name, "Nonna? Nonna? Are you here?" Zemry told of people seeing those they loved soon after they'd left the earth. Maybe she was sitting on her lemon tree, or maybe on a star, hidden from me in the daylight, but when night fell, I'd be able to see her there, waving to me, and she'd be glowing from the inside out. I followed her flower- and tree-lined path to her rock and water garden. There were koi, lily, and palms, and it was quiet, except for the bubbling water sounds. Sitting on her bench, I concentrated as hard as I could so she could find me there.

"Where are you?" No answer. I left the garden and went to her studio. When I opened the door and went inside, I was knocked back by everything that was my grandmother. She was everywhere in her painting room. The light filtered in and I stared. Canvases lined the walls of her studio, in order. With my heart flopping around in my chest, I went to each one and studied it, touched it.

She had painted herself from before she was born as a seed of herself in a round shape that looked like a flower bulb, and ending as an old woman with her old hand held over her lower stomach, her eyes staring out at me. In that last one, the largest of them all, I held in my breath. There, in her dark eyes, she had drawn the picture of her burning barn. The fire had all but eaten away the barn, until it was almost all fire. I could hear her breathing that sounded like fire rushing.

There was a note taped to the big painting.

I reached out and took it, my fingers warm and already full of whatever she had to say. It was as if the letter was heavy, and when I opened it, I imagined the words dripping down like paint.

Dear Melissa Rose, I knew you'd come here. Now, I don't want you to cry. Please, no tears. I knew exactly what I wanted and I had it all. I have no regrets, other than I left before I was able to see you again. I'll miss making cookies, and the pasta, and painting—all with you. Look for me in all the beautiful places you will find, *o chiacchere*. I will be with you always. I will never leave you, even if you think you do not feel me. I am in this room with you now, smiling down on you. Right now, as I write this, I feel you. I know you feel me looking at you.

Don't be upset with your parents. I know you will be angry that I didn't ask you to come. But how could I let you see me like this? I will speak frankly, little one. There is vomit, pain, cries, and the silly tears come willy nilly. There is trembling and weakness. There is the end. You know who I am. I am not that helpless shell of a woman. The hollowed out woman consumed by the flames was only a vessel to hold all that I will always be. The soul of me will whisper on the wind. I love you, my *nipotina*. Grow up strong. Be fearless. Always be fearless. And sweet one, do not be hard on your mother, for she loves you. She has done a brave thing to come to me and we have made our amends.

With love to you, *Nonna.*

I read the letter over and over so I'd remember the words, looked around the room, and said to her, "I feel you Nonna, I do." I left her studio to bury the letter under her rose bushes. Peter found me there, staring at the mound of dirt, trying not to cry.

He pulled me up, gave me a hug. I thought how brothers and sisters hardly ever hugged, unless something really bad happened. I thought of the times when he was home and he'd called me silly names, ones that would be hurtful if anyone else said them, but since he was my brother I gave it back as good as I got.

"I have to fly out in two hours. My cab will be here shortly."

"But you just got here."

"I'm sorry. I don't do well at these things. With our parents."

I looked across the garden towards Mother. She stood near the fountain, staring off towards the sea, her usual neat hair blowing wild all over her head like a Medusa. I couldn't see her expression, but her body looked sad and tired.

"Hey, sis? You going to be all right?"

I looked up at my brother, and nodded, afraid to say anything in the case I burst out crying again like a big fat baby.

He gave me a sad crooked smile, then said, "I feel like I'm deserting you. Don't be mad at your big old brother, okay?"

I hugged him tight and hard. "I'm not, Ugly Toad Face."

"Thanks, Booger-Head." He pinched my nose, then quickly turned and strode off, tall, dark haired, and square-shouldered like our father, except more handsome. He turned once and waved. His look said he was glad to be escaping.

I ran to Nonna's studio, looked inside to make sure no one was there, and then took the key from under the rock and locked the door. I didn't want anyone in there. I put the key in my shoe and walked to the house.

Back in the living room, a skinny old man put on Grandmother Rosetta's big band music. Mother frowned at him, but he stood in front of the stereo with his arms crossed over his chest. I knew some of the family, including Mother, wanted to be in a funeral home, with the flowers so strong they didn't smell like flowers anymore since all they were there for was to cover up the smell of death and fluids they use on a body. I knew what they did to the body. I read Father's books.

At regular funerals, they played organ music over the loudspeakers that didn't sound like anything anyone at all liked to hear. And then some preacher would pretend to know the one who died, telling the family things that made no sense to the ones who knew what their loved one was like. And they looked made up like some weird clown with their mouth drawn down in a frown and their body stiff and hard. People would say, "Oh, look how good they look," and it was nothing but a lie. I'd seen those kinds of funerals. So had Nonna. She instead made sure everyone remembered her just as she was.

I looked for my father, and found him standing across the room with a drink in his hand. The drink was full, the ice melted. He looked lost. I went to him, and touched his hands wrapped around the glass, and they were so cold, or maybe mine were, or both. He looked down at me and tried to smile. His two brothers and two sisters circled around him to make him feel safe and strong again, and to make themselves feel that way, too. One was inside the circle, and then they moved out and another in, until all five of them had each been inside the circle to be hugged and petted and held up.

My aunts and uncles touched my head and said how pretty I was. I figured they needed to lie since it was a Relative Rule, but I let them. They had all loved Grandmother Rosetta. Mother walked around checking people's drinks and food, with her black dress on and her stockings without runs and her high-heeled shoes clicking smartly on the floor. She nodded her head when people asked her questions, and told them all about Grandmother Rosetta's cancer. I passed by once to hear her say to a bleached out blonde in a tight navy blue dress, "It was her uterus, you know. She didn't find out until it was too far gone."

I decided I liked the woman, as she stood in her short dress, her red lipstick, her too-blonde hair. She took a sip of her drink with a lemon slice floating in it, looked at Mother and said, "Women get screwed all around. The unfairness of the gods. I mean, taking our breasts and wombs and tearing them apart, the very thing that makes us women. And don't get me started on how men screw us in every sense of the word. Yup, women get mightily *screwed*."

Mother stared at the woman and quickly walked away, but I stood by her and took in her spicy perfume smell. I wanted her to tell me more about women. To tell me how it would be when I grew up. What I should watch out for and what I should dream and be. How I could make sure that the gods were fair.

She looked down at me and said, "Hey, you look like Rosetta would look when she was a girl, all dark and pretty. She was a good friend to me." Then she handed me her drink with its red lip print on the rim. "Drink this up. It'll help you." She winked. "And don't tell on me. I mean, sometimes we all need a little help." She patted her purse. "I got a flask here. I'll just make me another one. I'm never around death without my flask."

I drank it down. It made me want to cough and spit, but I finished every last drop.

She took the empty glass and nodded at me. "I respect that. Yes ma'am. I respect that a lot." Then she walked off on her heels, her hips swaying. I wanted to follow her and see what she'd do next, but I didn't feel like moving. She disappeared behind a group of women, who all turned and watched her, and then whispered to each other with sour faces. As I stood rooted to the floor, I began to feel warm and glowing. The potion she gave me was working. I was light and heavy all at the same time. I looked for the blonde woman after that, to ask for more. From the window, I watched her drive off in a flashy red car, her bleached hair blowing in the wind. I went to lie on the couch, the sun warming me. From there, I saw Nonna's roses blooming, a fat bee climbing, a butterfly, a housefly batting the glass, *tap tap tap tap tap . . . tap tap.*

I awoke to Mother's voice. I said, "What? What?" Then realized she wasn't talking to me. I curled in on myself and stayed quiet, as if still asleep, so I could listen and watch by peeking from between my arms.

The house was quiet, except for Mother and my aunts and uncles standing in a group talking. Everyone else was gone.

Mother said, "Jack, I can take care of things here."

He said, "I don't know."

"Well, I know. Go home and rest. Your sisters and I will sort it all out."

Father pushed back his hair, and it stuck out wild all over his head. "Sort through her things?"

My uncle said, "We can't just leave it all here like this?"

My aunts and my mother looked at each other, as if they knew secrets no one else knew. Mother spoke up. "Your sisters and I will take care of it. It's what women do, what needs to be done." My aunts nodded, wiping their eyes with hankees.

Father wrung his hands. My uncles stood beside their brother, their hands hanging by their sides.

Mother put her hand on Father's shoulder. "Women know how to hold pain in good and tight so it doesn't get in the way. You go home and I'll call you when things are settled here."

I sat up. I didn't know if I wanted to be with the women who were going to hold in their pain. Or, with the men who could leave so they didn't have to feel the pain.

Mother looked at me as I half-sat up on the couch, and as if reading my mind, she asked, "Do you want to stay and help, Melissa?"

I decided, and shook my head. I didn't want to watch them undo what my nonna had done. I was not a woman who could hold her pain and help them do what needed to be done.

Later, when I told her I wanted the paintings in her studio. She said, "We have to consult with all the family before those things are decided."

I went to the studio with my satchel, a pillow and blanket, and refused to leave until it was time to get ready to fly home the next morning. Before I left, I took some of Nonna's paints and paint brushes and put them in my satchel. I made sure I had her favorite boar's hair brush. And I took one of her smaller barn-on-fire paintings, the one she'd painted while I'd visited and painted beside her.

I left the studio, put the key back where she kept it, and with one last look at all I loved, I walked away.

On the return flight home, I again sat and watched as things grew smaller and smaller until they were hidden by clouds and mists.

Father said, "I'm so sorry. I know how strong you've become and I didn't trust you enough." He touched my arm. "Princess, you have to believe I thought I was doing the right thing." He took one of those shuddery breaths, like little kids do, and said, "Or maybe I was just too afraid to face it." He pulled my chin so I had to look at him. "It consumed her. Consumed the very womb I grew in."

I jerked my face away from him.

SIXTEEN

I pretended Grandmother Rosetta was still alive. I pictured her in her studio painting. If my parents tried to talk to me about her, I'd leave the room.

Mother made it her mission to force me to admit she was dead, but I wouldn't. I'd smile at her and say, "Nonna is picking avocados for her salad right now." Or I'd shrug and say, "I bet she is painting a burning barn in a secret place no one knows about."

Father tried to talk to me, but I held my back stiff. He said, "She lived a full life. It's normal and natural for people to get sick and die."

"You don't know what you're talking about."

"Yes. Yes I do."

"Nonna loves her life. She's going to plant an orange tree this year."

"This isn't healthy. Your mother is worried."

I shrugged. But, I was only pretending to my parents, not to myself. I pretended to them that I was waiting for the day she'd take me to Italy. I knew I'd never go to Italy. Ever. I couldn't go to Italy without Grandmother Rosetta. I just didn't want to give my sad feelings to my parents. My feelings were all mine.

I knew Sweetie would be checking at Whale Back to see if I left another message, but I hadn't gone back since the morning I left her the note two weeks ago. It didn't seem right to be happy and run around on the mountain when Grandmother Rosetta couldn't do anything she liked to do ever again. I knew it wasn't what she wanted me to do, but I couldn't help it.

I was lying in bed, listening to Father typing while a cool soft wind blew across me. It was either very late or very early and the dark was both still and alive, like the mountains and valleys always were.

I heard a rustle in the bushes. Then: *tap tap tap tap tap . . . tap tap.*

I stared at the ceiling.

"Wake up."

I turned my head.

Sweetie leaned on the sill. "You about to stay in this here room the rest of your sorry life?"

"Maybe. What's it to you?"

"You got to get back to the mountain. Not right for you to stay inside all'a the time."

"Why not?"

"Huhn. I know *why not*. Mama does it and she gets sicker, she don't get better. She lays there and gets weak and cries and her soul gets tired of living. She's getting to be in her own world half the time. You are not like that."

"Maybe I am."

Sweetie pulled herself in and stood over my bed. She shoved her hands on her hips. "Nuh uh. You are *not*."

"*Shh*! You're going to wake up my mother."

She sat on the side of the bed. "I know how you hurt over your grandmaw. Heck, I miss my Grandpaw ever-day. I miss him and it don't ever leave. But, you can't let that stop you from living. You got to get up and get living ever-day you can."

"But you said you don't hurt." I was crying, but not aloud. It was one of those kinds of crying where the tears are real hot, and they come out slow, like lava. They ooze down the cheeks and into the creases of the neck, spreading on the pillow.

"That's the wrong kind of hurt and you orter know it." She stood.

I turned my head away from her. "Why should you care what I do?"

"I miss having you around, just a bit, I reckon."

When I finally turned my head back to her, Sweetie was gone.

I let the tears give way. My pillow soaked, then my nightgown, then the covers, and then my bed floated, and my whole room filled with my tears until everything, including me, gushed out of the window and on a giant wave followed Sweetie all the way to her mountain. I didn't dream, much.

When morning peeked over the mountains, I was tired of my bed. I pointed, flexed my toes, rose up out of bed, stretched my arms to the ceiling, lowered them out to the sides and turned right and left back and forth, did twenty-five jumping jacks. I washed my face, dressed, and left my room to do chores and eat breakfast.

Mother sipped coffee, and she had a piece of toast, along with strawberry jam from the cat lady, in a plate in front of her. She smiled and I stopped short at that smile. It was a big wide-open smile, one that let all the sunshine outside come through her lips and eyes and into the room. My mother looked beautiful then, beautiful and sweet and real and . . . so . . . so motherly. I wanted to run to her and throw my arms around her, but I felt weird, and I didn't want to move to break the spell.

She said, "Good Morning. Good to see you up. Want some toast?"

"Yes Ma'am, but I'll make it." I popped bread in the toaster, poured myself some orange juice, and when the toast popped up, I put it on a plate, took it to the table, and spread on strawberry jam.

My mother and I sat across from each other, eating. When the toast was gone, she said, "You look so much better today."

I picked up our dishes and took them to the sink.

"Don't worry about those, I'll get them," Mother said.

"Oh. Okay. Well, then, where's my chore list?"

"None today. I've done everything."

"You . . . what?"

She gave up a tiny shrug. "You've been through a lot."

I went to her and hugged her and when she hugged me back, I admitted how good it felt. "Thank you, Mother."

Her voice sounded funny when she said, "Go on. Out. Before I think of something I forgot to do."

I left the house as fast as I could.

I carried in my satchel a picture of my grandmother when she was young. She stood with her foot on the running board of an old truck, her grin spoke joy. It was a favorite photo of mine. She always looked fearless and ready to take on the whole world.

Sweetie was already at Whale Back waiting for me. She smiled a little shy. She didn't say, *I'm glad you're here*, or *I'm sorry about your nonna*. She didn't have to say it, I knew she felt these things without her opening her mouth.

We slowly walked to Jabbering Creek. I took off my socks and shoes; Sweetie took off her boots. We put our feet into the cool water. I showed her the photo.

Sweetie took it from me and studied it. "You look like two peas sleeping in a pod." She handed the photo back to me. "Me and your grandmaw would be friends. I can tell."

"I want to be just like her."

Out of her pocket she pulled the wooden bird Zemry had whittled and painted. "This here's for you to keep for a while. It makes me smile, so it will make you smile."

"But Zemry made that for you."

"And since he made it for me, I can do what I want with it, right?"

I smiled thank you to her and put the bird into my pocket.

Our shoulders touched, our arms touched, and every now and then our little toes touched together in the water. I leaned my head on Sweetie's head and she didn't move away.

I didn't want anything else to change. I wanted everything to stay just as it was right then. Forever.

SEVENTEEN

It was well into summer, and the days weren't as hot as I thought they'd be. Sweetie said the mountains always had just right weather. I didn't sweat as I did in other places I'd lived, like Georgia, Florida, and Louisiana. Way down south, the air was so thick and wet, I couldn't breathe right, and had to take in little bits of air so I wouldn't feel as if I was drowning. Sometimes it'd get so hot, I'd have to stay inside with glass after glass of lemon-iced tea. Back then, I'd loved staying inside and watching television all day.

The cat lady said we were having a cooler summer than usual, and we had better enjoy it. In the spring we'd had what she called a Blackberry Winter, when all the blackberry blooms were out and a late frost sneaked through. Zemry, Sweetie, and the cat lady seemed to know things about weather that I didn't unless I watched a weather report. I wanted to ask Father what he thought about that in his scientific mind, but I never did.

Some places Sweetie and I explored on the mountain were so thick with trees and bushes, that if it rained gentle enough, I didn't know it at first. I'd sit in the shade and hear the pattering as it hit the leaves and wait for it to reach my face. The creek water was cool, and just right for sitting by and eating a picnic lunch, and that's just what Sweetie and I did many times.

My thirteenth birthday was a few weeks away and I had been feeling restless. I couldn't sleep right. Even with the cool breeze, I was too hot. I'd throw off the covers, then I'd get cold, and put them back on. I had nightmares about falling off the ridge and the ghost boy that Sweetie called a haint taking me away from my family, or a bear ripping my face open, or that I died and couldn't find Grandmother Rosetta. I dreamed other people died—my parents, Sweetie, Peter. I couldn't stand it.

To make things worse, Mother had taken me to the store to buy my first bra and I hated how it pinched. Sweetie had laughed at it, and that made me itchy-hot mad. She had nothing to put in a bra and said she was glad about it, but mine seemed to grow overnight. I'd picked out a blue bra and a white one. The saleslady had measured me while I stood with my face burning.

After a week of all that weirdness, I woke up feeling fat and cranky, and I had a pimple rearing up out of my forehead and another on my chin. My stomach hurt, my legs hurt, and my head hurt. I moped around the breakfast table, crabby as can be. My new breasts were sore and the bra mashed them. After breakfast, I went to the bathroom, and while I peed, I looked at my panties. Blood. It had happened to me. I didn't want it to, but there it was. Bright red against my white cotton underwear. I took them off, careful not to get any nasty blood on my leg. I stood half-naked at the sink and scrubbed at the red, watching the blood go from red to pink and then finally run clear. Down the drain it went, away from me.

There was more. I grabbed a wad of toilet paper and wiped my leg, wondered how much of it would come out. I ran a tub of hot water, and climbed in. After the water turned lukewarm, I turned on the hot, and laid my head against the faucet. I stayed in there long enough for Mother to knock on the door to see what I was up to.

"I'm taking a bath, Mother."

"In the morning? And for this long?"

"What's wrong with that?"

"Well, you usually take off to the mountain and bathe when you get back, before dinner."

"Well, today is different. Why can't I do something different? Why do you care?" I knew sassing her would get me in trouble, but the crabby feeling took over. "Can't I have some privacy around here?"

"Are you sick? You've been acting strangely."

"I'm not sick. I'm . . . just . . . it's nothing."

She didn't say anything back, at first; I thought she left. Then she said, "Dry off and come see me in my bedroom."

"Yes Ma'am." I stepped out of the tub, toweled off. I'd read the books Mother had given me, but I still felt weird. I wadded up some toilet paper and stuffed it between my legs. After pulling on clean panties, I pushed the wad in as far as I could to stop the flow. I stared at myself in the mirror and didn't see anything different. But behind my eyes, I was different.

In my parent's room, my mother sat on her bed with a bag beside her. She patted the bedspread and I carefully sat next to her, hoping nothing gooshed out.

"Well, it's happened, hasn't it?"

"What?" I didn't want to say it. I was too embarrassed.

"Your monthly period. I knew something was up."

I shrugged.

"It's earlier than I had mine. I was fourteen. But, my sister, well, she was early with everything. Had more trouble out of that girl." She eyed me. "But, I know you won't be like her, will you?"

"I don't know what you're talking about. I hardly know Aunt Beth."

"Who does? She lives in Paris and . . . oh never mind." She handed me the bag. "I trust you know what to do? You read the books I gave you?"

"Yes Ma'am."

"Read them again."

"Yes Ma'am." I stood up and there was a gush between my legs. I squeezed my legs together.

"You know what this means, don't you?"

I nodded, even though I wasn't sure what she was talking about.

"You're a young woman now. And certain responsibilities come with being a young woman. I want you to think about that. Now, go get fixed up." She waved me away.

I grabbed the bag, went to the door, and stopped with my hand on the knob. "How did you know?"

"Mothers know these things. At least some of them do. Be glad you didn't have *my* mother. She never told me a thing about anything. I had to find out about life and men and womanly happenings all on my own. It was excruciating. That's why I gave you the books ahead of time. So you wouldn't be afraid. My mother made it into something dirty. I don't want you to see any of this as dirty. It's not." She looked at me. "Okay?"

"Okay." I turned the knob, ready to make my escape.

"Melissa?"

I didn't bother to hide my sigh or to turn back around to her. "Yes Ma'am."

"You've gotten taller, and thinner. I don't want you to think I haven't noticed how you've grown and how pretty you look."

I turned to face her.

She picked at her bedspread. I all of a sudden noticed that her hair, which usually looked perfect, was untidy, and her face was flushed. She didn't even have her stockings on yet. She stared at the squares she made with her finger on the bedspread. "I wanted to let you know that I've grown used to your hair. It becomes you. I've just been stubborn about it."

"You okay, Mother?"

She brushed back her hair, looked at me. "Your father. He's been acting strange, don't you think?"

"How do you mean?"

"Oh, I don't know. I mean, he's been, well, distracted."

"He's working on his novels. Like he always does, isn't he? I mean . . . " I tried to think about how Father had been acting, but I hadn't been paying much attention to him. "Maybe he misses Nonna."

She raised her eyebrows in a way that said *oh, I'm so glad you finally admit your Grandmother Rosetta is gone.*

I looked at her in a way that said *don't talk about it, please, don't talk about Nonna to me.*

"Yes. I know he misses her, but it's more than that. He bought a new aftershave. And some new shirts that he's never worn before. The kind he said he hated. And those boots. Why would he wear boots like that? Teenager kind of boots?" Her eyes were red-rimmed and her lashes wet. "And he's growing a mustache. He said it makes him look younger."

"Maybe he's just trying new things. Like you do with your recipe books."

She smiled, but it wasn't much of a smile, and said, "Maybe you're right. Well." When she said, "well," she said it in the *I have things to do* way, with a clap of her hands on her thighs. She stood up. "Go on, get yourself fixed. There's aspirin in the cabinet. I suggest you take a few of them." She turned away and fiddled with the pillows, plumping them up and straightening the lace.

"Mother?"

Without looking at me, she waved me away. "Close the door behind you, please, dear."

I wanted to go to her. Put my arms around her and pat her back. But I didn't. I left, closed the door behind me, and then hurried to the bathroom with the bag. I hated becoming a young woman, hated the feeling of blood coming out of me there. I hated that my breasts were growing. I hated the changes in me that were already either there or fast coming. I wanted things to always stay as they were, as they had been before Grandmother died and before blood flowed and before my body changed.

Inside the bag was a box. I sighed, opened the box, took out a pad, and fiddled with it until it was fixed right to my panties. I'd seen the commercials for tampons, and though I'd thought it was gross, I wished I had those. As I walked, the thick pad was like I wore a little saddle. I swallowed the aspirin, and put on a pair of my old baggy red pedal pushers, just in case. Over that I wore Peter's button-down shirt, long enough to reach past my behind, so no one could see any bulge.

On the way to Tablet Rock, I almost turned around and went home. Sweetie was already there with her back against the poplar. Her legs were straight out in front of her, and she had her head back, looking up at the sky. I flopped down next to her without saying anything. She said, "How many times that makes me not late!" She grinned.

I shrugged.

After a while she said, "You sure a quiet one today."

I finally told Sweetie about all the changes. I wanted to talk to a friend about them, wanted her to say, *Oh, I know! The same things happened to me and I hate it.*

She looked at me with her eyes big and round. "That happening to you right now?"

"Yeah."

"Well, I am willing it not to happen to me." She nodded towards my chest. "I don't want them titties bound up like that, either."

"Don't call them that," I said. "That's *gross*."

"Well, them teats then."

"They're *breasts*. Girls have *breasts*, not what you said."

"Animals have teats, and they don't be worried about what I call them."

"We are *humans*. That's why we *evolved* and they didn't, so we can call things by their *proper* names."

"Whatever you call them, and that other stuff, I *will not* get that disease."

"It's not a *disease*. God, Sweetie!"

Sweetie crossed her arms over her chest. "Willing it all away."

"You can't do that. You can't force natural orders of things to happen or not happen."

"Huh. Maybe I can. Maybe this magic I got will make it where I don't got to do anything I don't want to." She raised up an eyebrow and pointed to my crotch. "Especially that."

I rolled my eyes and stood up. "I'm going home. I don't feel well."

"It's that stuff. Makes a body ornery and strange."

"I'll see you later." Right then, she looked like a little girl to me.

She asked, "We're still like we was, right? I didn't mean to speak so sharp. Just don't think sometimes, I reckon."

"I better go."

She didn't ask me to stay, but the hurt seeped out of her pores.

As I walked home, I wondered if things were changing too fast for me to keep up. I wondered what it all meant. Grandmother Rosetta dying, the blood coming, Mother's talking to me as she had, all signs of the wind changing direction. No matter what I wished for, it didn't make a difference, change still came because the world was always changing and evolving, even if we couldn't see all of it until we looked back in time. Father was right about that.

At the bottom of the mountain, I stood still in the grass with the sun full on my face and I didn't want the day to end, even if I hated the day in my cranky mood. Each day that passed meant I was closer to summer's end. I didn't want the fall to come, and then cold dark winter, all the leaves dropping to the ground, leaving the bare sticks whistling in the wind.

EIGHTEEN

I felt like my old self again, almost. I woke, made my bed, stretched and touched my toes, turned side to side, but didn't do my jumping jacks in case that made the blood come back. In the bathroom, I checked my panties. Nothing there for the second day, so I was free. Over a breakfast of eggs and toast, I thought about the rest of the summer, thought about two days ago when Mother took me to the drugstore and I saw the ice cream shop that just opened. As we drove by, I'd wanted one of those ice creams more than anything.

We'd gone to the drugstore so Mother could teach me how to buy my own sanitary napkins, as if I needed a lesson in front of everyone. I told her I was not using any more of those little saddles. She said I could lose my innocence if I used tampons, and when I asked her what she meant by that, she blushed and said, "I think you know what I mean." I wasn't stupid, but I just wanted to hear her say it. She was in the dark ages, for I'd read in magazines how things like that didn't happen.

She pointed to the pads, and not wanting to draw any attention with her there, I took the box from the shelf. I'd come back later and get what I wanted with my own money. While the man rang up the napkins, I stood at the counter and thought I'd pass out and die right there on the spot. What if any of the Circle Girls saw me buying pads? Or worse, T. J. and his Posse?

Mother stood beside me, her hand on my shoulder. Her hand was so heavy, it was as if I were pushing through the linoleum floor. I wished she *would* push me through a hole in the floor where I could disappear. When we were back in the car and driving away, she turned to me and said, "That wasn't so bad, was it?"

I stared out the car window.

She stopped the car across the street from the sign that read, *New! Ice Cream Delights! Open for Business!* and it was all I could do to stay seated in the car while Mother bought flowers from an old woman who peddled them from a cart. I watched kids walk out of the door, licking their cold treats and I was filled with want. Ice cream wasn't all I wanted. Jeremy stood with his back to the wall, drinking a Coca-Cola.

He wore a white shirt and jeans and was so handsome I couldn't breathe. I wondered what he'd been doing all summer, and with whom. I decided right then I would talk Sweetie into having ice cream. In town.

Since then, all I could think of was Jeremy and ice cream and town, Jeremy ice cream town. Jeremy eating ice cream in town. I even had a dream where we held hands, and then he leaned over and kissed me right on the lips, long and slow. I woke up with my hand between my legs and was so embarrassed, I went to the bathroom and washed my hands twice. I couldn't ever tell Sweetie about that. It was a secret that would stay out of our locked secrets box, out of the diary, and inside my own head.

I met Sweetie at Turtlehead Rock, filled with excitement over Jeremy and ice-cream and town—normal almost-teenaged things. I'd first need to make things easy between us again, since I'd been so smart with her before. We picked wildflowers for Miss Mae and Mother, and I talked about old television shows I used to watch, especially ones that had ice cream parlors in them, like Mayberry RFD with Sheriff Taylor and Aunt Bee.

Sweetie kept looking at me sideways until I finally asked, "What?"

"You sure are itchy over something."

"Am not."

"I know you."

"What do *you* know? You think you know everything. Well, you don't."

Sweetie turned away from me.

I was ashamed and not doing a good job of making things right. I picked an especially pretty flower in different shades of orange, red, yellow—the colors were so bright it made me dizzy to look at them, they swirled and danced and caused spots to float behind my eyes. It was a perfect Sweetie flower. I stuck it out to her. "I'm sorry. I haven't been a good friend, and a worse bound-sister."

She didn't even act stupid about it by slapping the flower away, or telling me to leave her alone or anything like that. She took the flower, held it up, and I saw it reflected in her eyes, swirling bright colors, and I became dizzy all over again. She said, "I spoke sharp to you more'n once, right? I surely have."

After that, we picked flowers without saying much, until we had thick bouquets.

Sweetie sat on a log and put her flowers on the ground beside her.

She whispered, "You over that stuff yet?"

"Yeah."

"What's it like?"

"Well, it kind of hurts, and it's gross. And Mother made me buy *pads* in front of a man. It was *so* embarrassing."

She looked down at the ground. "Mama has that ever now and again. I got to make them pads and burn them when they's full." She made a disgusted face. "I just don't want it, Lissa. I don't want them kinds of things to happen to me. That's why I got to will that stuff away with magic."

"Well, it's a fact; us women are mightily *screwed*."

Sweetie's jaw slung open in the first wide-eyed surprised look I'd ever seen from her. Then she laughed so hard, tears ran down her cheeks. I began laughing with her. We sat on the log and laughed until the whole mountain echoed with it. Nonna swooped down and sat on the log with us and laughed just as hard as we did. The joke was on all us women.

When it was time for Sweetie to go home, we stopped at Whale Back to plan our next meeting place. I took a deep breath. I hated to ruin all the laughing and fun but hoped Sweetie would surprise me and be happy about things. I wrote in the ground, *ice cream in town.*

She looked at me as if I had lost my mind.

I underlined it.

"No!" She stamped her foot. "You done lost your pea-picking mind?"

"Why not?"

"No town. I got to brand your hide with that message?"

"I don't get it. What's the difference? If you go to school and get stuff from the church, why not town?"

She stomped on *ice cream in town.* "If I do not go to school, the school police come looking for me, and if they come, Mama gets the shotgun, and if she does that, they will take her away. Then what will come of me?" She scuffled over the stomp marks until no letters were showing. "And I told you why I got to go to that church." She slit her eyes at me. "No laws or sick mama's say anything about ice cream in town."

"I'm just saying it will be fun." I smiled big enough to show a mouthful of teeth, then said, "Don't you want some ice cream? It's my treat; I have an allowance."

"Not about money. Don't you know me by now, Silly Goose

Head?" She turned on her heel and ran off into the woods.

"Wait, Sweetie! Don't run away." I ran after her halfway down the trail, then stopped. I called out, "Well, if you don't want to go, fine! I'm going. I want some ice cream." I waited. I didn't hear anything, so I tried again. "We can't spend the whole summer running around here. I'd like to try something different. A movie, some ice cream, that amusement park up in the sky. *Something.*"

Up ahead, I saw her blonde head appear then disappear behind the trees. I turned around and stomped home, forgetting the wildflowers, including the swirly colored one, on the ground.

***

I woke the next day, jumped a few jacks, then cleaned up and headed to town. I wore a yellow and white sundress Mother bought me that wasn't too bad. It was a long walk from my house, but walking was a lot easier since Sweetie and I had run all over the mountain almost every day. It was strange not heading up to the mountain to see her, but in a way I felt free and easy. I swung my arms back and forth and thought about ice cream, but mostly about Jeremy.

At the ice cream shop, my stomach did a flip. Through the glass, I saw T. J. sitting at a table with Deidra. I sucked in a good breath, made myself stand up tall, and walked bold as anyone pleased through the door. A little bell rang as I entered and I liked how happy it sounded. In the corner, a big Wurlitzer jukebox played "Tutti Fruity." T. J. and Deidra turned to look at me and it was all I could do to keep walking to the counter. My legs were jiggly and jerkity when I passed them. I expected to feel T. J.'s fist in my back, and a tingle shot up my spine.

What was so strange or wrong about ice cream on a summer's day? Peter said he used to do it with his friends during summer vacation. He said they'd take towels and run outside and be drenched by the rain, then hit each other with the wet towels. He said when they lived in Baton Rouge, they ran behind the mosquito trucks or rode their bikes behind them, and never worried about growing two heads or their fingers falling off. Sometimes he'd lie pretend-dead on his back with his feet in the air while his friends pointed at him and laughed. He said to earn money they'd do chores for old ladies, or pick up bottles to return to the store. With the money they'd go to the movies, buy popcorn, Milk Duds, Sugar Babies, Zero's, Snickers, and something cold to drink.

I'd dreamed of doing those things myself one day with a friend. Sweetie didn't want to do anything. For almost the whole summer, I'd been running around on a mountain and hadn't once ridden a bike behind a mosquito truck, or slapped someone with a wet towel, or swam in a pool.

The man in the apron cleared his throat, asked, "Have you made up your mind yet, Miss?"

"*Oh.* Yes. I mean, no, I was thinking." I smiled at him.

"Take your time." He began washing glasses and spoons.

The treats were listed on a board tacked to the wall. Lemonade, limeade, root beer floats, sodas, cherry smash, banana split, egg cream, cones, shakes, malteds, and if I wanted, sprinkles and cherries to put on top. My mouth watered and my eyeballs bulged with the choices. I said, "I think I'm ready."

The man smiled as he wiped the counter in front of me.

I hesitated, waiting to hear T. J. say, "Fat Ass don't need any treats, she's fat enough already." He wasn't saying a thing. I gave my order. "I'll have a vanilla cone, please. With sprinkles."

"That'll be all for you?"

"And a cherry on top?"

"Coming right up."

I sat on the stool at the counter and watched the man swirl my ice cream into the cone, spoon multi-colored sprinkles on top, and with a pair of tongs, pluck a cherry from a bowl. He stuck it on top, winked at me, and then plucked out another cherry and put it next to the first one. When he handed it to me, I gave him my money, and immediately ate one of the cherries. It popped inside my mouth with a big burst of sweet. I chewed it, thinking about Sweetie's cherry pie. It made me both mad and sad. I told the man, "Thank you."

"You're welcome. Come back again."

I slid off the stool and walked to the door to wait outside for Jeremy.

T. J. said, "Where's that weirdo friend of yours?"

I licked the sprinkles around the other cherry and kept walking.

I was at the door when he called after me louder, "You got tired of all her stupid shit, huh? No more weird birds of a feather weirding together?"

With my hand on the doorknob, I stopped and wondered what I should say, or if I should get out before it turned ugly.

The man in the apron said, "No cussing in here, boy. Get out if you want to flavor the ice cream with any of that language."

I turned to face T. J., "I *am not* tired of her. She's my friend." I was not a good friend, and certainly not a bound sister. Why else would I be having ice cream hoping a boy would come by, instead of finding out where Sweetie was right then? Was she waiting at Whale Back Rock? Would she give in and meet me for ice cream? I wanted to defend myself. I wanted more to defend Sweetie.

Deidra giggled, of course.

I said, "She's caring for her sick mother."

Deidra smoothed her hair. "My mom says that girl is nutso from having no dad and a crazy mom. She said Sweetie belongs in the nut house instead of running all over like a wild animal."

"We never seen where she goes." T. J. eyed me up and down with his lip curled as he always curled it when he thought he was smart. "Does she live in a cave with bears?" He screeched like a hyena. "Do they have a black cauldron where they boil children?"

Deidra's mouth puckered. "Mom said no telling what made them *that way.*" She said *that way* as if it was something nasty in her mouth. "She said Sweetie's mom was nothing but a tart swinging her hips around when they went to school together."

My ice cream melted onto my hand as I stood there. The other cherry slid off to the floor. I didn't stoop to pick it up. I said, with too much pride for the wrong reasons, "Sweetie and Miss Mae have a nice clean house. I've been there plenty of times." I liked how their eyes got wide and curious looking. "And Miss Mae is beautiful. And it's quiet there." I wanted to say more, but I imagined Sweetie's face if she heard me talking about them.

"Goody goody gumdrop for you," Deidra said.

T. J. curled up both sides of his mouth, said, "I bet they hunch in their cave and cast spells. *Wiiitchesssss.*" He cackled like a cartoon witch and made his fingers into claws.

The heat started in my chest and worked its way to my face. "Both you shut your fat mouths!"

T. J. laughed an ugly laugh. Deidra looked at me as if she thought I was as crazy as she thought Sweetie was.

"Kids, I'm going to have to ask you to leave if you can't behave in my shop." The man had both hands on the counter and leaned forward. "Miss, go on outside with your ice cream, it's dripping all over the floor." He shook his head at me. "Kids, they don't ever change. I'll need a mop now." He turned and went through a door to the back.

T. J. turned to me, crossed his eyes, and whispered. "*Craazzzzy* people."

Deidra snickered.

I hesitated. Nobody wanted to be branded as crazy. It was bad enough to be fat and four eyed, but to be crazy was an even worse fate. I opened the door and hurried outside. They didn't follow me and I was so filled with relief I almost forgot why I was there, to wait for Jeremy. I ate what was left of my ice cream with my back against the wall. I ate without feeling any joy and that made me mad.

I was still there when a group of kids from school herded through the door. They didn't act as if they noticed me. Jeremy wasn't with them, so I eased down the wall until I was folded into a tight ball, my arms around my knees and my head resting on my arms. I thought about what T. J. and Deidra said. Maybe Miss Mae *was* crazy. I had never met a crazy person before. I'd never known a mother to stay in bed all the time while her daughter had to do all the work and cooking, and ran out in the middle of the night.

It wasn't long before the kids stampeded out, and still no one bothered to say a word to me. A few of the girls looked down at me and then quickly away, but not before I saw their smirks. When T. J. and Deidra came out, they whispered to each other, laughed, and then walked down the street. T. J. picked up a rock and threw it at the side of the building, so close to my head, I jumped up. This made him laugh even louder while Deidra giggled behind her hand.

T. J. called out, "Better be careful. That old witch might shoot at you, too." They both ran off after the herd.

The magic of the day had left me. I thought if Jeremy could just come by and see me sitting there, his heart would melt. I could tell him about Sweetie and they could become friends. The three of us would explore the mountain together and one day, when Sweetie wasn't around, I could kiss Jeremy's lips for real.

I sat for another eleven minutes before I gave up and ran to the mountain. I ran to Whale Back, my stupid dress catching on twigs and stickers, and called out for Sweetie. No message was scribbled in the dirt, no moccasin message under the rock. I waited for an hour and three minutes for her to come, but she never did. All the way home, I mumbled to myself about how selfish she was. How she never wanted to do anything other than run on the mountain. I stomped through the trail and fussed about how she should understand I wanted to go to stupid town some-stupid-time. All the way home, I made myself feel as if I was the good one and Sweetie was the mean one.

Back at the house, I cleaned up and thought about things. Once clean, I went to the living room and asked Mother for more new clothes. She was so surprised; she closed her poetry notebook, looked at me, and said, "I think we can go to my dress shop first thing tomorrow." She stood up and smoothed her skirts. "This is so exciting, isn't it?"

"Yeah. I guess so."

"We can have lunch while we're out."

"That's fine, Mother."

***

The next day, I tried on lots of outfits before picking a dress, different colored tops, jeans, shorts, sandals, flip flops, boots, and t-shirts. Mother jabbered all the way home about the exquisite dresses and the exquisite taste and the exquisite who cares exquisite *blah bleah blork bleep*. I didn't care one exquisite bit.

The day after that, before I could let myself feel shame over my need to see Jeremy, I spilled more money from my bank to use at the ice cream shop. I wore my new jeans and royal blue pullover shirt, so I wouldn't look as if I was trying too hard to look any certain way but a girl going to get ice cream.

Mother stopped me at the door. "Where are you off to in your new outfit?"

"To the ice cream shop."

"Oh no, Melissa. You've lost weight."

"All the kids go there."

"Sweet-tea, too?"

I swallowed my guilty feelings. "No, she's not going."

"Well, I suppose if it's a kids' hangout, there's nothing wrong with a tiny bit of ice cream." She reached for her gloves on the hall table and put them on. "I'll drop you there and do a little shopping for me this time."

Waiting for Mother to get ready, I had an argument in my head. Jeremy and I could walk hand in hand and then he might kiss me, more than once. Yet, I wanted to put on my boy's clothes and run wild in the woods with Sweetie, never caring about becoming-a-woman kinds of things.

Mother picked up her purse and keys, humming with such a happy sound that I almost felt sorry for all the trouble I'd caused her all my life.

In the car, she tapped her nails on the steering wheel.

"Mother?"

"Yes, dear?" With her right hand, she searched through her purse for her lipstick.

"Why don't you like Sweetie?"

"Now what kind of question is that?"

"I don't know."

"That girl is trouble. You see all those scars? Someone's getting to that girl, and I don't want you in the middle of it."

"That's not how it is."

"Then how is it?"

I didn't know how to explain it without giving away Sweetie's secrets. Besides, it was all sounding weird to me, being away from it as I had been lately. "She has accidents is all."

"Oh, Melissa. You are so naïve. You always have been." She smeared pink lipstick across her mouth, smacked her lips together, then asked, "How long do you need with your little friends?"

I wanted to shout that they were not my *little friends*, but instead I answered, "Is an hour and a half too long?"

"No, not at all. I need some stockings and a new scarf. Yes, and a new dress will turn your father's eye again, don't you think?"

"I guess so."

"I saw a rather modern one the other day. I may try it. And maybe I'll get my hair cut into one of those new hair do's like I saw on one of your television shows. And some go-go boots, you think? I bet he notices me then."

I stared at her as if she were an alien.

She glanced at me. "What?"

"Nothing."

"Sometimes a woman has to do things, that's all. You'll understand one day."

I didn't tell her that maybe I understood a little bit. Maybe I felt some of those things about Jeremy. It was weird to think I could compare myself to my mother, but at the same time, it made me feel closer to her. I couldn't sort through all the thoughts rushing around in my brain so fast I couldn't keep them straight. My brain was the most alive part of my whole body.

She dropped me in front of the ice cream shop and after I peeked in and saw Jeremy wasn't there, I didn't even bother going inside. I again stood with my back against the wall and hoped the other kids would stay away. After twenty-one minutes of waiting, I saw him before he saw me and my heart beat so hard I was sure he'd see it through my shirt.

I timed it so that when he was at the door, I was there, too. Without looking at me, he said, "Have you seen Beatrice?"

"N-n-n-no. I h-h-haven't." I tried to control my tongue, but it didn't listen. I tried to breathe, but my breath caught. "I was g-g-going to g-g-get some ice cream." I swallowed hard, swallowed the old Melissa down and smiled in the way I saw Mother smile at Father. Breathe. In. Out. "Are you g-going to get some ice dream, Jeremy?" I couldn't believe I said ice dream. I was an idiot.

His eyes glittered and he suddenly looked happy. My heart jumped out and landed right on his lips, but his lips shouted out, "There she comes!" He pushed me out of the way. My shoulder burned where he touched me. He shouted again as he waved his hand in the air, "Hey, you, over here!"

Beatrice skipped to him, her red ponytail swinging from side-to-side in a way mine never, ever would, even if it were still long instead of chopped short. Jeremy stood with his thumbs hooked into his back pockets, and his chest stuck out in that way boys do when they're showing off. I never had a boy stick out his chest and put his hands in his pockets like that for me. When she was near him, she stopped, put her hands behind her back, and looked down at the ground. Jeremy reached out and pulled her ponytail. Beatrice screeched a silly giggle. They stood like that for a while, until they finally walked into the ice cream parlor, their hands almost touching, but not quite. That almost touch pierced my heart more than if they had held hands.

When Mother came to get me, I had gobbled three ice cream cones with extra sprinkles and a napkin full of cherries, not bothering to hide my piggy ways from Jeremy and Beatrice. They didn't notice anyway, as Jeremy drank his chocolate malted, and Beatrice an egg cream. I didn't even care if T. J. walked in and called me a fat fool. That was surely what I was.

That night I lay in bed thinking how I'd torn apart the bond between Sweetie and me. All over silly things like a silly boy and silly cold ice cream and silly everything. I hurt Sweetie for the stupid reason I thought Jeremy was handsome. I had always thought I wasn't pretty enough, good enough, skinny enough, anything enough, to have anyone like Jeremy. But as I sat in that ice cream parlor slurping ice cream and watching him, I saw how he really was. How he giggled like a girl, and how his teeth didn't look clean. And when he said he didn't understand why people thought the mountains were so great, he liked the flattest part of Kansas better, I knew I was a fool for thinking I loved him. I was stupid enough to lose someone like Sweetie, the best friend I ever had, my very own bound blood sister, over a boy, and worse, a boy like Jeremy.

I fell asleep and the dream took over. I was covered in mist. My body could not move. My brain did all the work. *Sweetie sang as she sat in a tree. She turned into a bird and flew away from me.* When I woke, a storm blew. Tree limbs whipped and rain hit the roof loud and hard. When it thundered, the floor shook. Lightning ripped the sky. I hid in my room, not aware of the time or caring. I was shamed. I'd told Miss Mae I'd watch after Sweetie and all I'd done was be mean to her and desert her.

Father tapped on his typewriter.

Mother breezed in with a bowl of grapes. "Snack time."

"I'm not hungry right now."

"Well . . . "

"I just want to read a while." I knew Mother wouldn't take the hint, not when she had the look that said she had something to tell me.

She sat on the side of the bed with her hair in the new cut. It was to her chin, and the two sides slid to points that fell forward over her cheeks when she bent down. The back of the cut was a bit shorter than the front. Her new dress smelled like rosewater from the iron, and was too short for her, in colors too loud for her. Yet, when she didn't open her mouth and say ugly things, she almost looked like a mother I could snuggle up to and giggle with about girl things. I thought about the days before, when she'd almost seemed like the kind of mother I dreamed about having. But she always ruined it.

"I was at my ladies' club and heard more news about that Sweet-tea and her mother."

I pretended I didn't care, but inside I became very still.

"You can do what you want with this information, but I'm just letting you know." Mother sighed, and in that sigh I thought maybe she didn't really want to tell me, but I wasn't sure. "I told you how there's a rumor that girl's father lives here in town. Seems Sweet-tea's mother ran around when she was younger. You know, kind of loose. And she had her baby out of wedlock, with a married man." She pushed back her hair. "Wasn't all her fault. Sweetie's grandmother was a piece of work. Ran off and left her when she was so small. And that grandfather—he was a strange one."

"Sweetie's father is dead."

"No, he's not. He, a married man, and Sweet-tea's mother had a torrid affair when she was still a teenager. Sweet-tea is the product of that. Her grandfather took care of them both, I give him that. But there's a long line of strange behavior up there where they live on that mountain. All kinds of stories."

My smile dropped bit by bit into a frown, and then I asked, "If Sweetie's father is here, why doesn't he go see her?"

"Besides the fact that who knows why men do the things they do?" She squared her shoulders. "Anyway, they say her mother most times can't get out of bed with her dark moods and some phantom sickness," she said. "And, I hear there's been shooting up there? That is unacceptable. You could be hurt, or worse."

I watched Mother's dark red lipsticked mouth move. I saw the ugly words spill out and fall on my bedspread. She still had the bowl of grapes held out to me, and her perfect red-tipped fingernails looked like vulture talons. I wanted to stop her from spilling out those awful words, but my jaws locked down.

"Sweat-tea's mother is trash. No wonder Sweat-tea's father walked away from them for another woman. Some women can't hold onto their man . . . men." She tilted up her chin.

I faced Mother with a fury. "Don't say that about Sweetie's mother! She's good. I've seen her, and I like her and you don't know anything. You don't know *anything*. It's not like that. Sweetie's father is a war hero. He sailed the ocean for treasures! It's romantic and sweet and I won't have you talk like that about them!"

Mother stood and pointed her finger at me. "Why, don't you yell at me, young lady. You're too intelligent to believe that rubbish or you wouldn't be leaving Sweet-tea to go traipsing off to ice cream parlors to find new friends."

The last part stung. I buried my head in my pillow. As her heels clicked out of my room, I said into the starched cotton pillowcase, "You don't know anything. It's not l-like that."

All that day, I lay thinking, reading, wondering, listening to the storm until late afternoon, then I rose and went to Father's study, knocked and went in. He sat in his leather chair reading pages from his book.

"Can I talk to you?"

"What is it, Princess?" He put down the pages as if he couldn't bare to look away from them.

"It's about Sweetie, and her parents."

"I heard all that from you mother. I don't care about gossip."

"It's not that." I stood by his chair and tried to get him to look at me, instead of glancing down. "I think Sweetie's cursed or has magical powers or something. I mean, I know you say everything is science, but some things aren't making sense."

"Huh?" He wrote something on the paper. "What's that?"

"I don't know. She isn't like other kids. And I'm confused. I want to be her friend, but sometimes I want to be like other kids, like the popular ones, or even the not-so-popular ones."

He cleared his throat and said, "Look, I know you're going through *things* right now. Your mother talked to me. Those are natural things. Nothing to worry over. Why, in some tribal communities—"

"*What?* No! That's not what I'm talking about." I looked down at my shoes. "I mean. I'm trying to talk to you about Sweetie. There's something not right." I whispered, "She doesn't feel pain. She says she'll never die."

He was reading. "It'll all work out." He patted my hand. "Right now, your father needs to finish this scene. I'm stumped. You see, there's this girl and—"

I left his study before he could finish telling me, and went to the kitchen. Mother was at the stove, stirring something. She ignored me and I knew I was getting the silent treatment. The ignoring would go on until I gave her a proper apology.

I stared at her back until she finally turned around. With her hands on her hips, she raised an eyebrow that said, *Well, I'm waiting.*

"All you know how to d-do is make things ugly. Even yourself. You're buying new s-stuff and have a new hairdo, but you're still the same inside. No wonder Father stays in his study or off d-doing whatever he does. He wants to be away from you."

Mother's face folded in on itself, as if I'd punched it with my fist instead of my words. She stood, her feet planted on the kitchen floor, her new hairdo not quite perfect as before, her short dress showing dimpled knees, her face flushed.

I wanted to take it back, but my angry feelings pressed out of the marrow of my bones and right out of my pores. "All you do is make us unhappy. When you were g-gone to Grandmother Rosetta's, Father and I were so happy. Happier than ever. The house was quiet and nice and we l-loved it without you."

"How dare you speak to me that way." Mother's chest heaved,

and her voice trembled. With a stiff arm, she pointed to my room. "Go. Go now, please."

I turned to walk away, the victory I thought I'd feel didn't feel so good after all. Instead of feeling bigger and stronger, I grew smaller and smaller. I was a tiny girl by time I lay on my bed. Tiny as the tiniest germiest molecule.

Outside my door, Mother's voice broke through, thick and heavy. "No more Sweetie. You hear? No more. I've had enough. No more." There was a sob.

From down the hall, Mother's bedroom door closed with a *click*, then, more sobs. I'd never heard her cry so hard before. I wondered, did she cry for me, for losing the Melissa she knew to the Lissa I'd become? Or, was she crying for Father? Both of us? Herself? I lay on my bed and wished for things back as they'd been earlier that summer. But it was too late to go back. Everything was rolling down the mountain, faster and faster and faster like a gigantic ice cream snow ball.

NINETEEN

When the timer sounded to let us know dinner was ready, we marched into the dining room, our faces pinchy. I didn't dare even clink my fork against my plate and draw attention to myself. Father ate while reading his pages. Mother kept her attention on her food. She'd posted the menu on the refrigerator, as she sometimes did, and called her latest creation *Don't Kiss Me Darling Beef,* which meant roast beef with a whole lot of garlic and onions and some kind of strong spice rub. It was really one of the best meals she'd ever made. And if I let myself be honest about it, her cooking had gotten better, and even her poetry wasn't as sappy and terrible.

It was hard to think of Mother changing. It was hard to think of her as a person.

"After you do the dishes, Melissa, I want to have a family meeting. We need to straighten this out. We're a family." She patted her lips with her ironed and starched and perfect napkin.

I let my sigh escape loud and long.

"And don't go sighing like a martyr. I am your mother. What I do is for your own good, Melissa Rose."

Father sipped his wine. He put the glass down on the placemat, looked across the table at Mother, and said, "Melissa is growing up and you treat her like a child."

"She *is* still a child and needs our guidance. A child is not an amoeba you find under your microscope. You don't study them; you raise them."

"Your nagging could peel the bark off a tree." Father drank the rest of his wine in one gulp. He looked triumphant as he set the glass on the table, refilled his glass, and let some dribble onto the white tablecloth. "Naggity nag nag nag."

I stared at the wine stain on the white tablecloth, waited for what would happen next. Mother hadn't said anything.

Father went on, "Sure could. Right off the tree in one long strip." He made a *ripppping* sound, then, "Nag nag and nag some more. You'd think you'd get tired of hearing the sound of your own voice, for pity's sake."

I'd never heard Father speak to Mother in that way. I chanced a look at her.

Tears wet Mother's eyes and her chin trembled. She stood up from the table, turned as graceful as a dancer, and just as graceful, she left the dining room. I heard her bedroom door close, and the sound of the lock snapping.

I knew Father would be sleeping in the extra bedroom. It had happened before, those separations between my parents; although, Father had never acted as mean before. What usually happened would be arguing, then slammed doors, then after a week, or two, once it was three, Father went crying back to Mother. She'd rock him to her and he'd tell her how stupid and foolish a man he was, how his brain couldn't always connect to his heart. She'd pat him on the back and say how she just wanted to have a contented family, a nice home, not like her family life had been. Then things would go back to normal for a while.

Father looked at me. "You go on like you've been doing. That's the end of that." He rose, grabbed his glass and the second bottle of wine that was half-empty. He then said, "Wait. What were you saying about your friend? Something about pain and dying or something?"

"You must have dreamed it or thought it up in your books, Father."

He looked confused, and then walked heel-to-toe-heel-to-toe to his study. That door clicked and locked, too.

I gathered the dishes to wash. Maybe after this fuss was over, Father wouldn't pretend to be a pushover to Mother and then take it out on her in other ways, and instead he'd pay more attention to her. Maybe she'd soften up some, because Father would show he loved her more than his science and his books. Maybe we'd stay in the mountain valley and not have to move again. I poured dishsoap into the sink, watched the bubbles rise.

One huge bubble lifted into the air and stayed right at eye level. I tried to see to the other side; the other side was wavery and blurred but beautiful. I wanted to step through to the other side of the bubble, step through and see what things were like there. The bubble lifted, lifted, hit the ceiling and disappeared.

***

On the way to Whale Back early the next morning, I hummed the theme to Flipper. I wondered if Sweetie would be there already, hiding behind a tree or thicket to jump out and say, "Hah!" I was ready for us to be the *old* us—best friends and blood-bound sisters. Sweetie was right. The mountain and creatures were the important things. I would stay a girl instead of a woman for as long as I could. Maybe forever. The summer lasted forever in books and in dreams, why not for me?

I ran along the path, in my new shorts and t-shirt. The inseam of the shorts didn't ride up. At the old mossy rock, I sat and waited. After thirty-one minutes, I slapped my forehead. We hadn't written where to meet. Our plans were messed up with all that had been going on. Maybe she'd left a moccasin mail. Hidden in the thicket under our rock was the plastic bag I'd put my note to Sweetie in about Grandmother Rosetta. And, I hadn't noticed before, but there was also red yarn tied to the branches, and more leading away down the trail.

"Sweetie! You did it!" I laughed and clapped. She'd remembered what I'd asked her about: tying yarn to mark the way. I opened the bag and slipped out Sweetie's note and a map. I looked at the map first. There were circles with "yarn" written in them. I thought it was a nice touch. But as I read her note, my happiness faded away, across the mountains, and off a high ridge, lost, floating up and away like the bubble.

> *mama got bad sick. worser than she ever been. got you a map. tied yarn on them branch like you said. guess i need you come since i'm a bit ~~skart~~ skared and need help.*

I grabbed my satchel, ran then, fast as I could go and still read the map and search for the yarn Sweetie left for me to find her place. The red threads were tied here and there, wet and dripping from the storm. Things looked familiar, but sometimes they looked all the same. I passed rocks and boulders we named, trees we carved our initials into, following those strings of red yarn, checked the map when I couldn't see yarn.

Below Sweetie's cabin, I ran up the hill, breathing hard, sweaty, dirty. I knocked once, and then just turned the knob and let myself in, threw my satchel on the floor by the door. I smelled the sick right off, and something else, like something was rotting. I gagged, ran up to Sweetie's room first, but her bed hadn't been slept in. I didn't want to go in Miss Mae's room, but I had to.

I hurried down the stairs and called outside her mother's door. "Sweetie?" There was no answer. My stomach knotted and twisted. I took a deep breath, let it out, and opened the door. Sweetie lay in bed with her mother, and they were both very still. The room smelled like vomit and sweat, but the rotted smell wasn't in there, so I hoped it was something else, something in the kitchen or a mouse or something that'd died. I went to the bed, still scared of what I would find. Their eyes were closed.

"Sweetie?" I reached out and touched her. She didn't move, so I pushed her shoulder, saying, "Please please please please."

She raised her head from the pillow, and I almost fainted with relief. She said, "Lissa?"

She struggled to sit up and as I helped her, I asked, "Are you sick?"

She rubbed her eyes. "Mama's bad sick. Not me."

She was wearing an army jacket that was three sizes too big for her. It made her look smaller, pitiful, and sad. I asked, "Are you sure you aren't sick?"

She shook her head. "Just Mama."

My stomach hurt from all the guilt and foolish feelings curdled deep inside. "I'm so sorry. I'm so sorry."

"Didn't I learn you nothing?"

"I wanted to see Jeremy and that's why I went to town. I wanted to do what my brother used to do. He made it all sound so fun and happy. Then Mother punished me over my smart mouth. And then the storm. It's all so stupid. I'm a stupid idiot. I'm sorry."

"This is not about what you been feeling or doing, Miss-Lissa, not this time." She let out a sigh, said, "We will worry over you being a stupid-idiot later." She stumbled out of bed and stood wobbling.

I shrank to a tiny size. I remembered a teacher once telling me that not everything was about me. How I needed to see the world from other's perspectives and that was what growing up was about. Or maybe Mother told me that. Or Father. Someone . . . someone.

"I'm losing my mind, Lissa. Preacher didn't give me no more them pills and they's almost gone." She shook her head, as if to sling the preacher's words from her ears. "He said my heathen ways was hurting her not helping." Her mouth trembled.

"The preacher said that?"

"When I went to fetch Mama's medicine, he told me she had to quit them pills. He said if I really wanted to help her, I'd try God's way, even if I didn't believe in it."

"God's way?"

"She's been getting sicker and sicker without them pills. I been trying to help her." She picked at thread on the quilt. "He told me I got to think of her and let her be healed proper. Maybe this time it's true."

"Healed proper? What's he mean?"

"He said they's a faith healer in a tent come to town. Said my mama believed in faith healing even if I was an ornery mule and didn't believe in nothing but mountain evil ways." Her face reddened.

"Hey! I bet that's what Mother and her ladies' group were gossiping about the other day. They went on and on about a tent at the edge of town, and all kinds of singing and yelling going on. We passed it the other day. I saw it, Sweetie; I saw it!"

Sweetie took a cloth from a basin of water and washed her mother's face. Her mother groaned and tossed her head, then went still again. "I will do whatever I got to do to help Mama. Even listen to that toady preacher." Her face hardened until it was almost like one of Zemry's masks.

"I know exactly where that tent is, too."

She raised her eyebrows at me.

"I saw it. Mother said the preacher was up to strange shenanigans. She told me to keep away from it. It's got to be the same thing. How many church tents could there be?"

"My magic tea don't seem to be working. Maybe the preacher is right. I don't know, Lissa. What about how Grandpaw taught me? I can't set my mind straight." She rubbed her eyes again. "I'm wore out."

I followed her to the kitchen. With a long match, she lit the stove, and put a kettle of water on to boil. Her hands were shaking. She then picked up a nasty rotten potato, stepped to the opened window, and threw it out.

"I still don't get this healing stuff. If the preacher has medicine, then he should give it to you."

She lowered her head as she chopped a root, her tangled hair falling over her face. "He said she left the church cause of me. She was shamed. Said we got to release all the demons and then she'll be better."

"Release the demons?"

She bit her lip, hard. Blood beaded. "He said her head hurt because the devil was in there biting her brain." She let out a sob, but she didn't cry. I'd never seen her cry.

I touched Sweetie's shoulder, her bones were sharp against my hand. "He's a liar and he's mean. Don't listen to that stuff."

"Then who I got to listen to? I done all I can for Mama and it is not working no more."

"What about a doctor?"

She shook her head as she cut up leaves. "Can't go to no doctor."

"Why not? That doesn't make sense."

She looked at me. "Life don't all'a time got to make sense, Lissa. Sometimes it just don't."

"What about Zemry? He'd do anything for you and your mother."

"I done tried. He weren't home."

"Maybe he's home now."

She put the roots and leaves in a strainer. "I left Mama to put the note and yarn and when I got back, she was walking outside without no clothes on." She bit her lip again, drawing more blood, then said, "Oh, it was pitiful, Lissa. She was looking for some little kitty she had when she was a girl. I likened to never got her back inside and in the bed." The water bubbled and boiled. Sweetie poured it over the leaves and root shavings, and then put a dishcloth over it. "When I got to leave her, it'll be to see that healer. Got to be done. Much as it leaves my tongue bitter."

"Then we'll go to the tent."

"You stay with Mama while I go."

Cold fingers fisted my stomach. Stay here with Miss Mae? With her so sick and acting crazy, with a shotgun somewhere around? Maybe it was under her pillow, or in the closet, and was it loaded, ready to blast my guts out? Or if not that, what if she did something really weird? Like running out naked again, off into the woods where I couldn't find her? Mother's warnings rushed up to me. I said, "Those pills help her to sleep. You could give her extra so she'd sleep while we were gone."

She checked the tea, put the towel back over it. "Well . . . "

"If we go together, then you won't be alone."

"But Mama will."

"But you leave her by herself all the time."

"Never this sick before. And she never went out without no clothes on."

"Well, that tent's way off past the ice cream shop."

She stomped her foot. "I don't know about no ice cream!"

"I know, that's what I'm saying. Things have changed even in the last few months. They've built stuff and opened new places and all kinds of stuff.'"

Sweetie took the towel off the tea. "My brain is full of cotton and clouds." She reached into a cupboard for a cup, then stopped, said, as if talking to herself, "Seems I recollect Mama telling me about a healer come through town long back when she was a girl. Cured her own mama of the bad stomach and made another woman's skin stop itching and welling up with sores and pus, and one man had hiccups for three months straight and after the healer his hiccups was gone." She rubbed her right eye. "I hadn't thought of that in a long while. Grandpaw said it was all a bunch of hen's pecking after seed that wasn't there." She took the cup and put it on the counter, poured the tea.

"All that sounds weird to me."

"You thought my magic tea was weird at first, right?" Sweetie took a small sip of the tea, then said, "I been studying on it and one day I'll be a Granny Woman. I will. But I guess I'm not ready yet. Or else Momma'd be well."

"Mother's friend said those tent people talk weird and fall on the floor wiggling around."

While reaching for the honey, Sweetie knocked over a bowl of blackberries. She stared at the berries rolling onto the floor, then said, "Well, shit-fire."

I picked up berries, thinking of what to do that would mean I didn't have to stay with Miss Mae. I put the berries on the counter.

Sweetie was grinding up pills with a spoon. "This is the last of them pills." She poured half the pill dust into the cup. "I been trying to make them last." She added a little more to the cup. "I think that'll do it."

The tea was nasty looking.

"I'll go see what's what even if I got to eat a snake's head off or dance and talk craziness. It's for Mama."

I couldn't decide which was worse—staying here with Miss Mae, or going to some tent where people might be falling on the floor and talking crazy and eating snake's heads off. All of a sudden, I wanted my Father. I wanted to smell his shirts when he'd been outside in the sunshine, wanted him to tell me how the world was structured and how everything had a scientific answer. I wanted to be in my room with my stuffed animals. I wanted Mother to lecture me on manners. I wanted to be plain old Melissa again. It was all too much.

She picked up the tea. "Grandpaw didn't like how them preachers pass around the hat asking for money from poor people. He said people shouldn't have to pay they's way to heaven when they don't got two nickels to slam together for meat."

"Sounds like my grandmother."

She put the cup on a tray and stood before me. "What you think, Lissa?"

I felt important. "I think you have to try it. If it doesn't work, at least you tried. Didn't you say your mother loved God and Jesus and all that?"

She nodded.

"Well, then maybe that'll be enough to help her."

She nodded again, headed to her mother's door and went inside.

I heard her mother say, "Don't. Don't. Don't. Don't. *Stop it. Get away from me.* You're trying to kill me! Where's Mathew? Mathew! Mathew!"

Sweetie's voice was soft, gentle. "Mama, drink it down. It will help you rest. Mama? This here's me. Your girl. Your daughter. Sweet Mama. Sweet Mama."

I couldn't hardly stand it.

She came out, put down the tray.

"Who's Matthew?" I asked.

"I do not know." She turned to me. "I made up my mind. I got something to ask Mama's God and the Mountain Spirit together. I figured a way to help Mama." She seemed to grow taller. "You show me where that healer tent is. You're right; it'll be faster." She went to the front door, grabbed her boots, and sat to put them on. As she laced the right one, she said, "I never had trouble finding nothing ever before. But I got to stop being ornery and trust my bound sister."

I nodded.

She laced the other boot, and then stood up. "I will see about her real quick and then we best get moving on. The extra pills will help her sleep longer, I reckon."

While she checked on her mother, from the window I watched a cardinal fly from branch to branch.

Behind me I heard, "Mama's sleeping so good."

She touched the bracelet I made her, glanced back at the closed door where her mother lay, then squared her shoulders. "You are the town person just like I am the mountain person. I showed you through the mountains, now you show me through the town."

I hesitated. "Are you sure, Sweetie?"

"I got to learn to trust my friend sometimes, right?"

We hurried out the door. But as we went through the woods, I questioned again whether I should have tried harder to tell her where the tent was and stayed with Miss Mae. She'd asked me to take care of Sweetie, to help her, and that's what I was doing. I couldn't help but feel full of importance that I could lead Sweetie. For once, I was in charge, I was the one who knew the way.

The worst part of it was the deeper secret part that I tried not to let scald up my throat. I didn't like the hidden part. Didn't like how it thick-oozed inside of me, making me queasy.

The hidden secret part inside me said, *I have to see. What will Sweetie do? What's all this healer stuff? Will they dance with snakes? Or faint on the floor? What's going to happen?* My secret thoughts became a hard knot inside my stomach.

The hard knot made a twin. It divided itself just as cells do. The twin knot said I was scared. Scared that if I stayed with Miss Mae, I wouldn't know what to do when she screamed and rolled around in bed and thought I was trying to poison her. What if she went crazy and shot me like T.J. said? I hated the twin hard knots, hated how they sat heavy inside me. I told myself Sweetie's mother would be fine, but as we ran though the woods, my stomach rolled the hard knots around while my head pounded with every step I took.

When I stopped to catch my breath, Sweetie didn't fuss at me. We splashed creek water on our necks. I said, "I don't get why the preacher said they can heal her when she's not coming with us."

"He said I was the cause of her sickness."

"Oh."

"I got to trade Even Steven between me and Mama. I'll take her hurt, and she'll take what I got. Then she won't hurt no more. I got to give up my powerful magic for Mama."

"But then you'll hurt. Everything will be different for you."

She grabbed my arm, and pulled me. "No more rest. We got to go."

My sides were splitting open and my throat hurt from breathing so hard. I thought about what she said. She'd give up her magic, feel all the pain again and all the other things she said she didn't want to happen to her, just so her mother would be well. Would I do something like that? My answer rushed up like vomit.

When we were to the bottom of the mountain, where the grass met the road, Sweetie stopped and looked around. She looked afraid, and my important feelings rose up again. I wasn't afraid, not in town. I said, "It's okay, Sweetie. We'll stay back behind the houses and buildings and keep away from everyone."

"I am not scared." She put her shoulders back.

We threaded through yards, past the ice cream shop, past the pancake place, past barking dogs, past the big amusement park way up in the sky, past a few curious stares. At the edge of town, right before the tent came into view, I heard singing and tambourine playing. "You hear that, Sweetie?" I pointed through the trees. "It's right through there."

Her marble-eyes searched mine and looked deep inside my heart. She took off while I stared after her, feeling as if my stupid selfish self should be swallowed up by the ancient mountain dirt underneath my tired feet. She knew about the twin hard knots inside of me.

Even then, I didn't run back to Sweetie's cabin to look after her mother. I let the twin hard knots bubble up to my throat and I burped the sour. I had to see what she'd do. I had to see what would happen. I hurried through the trees after her.

I had to see.

TWENTY

The gray-white tent was as big as Sweetie's cabin. It stretched across the field, just out of the edge of town. The license plates on the cars were from other states, along with some from North Carolina, and there were also people walking down the road. Outside the tent, I listened to the people inside singing about blood of the lamb. When I felt brave enough—I kept thinking about the Cowardly Lion and how afraid he was to see the Wizard no matter how far they'd traveled the yellow brick road to do it and how he finally went inside and the wizard was nothing but a little old man—I went inside.

The Methodist churches Mother used to take me to were quiet and stuffy. When Grandmother Rosetta stopped being Catholic, she went to a church by a pond. She said it gave her a peaceful feeling every Sunday. I went with her once. It was a little building on a hill overlooking the pond where swans swam around dipping their beaks into the water. One of the swans was different from the others, black with a red beak. I liked him the best. The church there wasn't any one kind of religion, but lots of them, or none of them at all, everyone mixed together.

The tent church was loud and smelled like sweat, perfume, hot hay, cigarette smoke, and old lady powder. Some of the people were dressed up, but many of them were in regular clothes or maybe work clothes. Some had their hats in their hands, turning it over and over with nervous fingers. People sat on metal chairs that were placed right on the ground. It was hot and stuffy inside, and some of the women fanned themselves with fans from funeral homes with a picture of Jesus knocking on a door. Some had big black Bibles, and others little white ones. Some stood with their hands raised up in the air, swaying and singing. I didn't see any snakes, so far.

Mother's friend Beula had said not many town people would come. Her friend Margaret said that Reverend Seth was shifty, and that he cared more about the money on the plate than he did his soul in the fire. And then the ladies' club hens pecked about how he spent too much time and money on the races and thought no one knew. When Mother and the women had seen me standing in the doorway, they'd shut up their clucking about the preacher and pecked instead over the snacks they'd had at Pitty-Sue's house and how her bread was always stale.

I walked down the middle aisle towards a platform at the other end of the tent, where four men and a woman stood. One of the men was the preacher. Sweetie once told me that he looked at her as if he were scared of her or wanted to hit her, and all she ever did was be a kid. I didn't like him. Even though he did look grandfatherly and he was a preacher, his eyes looked as though he had bad thoughts squirming in there.

Someone called out, "A-*men*, Reverend Seth!"

It was the other man who grabbed my attention more than Reverend Seth. He wore a white robe, white shoes, and had a big wood cross around his neck. He was bald, and his skin was so white, it almost matched his robe. Creepy chills crept up my spine. I figured he had to be the healer Sweetie talked about. Off to the side by a curtain, two other men in dark suits stood with their arms crossed over their chests. They looked like mean guard dogs as they watched the woman on the platform.

The woman had her arms by her sides, her head thrown back. Reverend Seth stood behind her. The pale man with the cross stood in front of her. He held his palm up to the woman, and said, "Thy affliction will be taken from thee by the will of God, through me." He lowered his hand and kissed the wood cross. Then he opened the Bible and began reading from it.

I tore my eyes from the sights and looked for Sweetie. She stood off to the side of the platform, in front of the steps that led up to it. I hurried to her, asked, "What's happening?"

She looked as though she was off in another world where I didn't matter.

"I've never seen anything like this before. Ever."

She turned towards me, and her breath raged in and out of her, so hot I worried she had fever. Pale white blood cells marching marching, *onward Christian soldiers* . . . someone was singing.

"What's wrong with the woman?"

Sweetie turned her blank face back to the stage.

"The pale man gives me the creepy crawlies," I said.

Someone behind me said, "He calls himself a *healer*."

I turned around to see a man spit on the floor, then he said, "All these here people are listening to ever-thang he says like he's God hisself. Hit's disgraceful. You'uns better keep your money in your pockets and run on home." He turned and walked away, slamming his hat on his head, then out the tent he went.

I turned back to the platform. The healer had stopped reading and had stepped up to the woman and raised his palm again.

Sweetie stared, her chest rising and falling fast, her hands clenched in fists.

The healer put his hand on the woman's forehead, and when he pushed, she swayed back into Reverend Seth's arms. When Reverend Seth laid her down on the floor, she jerked around, and then lay still. Other than a crying baby, it was quiet until the woman on the floor rose onto her knees, raised her arms, and cried out, "Praise Jesus! Praise Jesus! I'm healed! I'm healed!" Then she began spouting off words that made no sense, and some of the others in the tent did the same.

The tent exploded with clapping, singing, and Amen-ing.

The healer raised his wooden cross, waved it in front of the woman, and then kissed it again. The crowd grew quiet. The pale man said, "Her affliction has left her because of her strong faith, and my connection to Him."

The people shouted and Amen-ed some more.

Reverend Seth stood at the edge of the platform with his hands held out. "Brothers and Sisters. Hush. Hush now. You have witnessed the healing of Mrs. Georgia Marie St. Cloud. Her demons have left her. A-*Men*."

"Amen!"

"We are all one in the Lord." Reverend Seth took a small Bible from his pocket. "The Good Book tells us to thank the Lord for all he does. So I want each and every one of you to thank the Lord by giving. You see the gentlemen passing around the hats? Empty your pockets as you fill your souls. A-*Men*." He grinned about the tent, then said, "As I told my followers, I have a *special* healing tonight. Many of you have caught wind of it and come to witness, as evidenced by our full tent!" He shot his eyes over to Sweetie and then back to the people. "Yes, I knew this would draw a *full house* . . . to the Lord."

I looked back, there stood my neighbor. Mr. Tanner saw me, and shouted out, "Hey! Your parents wouldn't want you in here. Get yourself on home, you hear?"

I smiled at him, shrugged, and turned to say something to Sweetie, but she was already on her way up the stairs to the platform. Reverend

Seth looked down at her and smiled a smile sweeter than the syrup I poured on my pancakes. The healer looked over at Sweetie and smiled just as Reverend Seth had, except worse. I didn't like those grins, they reminded me of T. J.'s when he thought up a new way to torture me or some other victim.

Sweetie went straight up to the pale healer and stood in front of him. She said something I couldn't hear.

An old woman near me said, "Who's that now?"

Her friend said, "That's the child Reverend Seth talked about."

"Oh! Glory be!"

"A-men to that."

"He said she's been touched by the devil."

"Oh, poor child. Praise Jesus!"

I wanted to tell them how wrong they were, but I had to watch Sweetie.

The healer faced the audience. "Flocks of Our Lord, we have a special, special daughter here today. God has sensed a need and he has provided. Here, right in front of us."

Reverend Seth put his hands on Sweetie's shoulders and turned her to face the crowd.

She looked down at me, frowned, shook off the preacher's hands, and turned back to the healer.

The healer said, "Brothers and Sisters, you will witness today the powerful hand of God through me." The healer went to Reverend Seth and clapped him on the back. "Reverend Seth here has told me how this young woman has been branded by God with a *strange* affliction."

The tent became very quiet. Not even the baby cried.

Sweetie swung around to Reverend Seth. "I come to heal my mama like you said. Now you talk to God and tell him what I want so Mama will not die."

Reverend Seth said, "If you act out, God will leave us and your mama won't get well, now will she?"

The healer raised his cross. "Lord God on High! See this child's need! Heal this child's affliction!"

Sweetie turned to the healer and said something, but her words were lost as the crowd prayed.

I waved my hands in the air. "Sweetie! Sweetie!"

She stood in front of the healer. Through the crowd's prayers, I heard pieces of what she said, " . . . didn't . . . to tell ever-body . . . my mama . . . Even Steven . . .mountain spirit and God . . . "

The healer took Sweetie by the arm, and shouted, "Yes, my friends of Our Lord! This child will be healed!"

"Not me! Mama!" Sweetie shouted. "She has to be healed. I *am not* sick!"

The healer crooked his finger and the two giant men slinked out of the shadows and grabbed Sweetie. Sweetie tried to jerk away.

The healer continued, "She has an affliction such as never been seen amongst us. God marked her. Let her affliction be a warning! Let her healing be witness to God's almighty power!"

Sweetie kicked at the men, but she may as well have been kicking two stumps. Her face turned purple as she screamed, "You nasty bastards! You assholes! Let me go, you stinking shitters!"

The healer pointed his finger. "She bellows like Satan!" He kissed the cross and turned back to the crowd, pushing his palms at them to quiet the noise. "Her mother prayed for the soul of her daughter, to no availing. Prayed for a healing. Alas, her faith was not strong enough."

Reverend Seth said, "That's right. She told me all about the child's *secret name* that cannot be spoken—heathen talk! From a heathen old woman who used magic from the devil and passed it to this poor innocent child!"

The crowd was quiet.

Sweetie stopped her mad kicking and screaming, and stared at Reverend Seth like a wounded and trapped animal. She shouted, "Who told you? Mama wouldn't tell! She wouldn't!" But when Sweetie turned to me, her eyes said she knew her mother would tell, if that meant saving the soul of her daughter.

I turned to the tent people, put out my hands. "Someone help her." Their eyes stayed fixed on the platform. I looked for Mr. Tanner, but he was no longer there.

A man said, "They ain't using no snakes? Well, Shee-it."

A red-haired woman turned to me and said, "Shush, hon. It'll be all right."

I couldn't be the Cowardly Lion. I had to be brave, like Sweetie was. I ran up the stairs to her. "Sweetie! Sweetie!" A third guard-dog man appeared out of the shadows and grabbed me. I whipped my head around, back and forth, at Sweetie, at the healer, at the crowd, and at the big hands holding me so I couldn't go to my friend. I yelled again, "Sweetie!"

Sweetie had spit coming out of her mouth, and her hair was flying wild around her head as she fought. She turned her furious eyes on Reverend Seth. She arched her back. "Let me be! Where's God? Where is he? God, if you are real, then you get down here!"

The healer said, "See how she fights. Satan has been tormenting this poor child. Look at the marks upon her pitiful little body!"

The tent people said, "Oh yes . . . Amen . . . Poor child." Their voices melted together, louder, faster, bigger, electrifying the hot damp air inside the tent.

Reverend Seth raced back and forth on the stage, pounding his Bible, yelling about God and Jesus and Sweetie's mother's sin of the flesh and magic and the devil and afflictions and evil.

The healer looked out over the crowd. "You, there." He pointed to a woman wearing a big flowered hat. "Come up here."

As the woman stepped up to the stage, I felt as if I was trapped in the scariest nightmare I'd ever had, one that I was so glad to wake up from and see I was really in my soft bed. A trickle of sweat fell into my right eye, stinging. The guard-dog man's fingers hurt my arms. I imagined I felt and smelled the fire and brimstone I used to hear about at an old church long ago. It was as if Sweetie and I were really in hell and not in a church at all.

The healer said something to the woman. She woman reached into her hat and then handed the healer a long sharp hatpin. My stomach fisted and reared up. I was afraid the hard knots of my secret shame would come flying out of my mouth and land on the platform for everyone to see.

The healer pushed against the hatpin woman's head. She fell back, just as Marie St. Cloud had done. A gang of women crowded around her, helping her back to her seat, some of them speaking the gibberish again.

The healer held the hatpin out for the crowd to see. "Behold the affliction of this young child." He went to Sweetie, grabbed her hand, and stuck the hatpin deep into her palm.

I screamed, and my screams were mixed with other screams in the crowd.

The healer lifted his Bible. "Hush! Hush! There is not cruelty here. See how the child doesn't flinch? See how she stands unharmed?"

Sweetie wasn't fighting anymore as blood trickled onto the wood platform. I thought she would curse, scream, and fight more, but she didn't. She turned to me, kept her bright burning eyes pierced into mine.

Through the thick clogging in my throat, I shouted, "Leave her alone!" I struggled against the man holding me, but he didn't let go.

Sweetie didn't blink and her marble colored eyes glowed brighter, burning just as Grandmother Rosetta's had in the painting. I saw a burning in the pupils, saw the fire there, leaping up, hot and full of rage. She gritted her teeth and I swore I could hear them grinding together above all the noise.

The healer held up Sweetie's palm and prayed over it.

Reverend Seth was about to foam at the mouth, lips covered in white spittle, his eyes wild and glazed. He was still pounding his Bible, telling people they best get right with the Lord, confess their sins, tithe the church, be children of God.

"Sweetie, I'm sorry. I'm sorry. I'm sorry." I didn't know or care if she could hear me. My voice croaked out, "I'm sorry. I'm sorry. I'm sorry—"

The healer slowly shook his head. "You see? Do you see brothers and sisters?" He put down his Bible, grabbed Sweetie's other palm.

She didn't try to stop him. She lifted her chin and stood with her feet apart.

The healer drove the sharp point deeper, kept it there, held up her palm to face the crowd. The pin had gone all the way through her hand. He then slowly withdrew the pin.

The tent people shouted and screamed. A woman fainted and someone carried her outside. A man called out, "This ain't the Lord's work! Hurting a child!" And another man cried out, "That's right! This looks more like Satan's work than Jesus' work!" People were rushing out, others rushing forward.

The healer quieted the crowd, pushing his palms towards them in a *hush hush hush* move. "Do you see how she doesn't feel the thrust of the weapon?" He lifted Sweetie's palms and wiped the blood with his robe. The white robe had an angry splotch of red and he showed it to the crowd. "She bleeds, but feels no pain. Her mother has kept the secret from all but your good reverend, who could no longer bear the secret alone. Her mother has held all the shame from whence the affliction was birthed; her dirty deeds with men. Her own father's blasphemy. Her own mother's witchery." He took both of Sweetie's hands and held them out to the tent people. "Stigmata! From her family's unnatural appetites! A generational curse upon the child for the sins of her mother and her mother's mother and her mother before her! Her father and his father and his father before him!"

The crowd rippled noises, took in gasps of breath.

Sweetie kept her lifted chin, her feet wide. She stared out into the crowd with her burning barn eyes.

Brother Seth pointed to Sweetie, shook his head oh so sadly. Oh so sadly. He said, "Yes, this child's mama revealed to me how she sinned. And in her sinning, this poor child bears hell's affliction and Satan's torment. A freak of nature. How has she coped so with her burdens on such small shoulders?" He wagged his head as if he was the most sorrowful of sorrowful men, patted Sweetie on the shoulder, wiped his sweat with a handkerchief.

The healer nodded, nodded, oh so sadly nodded.

Sweetie stayed still, as if she'd left the earth and gone somewhere else. As if she were a shell of a body and what made Sweetie herself was hovering above looking down on everyone and everything.

I twisted in the man's grip, feeling my own white-hot anger bubble up my blood. "It's not true! Her mother is beautiful. Her mother is an angel. I saw her. I know it. I know it. And Sweetie isn't a freak. *Let her go.*" I turned my head around to face the man holding me. He looked down at me with his mouth turned down. I thought he had to be good inside somewhere. "Please, mister. Please help my friend. Please."

He lowered his head, said, "This is just a job. Just a job."

The healer spoke, looking at Sweetie as if she were a stray kitty in the gutter. "Today, I will heal her affliction. I will release her from Satan! Brothers and Sisters, do you Be-*lieve*?"

"Yes! A-men!"

Sweetie turned her face to the healer, then spat at him, a big fat ball of spit that landed on the healer's face, dripped onto his lips. His spit-on lips tightened together, his face wet and red and blotchy. Without wiping off her spit, he kissed the cross again, drew it back, and struck Sweetie on the head. Someone in the crowd screamed or maybe it was only me.

Sweetie narrowed her eyes and I thought she was going to spit at him again.

The healer shouted, "Spare the rod, and spoil the child, it is written. This girl's mother has let her grow wild and wanton, just as the mother was."

Then, out of the sky it seemed, so that at first I thought it might be God, a booming voice rose over the crowd releasing only one word—"*ENOUGH!*"—and a big man with broad shoulders jumped up to the platform in a long leap and faced the healer with his hands balled into fists. "Let her go!" The guard-dog men holding Sweetie looked at each other and let Sweetie go.

The man holding me said, "I wasn't paid to get beat up." He let go of me and I ran to Sweetie. She had lit into the two who'd held onto her, kicking and hitting them as if she'd lost all the rest of her mind. "Sweetie!" She didn't hear me, didn't care.

The broad shouldered man turned to me, and when I looked up at him, he had the most beautiful green eyes I'd ever seen. Familiar eyes. "Get Sweetie out of here."

I stared at him as if I didn't understand anything in the world anymore.

The crowd had grown quiet, watching with widened eyes, as if they'd just awakened from the same bad dream I had. The healer and Brother Seth were trying to get them riled up again, but they began to walk out of the tent.

Green Eyes stepped close to me, and he smelled like pipe smoke. "Get your friend and go. Hurry now." He strode over to the healer, grabbed the cross, and ripped it from his neck. When the healer tried to take it back, Green Eyes punched him in the nose. The tent people who hadn't yet left began praying and swaying. Someone jumped up on the platform. Someone shot a gun in the air. A woman shrieked.

I ran to Sweetie and pulled at her arm. She was working on Reverend Seth, hollering and pounding him with her fists. Little blood prints from her fists were on the healer's white robe and on Reverend Seth's white shirt. Reverend Seth stood as if he was made of wood, taking her blows. I pulled her harder and she turned, socked me on my ribs before she saw it was me. She was breathing in and out so hard, I thought she might die if I didn't get her out of there.

"Come on, Sweetie! We got to get back to your mother!"

That did it. Her burning eyes went back to her regular Sweetie eyes.

We jumped off the platform, ran toward the way out. Hands reached out to us as we dodged and charged down the aisle. I didn't know if they were trying to help us, or grab us, or maybe just touch the freak of nature. When I glanced back one last time, Green Eyes stared after us, still holding the healer's cross in his fist, the healer flat on the floor.

We didn't stop running until we were to the split off by the creek. I leaned over into the bushes and vomited everything out. It was bitter-sour and nasty. Sweetie patted me on the back, took a palm of water and splashed the back of my neck. I wiped my mouth and couldn't look Sweetie in the eye.

"You got it all out now?"

I lowered myself to the ground and put my head in my hands.

"I got to go to Mama."

Without lifting my head, I said, "You go, don't—"

She took off running before I finished.

I listened for the sounds of the crowd coming to get us. I felt wet on my back from her blood and the creek water. There were only the birds singing and squirrels chattering, and the wind causing two limbs to rub together. The sounds were of a normal day, as if nothing strange had happened at all. As if the day were nothing but a bad dream and soon I'd wake up in my own bed, with the breeze pushing through the window.

I wondered how grown-ups could be so mean to kids. How they felt as if they could do whatever they wanted just because we had no say-so. I saw Sweetie on the platform again, how she fought the men, hitting, screaming, and spitting, and how brave she was. I hadn't been brave enough at all, vomiting in the bushes. Miss Mae would be angry with me for messing up the job she'd given me. I hadn't watched after Sweetie at all. Sweetie was right about me always having to know too much about what I didn't understand.

I sat in the woods with the animals and when I could get up without feeling dizzy, I found my way on the trail back to Whale Back, and from there the yarn led me back to Sweetie, the map left at Sweetie's house.

I wondered what Father would have to say about all that happened in that tent. I wonder what he'd think about his biological machines.

TWENTY-ONE

I climbed the hill to Sweetie's, ran into her little house, and straight to Miss Mae's room where Sweetie stood over her mother's bed. There was wet on her pillow and Miss Mae's lips were caked with white.

Sweetie looked up at me, her face a world of sorrows, a universe of sorrows, a whole galaxy where everything happy and good was sucked into a big black hole of space. She opened her mouth, closed it, then opened it again. Her voice croaked when she finally said, "She is gone. She left me."

I could only blink.

"I orter not gone off." Sweetie reached out and touched her mother's hair. Sweetie's hands were bandaged in white cloths and a bit of blood stained the palms.

I made my legs work, forced them to stand beside Sweetie. Miss Mae lay still, and she looked as if she were sleeping. But in that stillness, I knew. All I could think about was the time Father drove around a curve and accidentally hit a cat. When I jumped out to see what happened to it, the cat was lying on the ground. There were no blood or marks at all that I could see. Just the cat lying there still and quiet, its eyes staring, empty. It was just as Miss Mae was, the way her body didn't move at all, the way she lay there empty-looking. I tore my eyes from her and looked at Sweetie. "Close her eyes, Sweetie."

"Huh?"

"Close her eyes." I reached, but could not touch Sweetie's mother.

Sweetie covered her mother's face with her left hand, and closed her mother's eyes. She kept her hand there for a while, and then slowly pulled it back to let her arm dangle at her side. Sweetie looked at me then, and I wanted to lower my eyes, but I didn't, I couldn't. She said, "We will bathe her with them herbs and put some sweet oil on her. I already wiped up where she got sick." She stroked her mother's hair. "I done it all wrong."

I swallowed, and tried to think of something to say, but I remembered how I had been at Grandmother Rosetta's memorial. How nothing anyone said helped, and how sometimes what they said made me feel worse. I could only say, "You did everything right. Everything you could." It was me, I thought. Me, who did it all wrong.

Sweetie leaned over and kissed her mother right on the lips. She touched her lips where she'd kissed them, and then stroked and smoothed her mother's hair. I backed out of the room and waited in the kitchen.

When Sweetie came out, she almost looked like a ghost herself, and I understood that part of her. The way I'd felt as if I were floating when my nonna died. The way everything was dark and strange and cold. Sweetie lit the stove and put the kettle of water on to heat, as if it was a normal day and she was going to make some tea. From the cupboard she took a wide pan that was bent and dark from many uses over many years. Into the pan, she sprinkled herbs from a bowl, root shavings from a tiny burlap sack, and flower petals from a small basket.

On the counter was a glass bottle with a stopper. Inside was what looked like the yellow liquid that she'd poured onto the twigs the day we became bound-sisters. Floating in the liquid were more flower petals, and dark spicy-smelling cloves. When the water heated, the steam rising up like a misty ghost, she poured it over the dry mixture, and then added a bit of the yellow oil to the water. From a drawer, she took two small cotton towels and put them in the water. With a wooden spoon, she stirred it all around. The whole time she didn't say a word, and for once, I didn't say anything at all.

When she finished stirring, she at last turned to me. "I will go undress Mama. You don't have to come."

"I'll help you." I followed her back into the room, holding things in as tight as I could. If I didn't hold things tight, everything would release into the air, all the thoughts and feelings swirling inside of me. How I tricked Sweetie. How I'd been the worst friend in the world. I'd start babbling away and wouldn't be able to stop. The words and feelings would crowd the little house, fall on our heads and shoulders and weigh us both down until we'd never be able to crawl out from under the mess I'd helped make.

We undressed Miss Mae. She was heavy. I always pictured people who died as being lighter, since their souls were out of them. But the body was heavy and the skin was cold. It was like touching something that wasn't real. A doll in a bad dream.

Sweetie went to a big trunk and from it took out clean white sheets. She said, "She got to lay on clean sheets after we bathe her."

I nodded.

Sweetie left the room. I followed her again, as I didn't want to be alone with Miss Mae. What if she suddenly woke up and pointed and said, "I asked you to watch out for Sweetie and look what you did. Now I'm dead. Dead dead dead! And Sweetie is all alone. All alone all alone!"

In the kitchen, Sweetie took from the counter the pan of herbed mixture, and headed back to the bedroom, with me on her heels. I was like a puppy slinking. She set the pan on the side table, took one of the cotton cloths, wrung it out, and handed it to me. She wrung out the other, and with it began washing her mother's body. She was gentle, but used strong sure strokes. I copied her from the other side of the bed, washing her arms, hand, stomach, hip, leg, foot. We'd dip our cloth every so often and wring it out again. I tried not to stare at her mother's body as I washed her. It was as pale as the belly of a catfish, and there were no marks on her. Miss Mae was the opposite of Sweetie with all Sweetie's scars. I thought how weird that was, how strange, that Sweetie's mother felt all that pain and wore no scars to show it, but Sweetie felt no pain and had many scars.

When her whole body was cleaned, we took off the dirty sheets. I sweated, but Sweetie had no trouble, since she'd done it many times when her mother was too sick to rise. She'd done it alone, without anyone to help her. When Miss Mae lay on her clean sheets, Sweetie took off the wet bandages on her hands. She looked at her palms and I did, too. They weren't bleeding and the small holes were right in the center of her palms. She then took the bottle of sweet oil, poured a drop into her palm and rubbed her hands together. She put the oil in her mother's hair. I smelled the clove and the perfume from the flower petals. Sweetie poured a bit more onto her palm and again rubbed her hands together. She put more oil on her mother's hair, then touched her eyelids with it, and massaged her neck with it.

As Sweetie perfumed her mother, I watched one single tear drip from the corner of Sweetie's eye, and make a slow trail all the way down her cheek, down down until it found her chin, and it stayed there, hanging onto her face, until finally, in slow motion it dropped onto her mother's cheek. There it made the same kind of track, down her mother's face, until it disappeared. I watched Sweetie as she tried to keep herself from crying. As far as I knew, she never cried.

I thought how Sweetie had stood in that tent and begged to trade places with her mother. That she'd sacrifice her special ways and all she was so her mother would be well. She'd become a plain old girl so her mother could be a mother again. Mothers were supposed to take care of daughters, not the other way around. Wasn't that the way things were supposed to be?

Sweetie hitched her breath, went back to the trunk. From it, she took a long white dress with lace around the sleeves and hem. It had pearl buttons, and white on white embroidered flowers around the neck. We dressed her mother in it, then Sweetie tied the bracelet I made Miss Mae around her wrist, and clasped a pretty silver necklace in the shape of two hearts together around her neck.

She said, "Her own mama's necklace given by my grandpaw." Sweetie then took a hairbrush lying on the table next to the bed, and began brushing her mother's hair in long strokes. From the roots down to the end, she brushed her hair until it shone. Miss Mae looked even more like a beautiful sleeping angel. Sweetie put a Bible in her mother's hands. "She loved her Bible. I hate it, and won't ever read one again, but Mama loved Jesus and she believed in all this book says. And it did not do her a bit of good."

I reached out and touched Miss Mae's face, drew back. It was even colder and harder. She was turning into stone. One of those Greek goddesses that stood forever in the museums.

"We got to wrap her up in the sheet. I don't want no dirt on her face. She'd hate that."

"Dirt on her face?"

"From when we bury her."

"Oh."

We wrapped her in the clean white sheet, and Sweetie tucked it just so, then she hugged her mother tight. "They's kilt her. Or maybe I done it. Maybe I do got the devil in me."

"That's not true. It's *not*."

Sweetie leaned into me, put her head to mine. "I thought she would get well. I thought I was doing things right."

"You tried the best you could all the time. You took good care of her every day."

She said softly into my ear. "We'll bury her under the dogwood tree up there behind the house, where she let me read to her before her headaches come on her so bad. She loves it up there. When I was real little, we'd set ourselves down under the shade and she'd tell me stories."

I saw them there, sitting together, Miss Mae's hair blowing in the wind and mixing with Sweetie's. Their hair was like cotton candy whirling together. Miss Mae telling stories while Sweetie listened with a little smile on her face. The birds were singing, the tree leaves waving, the squirrels and coons and even the bears stopping to listen.

She looked down at her mama, and her face wrinkled in on itself. Then she fell over her mother, tore at the sheets, ripped them away from her face, pushed her face into her mother's hair. I heard her muffled, "Mama. Don't leave me. Don't leave. Don't leave. Don't leave."

I ran out of the room and stood in the middle of her little house, turning around, seeing everything I'd come to love and wanted to know more about, seeing Sweetie's home that wouldn't be a home anymore. My throat and chest ached with all the tears that wanted to come. I willed them back, willed them sucked back into my body. I had to be strong, for Sweetie.

She was in there a long time before she came out. She sat at the table and I did, too. She looked down at her hands. I looked down at mine. The minute hand on my watch circled four times before Sweetie said a word.

"It's time."

I swallowed, looked up at her.

"If you don't got the stomach for it, you don't got to help." She eyed me, in that way she had.

"I'm helping you."

She stood and went out of the front door.

I stared out at the woods. The leaves were waving in the wind as they always did. Except they were waving goodbye to Miss Mae. I imagined I saw her spirit in the trees, watching over Sweetie. I wondered if Grandmother Rosetta would see Miss Mae. If the two of them would meet and come to love each other. And they'd both watch over Sweetie and me for as long as we needed them to. Forever.

Sweetie soon was back with two shovels. She held one out to me.

I took the shovel.

We went up behind the house to a grassy spot where the dogwood tree grew.

As Sweetie looked up at the waving leaves, she hummed a song but didn't sing it aloud as she usually did. Every so often she'd sing a word, like, fare you well, and leaving a home, and distant roam.

An image of my mother lying still, hard, and cold, rose up like a scary shadow. It made me want to scream and tear out my hair, so I thought maybe I didn't hate her as much as I thought I did. I was afraid I'd be punished, that I'd go home and my mother would be gone, too. Or Father. Or both of them. And, I'd be an orphan. They'd have to put me in an orphanage. I sweated, my heart thumping out of my chest. I wondered what would become of Sweetie, without a mother or a father. My breath panted out in puffs and I was lightheaded. I swallowed back the vomit, and it burned my throat.

Sweetie dug the shovel into the dirt, pushed it in the ground with her foot, and pulled up a clump.

I did the same.

Without looking up from shoveling, she said, "Thank you."

I swallowed every last bit of my spit. I swallowed down the bad feelings I had. The feelings of how I made her leave her mother, so I could feel important. So I could see what she'd do next. I'd wanted to see her next trick, had treated her like a circus act, just as her grandfather said people would do. And I was her blood bound sister. I began digging harder and faster. The only sound was the shovel hitting the dirt and our hard breathing.

I would ask Father if Sweetie could stay with us, and if we could stay in the mountains forever as a family. I'd never had a real home before, not one where we stayed and made roots grow beneath our feet as Zemry talked about. She needed me, or maybe I needed her more. I couldn't figure it out. I looked over at Sweetie. She looked pale and tired. Underneath her eyes were purpled shadows. I'd never seen Sweetie without a big light shining from the inside out of her. What if the healer had taken away her magic and her mother had died anyway. I didn't want to think about it. I wanted her magic and light back.

I said, "You can come live with us."

She stopped shoveling, wiped her face with her shirt, and did not look up when she said, "Nuh uh."

"If you don't, they might put you in an orphanage."

Her head snapped up, and her eyes had the fire again. "I will not leave this here mountain. *Never.* It is my Home." She dug again, harder and faster.

I bit my lower lip so I would keep my mouth shut and went back to digging. When I thought I couldn't dig another shovelful, Sweetie stopped and stared down at what we'd done. The hole we made wasn't near deep enough. There were a lot of rocks and tree roots, too.

She said, "We best rest. Directly, I'll break us some cornbread."

"I can make us something to eat while you rest."

"We both'll just set here under the tree. Then we'll eat, and then dig until it's done."

I sat on the grass and she did the same. We wiped sweat from our faces and waved away buzzing bugs. My arms were tired and burning from digging into the hard ground. I was glad. I wanted to hurt, wanted to feel the pain in my arms. I wanted to take the shovel and beat myself over the head with it. Sweetie lay back on the grass, and I lay beside her. We looked up at the tops of the trees, and the blue sky peeking out from the leaves. I let myself pretend everything was fine, since it was such a beautiful day. I could pretend very well; I was a great dreamer.

That was the last I knew until I awoke to shouts coming from the other side of the trail beneath Sweetie's cabin. Someone said, "Over here!"

Someone else asked, "Do you see them?" It sounded like Father.

Sweetie jumped up and looked around like a wild animal. "They will not take me to no orphan place."

"I won't let them. It's my father. I'll talk to him." I stood up and held my hand out to her. "Come on. He'll help us, I promise."

She looked down at the hole in the ground. She rolled her eyes to me, then back to the hole we were digging, down towards the cabin, and then cocked her head towards the sound of old leaves crunching and the rustling of bushes as someone scrambled up. Sweetie's eyes bugged out. She pulled and yanked our some of her hair. Her body stiffened up. Through her gritted teeth she growled out, "Mama, I can't let them take me off and lock me away. I'll die, too." She took off into the woods, fast as any wild animal. The soles of her boots kicking up leaves and dirt as she ran.

"Wait! Sweetie!" I stood over the grave, my hands held out, as if I could draw her back to me just by the pull of my wanting her. She was like the deer we'd seen, beautiful even in their fright. I knew she wouldn't come back, and I knew if I ran after her, I wouldn't catch up to her. She wouldn't jump out from behind a tree and say, "Boo! Ha! Come on, I got something inneresting to show you." And she wouldn't say, "This here's how you do it, Lissa. Watch me, Silly Brains." She wouldn't say, "You got the fire inside you, Warrior of the Creek."

I let my arms fall to my sides. I'd never felt as tired and lonely as I did right then. I stood over the dirt pile, the hole, our shovels, the indents in the grass where we'd fallen asleep. I picked up the shovel and began digging again. That was what I had to do. I had to bury Sweetie's mother for her. That was what I needed to do. What they both wanted me to do.

TWENTY-TWO

Father walked up to where I was. I ignored him as I dug the shovel in the ground, pushed it far into the earth with my shoe, and lifted up a mound of dirt and rocks, then tossed it on the pile. He put his arms around me to hug me close. I tried to shake him off to keep digging, but he wouldn't let go.

"Melissa." Father tried to pull me away from the grave. "Melissa . . . stop it."

"I have to bury Sweetie's mom. I promised."

He tried to grab the shovel, but I jerked it away.

"It's against the law, Princess. And, well . . . the animals will get to her."

I kept digging.

"Your mother's been worried sick. Half the town's in an uproar over what happened at the revival. They've arrested that healer, or whatever he is. Nothing but a shyster, a common criminal. The Reverend has some explaining to do, as well." He pushed back his hair, and I noticed how long it was growing. He said, "And if it hadn't of been for those kids seeing you and Sweetie digging . . . well, they went inside and saw . . . saw her, and alerted the sheriff. This is unbelievable in a civilized society."

I dropped the shovel. "What're you talking about? What kids?"

"From your class, I guess, I don't know."

My stomach turned inside out with the thought that maybe T. J. and his Posse had been in Sweetie's house, seen her there. Maybe they'd followed the red yarn. I wanted to fall on the ground and never get up. I kicked a piece of root I'd dug up.

"Adults need to be involved now."

I thought how Father would find a way to write about everything in his books, or make it a science project for his students. He could go and examine Miss Mae's poor body and talk about how everything shut down, how even now her cells were decaying away. That's what he did; he watched people, studied them, used them.

"They won't let you put her here, love." He added, "And you know it."

I picked up the shovel and threw it as hard as I could. It landed on a rock and the sound of metal against rock echoed all around me. I sat on a log and put my head in my hands.

Father sat down next to me. "It's a wonder they let her stay up here with a mother as sick as she was. I guess they didn't know how bad things were."

I felt wet on my face, even though I didn't think I'd been crying. It seemed like with the sweat, snot, and tears, I'd be dry as the desert. That there'd be nothing moist left in me and I'd fall flat to the ground, nothing but dried up skin and bones.

More shouts from Sweetie's cabin. I asked, "Who's down there?"

"They're good people, Princess. Let them do what they can to help."

I gave my father a sour look. "Like they did at the tent?"

"That's a small part of the community, Melissa. It's not representative of the whole."

There was a part of me, an inside part of me, that felt safe with my father there. A part that knew he was right. A part that wanted him to fix everything and make it all better. Like when I tossed with fever and he brought me hot lemonade. I looked up at him. It was better to think of him as handsome and strong instead of the other way.

"Can't we just bury her here without them knowing it? You and me?"

He shook his head back and forth.

From below, I heard a horse whinny. I stood, began walking back down to Sweetie's place.

He followed alongside me. "Everything will be okay. We'll get it all sorted out."

"It's not like one of your books, Father."

He grabbed my arm to make me look at him. "What do you want me to do?"

"I want Sweetie to come stay with us. We can live here and not have to move again. That's what I want." I was strong. I was ten feet tall, taller than my father, taller than the trees. I felt as if I would get whatever I wanted right then.

"That's not something to decide right here and now."

"Why not?"

"When you're grown up, you'll understand better."

All that meant was he didn't understand either. I jerked from him and started down. I was going to get Miss Mae if I had to carry her all by myself back up to the dogwood tree.

Mr. Tanner was there, two women from mother's ladies club, and a couple of men I didn't recognize. There were hoof and tire track marks cut into the pretty garden. I pointed to them. "Look what they did!"

"They had to pull a wagon up here. It was the only way to get Sweetie's mother down to . . . take care of her properly."

I stopped and looked down at the tire grooves. "They ruined the garden."

Father put his arm around me. "They had to."

His arm was heavy on my shoulders, as if it would take all my strength to shrug it off. Maybe I'd go down down into the ground until I was buried far below. The dirt over my head, in my nose and ears, the worms eating my brain. I moved away from his arm.

He again ran his hands through his hair until it stuck up on end, and the long pieces flipped out like a woman's. He asked, "Do you know where Sweetie is?"

"No, I don't." Turning my face away from him and towards Sweetie's cabin, I closed my eyes. The people standing around and the ruined garden made me even sadder. The inside of my lids were red, shades of red, like blood. That's what I wanted to see, nothing but red, like Grandmother Rosetta's burning barns.

I let myself imagine how I could move up to the cabin, fix the garden, and wait for Sweetie to come back. Opening my eyes, I said, "I left something in Sweetie's house."

Father put his hands in his pockets and stared up at the trees. "Okay, be quick, though."

I went into the house and looked around. Already it felt too full of the townspeople, with their footprints, and someone's pipe smoke, pipe smoke that was familiar—the green-eyed man? In Miss Mae's room, the bed was stripped down to the feather mattress. I hated thinking about Sweetie coming back to see the empty bed, the bare mattress, the dirt all over their clean floor. I touched the hairbrush Sweetie used to brush her mother's hair. Long strands of the blonde were in the bristles and it made it seem as if she was still alive, as if she'd come in the room, pick up the brush and pull it through her hair. The brush smelled like sweet oil and herbs.

There was a broom in the corner, and I used it to sweep up the dirt that had been tracked in. I took the pan from the counter, poured out the herb water, wrung out the cotton cloths and hung them over the sink. After rinsing out the pan, I dried it and hung it on the hook. The sweet oil bottle was still uncorked, so I pushed the stopper back in and set it back on the counter. There was cornbread wrapped in a towel and I sliced up pieces of it, in case Sweetie came home hungry, all she'd have to do was pick it up and eat it. I thought maybe later I could bring some of Mother's food back to the mountain. And once she had eaten and rested, she would feel better, and be ready to live with us. I made plans all inside my head, where all kinds of things could grow into lives and people and places and things.

Father appeared at the door. "Let's go before your mother sends the rest of the town up here after us."

"What about Sweetie's things? Will they be safe?"

I knew from the way Father looked around that he didn't think there was anything worth taking. "I'm sure everything will be okay. Let the authorities take care of the rest."

"Wait, just one more thing."

"Melissa." Father sighed.

I grabbed my satchel, ran upstairs, and took out our diary and a pen. I tore out a page, and wrote Sweetie a note explaining everything, told her to come to my window, and put the note on her bed with one of her rocks to hold it down. Then I scooted the chest into the corner and put the quilt over it so maybe it would be out of sight in case T. J. and his Posse came snooping again. Maybe they'd miss it in the dim light, or if not, think it full of junk. Or not. I didn't know. It was all I could do right then, until I could figure out things.

Father climbed the stairs. He had to stoop over to fit in the small space. "Let's go. Now." He put his hand on my waist and gently pushed me towards the stairs.

Down the stairs, out of Sweetie's front door, and through the woods I let the day and what could have been and what I could have done and should have done and what others did, ran over and over in my head like a fast waterfall. And I had a burning anger rush through my bones, so that they creaked as I walked beside Father. My bones creaked and strained inside my skin. All the marrow had drained out. All my tears drained out and dried up. I was a creaky boned dried up stupid selfish girl.

None of us deserved Sweetie. I clenched my fists until my fingernails dug into my palms, then I pressed my nails in until I felt my skin puncture. Harder I pressed, until I knew I was bleeding. I wanted to feel pain, and at the same time, I wished I were like Sweetie and felt nothing. I heard Sweetie in my head. *That's not the same pain I'm feeling, Miss Lissa.*

$$***$$

Mother rushed up to hug me tight enough to push out all my air, then stepped back. "What in the world were you thinking?"

I didn't answer her.

"Look at our daughter." She grabbed my hands. "And she's bleeding! Can you explain this to me?"

"Just shut your mouth for once, will you?" Father answered.

"Don't you even think about using that tone of voice with me. Well, I tell you what's what. We're not staying here next semester. You can find another job."

"This town is fine. Just like the last one was. And the one before that. Yet, every time I find a little bit of heaven to write in, you find fault with it."

"Don't you place this on *my* shoulders! Don't you dare." Mother's face was flushed and her chest heaved. Her face turned blotchy. "Dear husband, what about the times some girl catches your eye, and I'm humiliated? You want to tell your adoring daughter about that? About your girls? Huh? Do you?"

I stared at Father.

Father reached out, grabbed Mother by the shoulders, and shook her. "That's quite enough."

Mother jerked away from him and slapped away his arms. "Get your hands off of me before I cut them off. Don't you *ever* touch me like that again!"

"*Stop it. Stop it. Stop it. Stop it.*"

"You think I like leaving places that inspire, just because you get embarrassed at your ladies' clubs and rose clubs and book clubs, and whatever kind of nose in the air society you're after?"

"Oh, but we've lived off my father's money and that's fine with you. What would your life be like if you had to work at regular jobs? Tell me that."

"You spend money faster than anyone could possibly earn it. My money would never be enough."

"All I got from you was promises about your novels making it big. Yeah, *big joke.*"

I turned and crept away. I was too tired to care. I went to my room and from my chest of drawers I took out pajamas, robe, and clean underwear.

In the bathroom, I drew a bath and from the basket of Mother's bath oils and soaps and beads, I took the lavender bubble bath and poured half of it under the running water. I undressed and climbed into the bathtub. My hands stung in the soapy water. As I soaked, I imagined Sweetie hiding, scared, sad, and alone.

A door slammed, and then another one. I lay in the tub thinking, until all was quiet. I then dried off with one of Mother's good guest towels she forbade me to use. I planned that if Sweetie didn't come, then I would find her. I'd go to Zemry's, he'd know what to do. I dried off with Mother's fancy guest towel, and hung it back up. I then put bandages on my hands without putting anything else on them. Maybe comas weren't so bad, after all. I put on my pajamas and robe, put my hand on the bathroom doorknob, but hesitated when I heard a door open, and then another. I listened as my parents made their way down the hall to the kitchen.

I padded to my room and put on my slippers, giving myself time to control my face. When I went into the living room, they were having cocktails, as if nothing at all had happened. I had an anger build up in my chest and push outward until I thought my heart would explode and spray the walls with blood and guts and bits of heart. My anger was bigger than the mountains that rose up all around us. Bigger than would fit inside of me. I burned with it, and I let it stay hot and heavy inside so I wouldn't be afraid to sneak out and find my bound-sister if she didn't come to me.

Mother looked at me. "Dinner will be sandwiches tonight. I wasn't up to cooking."

"I'm not hungry."

"Now, Melissa. Let's put all this behind us. We're family," Father said.

I turned and left them to their cocktails and lies, and went to bed.

They didn't know what was inside of me. They only knew what they thought they always saw.

TWENTY-THREE

I fell asleep waiting for Father to quit typing and go to bed. I dreamed Sweetie was calling to me as she ran through the forest. I ran through the woods, telling her to stay where she was so I could find her, but her cries became farther and farther away, until all I heard was a tiny whisper on the wind. It was dark in my dream and I ran faster and faster, until I ran right off the side of the mountain. I was in the air, still pumping my legs like in the cartoons, screaming for Sweetie to save me. My legs jerked in my sleep and I woke. Everything flashed back in that instant. I jumped from the covers and looked out into the night.

It was still and quiet as I put on my brother's jeans and old cotton t-shirt. The jeans were looser than ever, and I cinched his belt on the last notch. Peter's boots were a bit too big, but I'd stuffed newspaper in the toes so they'd fit me. His clothes smelled like the Old Spice he used to wear and I almost cried with missing him. Only on Thanksgiving and Christmas would I get to see him, other than when our nonna died.

He'd burst into the house, tall and loud and full of fun. He'd pick me up and swing me around the room, and even when I thought I was too heavy, he never did. He called me his favorite sister, and I called him my favorite brother. We thought it funny, even when Mother crossed her arms and told us to settle down before we broke something.

Peter'd been in school a long time and sent me pictures of his friends and him mugging for the camera. He told me that one day he would find the cure for heart disease and cancer and all the other things that made people suffer. He said no one should feel pain, and maybe he'd find a cure for that, too. I knew his back and legs hurt him from when he took that bad tackle. He'd been in the hospital for two weeks in traction. The doctor told us it was lucky he wasn't crippled for life. To me, he looked crippled when he limped around with his eyes tightened up with pain. He'd pace the floor, and swallow aspirin, and stronger white pills if it was bad enough. Even after all that, he was sad that he couldn't play football anymore. Then when his friends went off to the war, and he couldn't do that either, he felt ashamed. I was secretly glad he couldn't join the army or marines, even though our teacher said it was a privilege to serve our country and people who didn't serve were cowards or didn't love our country. I sat very still when she said that, knowing it wasn't true.

If Peter was in his room instead of far away at school, I could tell him everything that happened and he'd understand. He'd sneak out with me, watch over me, and help me find Sweetie. I knew I shouldn't, but I always begged him to come home, writing long sad letters with pressed flowers and pictures of the places we moved to. At Grandmother Rosetta's memorial, he had said I was old enough to understand that he hated how our parents made him feel as if he wasn't doing enough. That nothing he ever did was enough. He said Mother was overbearing and Father was weak.

I grabbed the framed photo of him in his graduation cap and gown, and put it in my satchel. Just in case I never returned, in case something bad happened, I had already written him a long letter and tucked it under my pillow. I'd told him he was the best brother any sister could wish for and that even though he was a big booger headed fool, I loved him with all my heart. I told him about Sweetie, and what I had to do to find her, and the places I'd go, just in case I didn't make it back. If something were to happen, I'd want him to know his sister could be brave. That his baby sister disobeyed rules when it was important, when she had to, just as he had. I wanted him to know where to look for my body if it came to that.

My satchel was full of what I needed. There was the diary with all of Sweetie's maps. I had to trust myself to follow them, just as Sweetie told me I could do. There was a note for Zemry, in case he still wasn't there. I hoped she was there, that she'd be sleeping in his bed, holding the porcelain-faced doll and dreaming all kinds of good things. There was a notepad and pencils, a banana I'd kept for a snack and never eaten, a Snickers candy bar, Father's heavy see-everywhere-in-the-dark-possible flashlight, a big sharpened kitchen knife wrapped in a dishcloth, the carved bird so I could give it back to Sweetie. I put the carved wolf from Zemry in my pocket.

Just like in the television shows, I put pillows under the covers to make it look as if I was there sleeping, and for good measure, I placed my old stuffed animals on the bed. The stuffed bears, dogs, and cats seemed baby-like now, but with them back on my bed, if Mother looked she would think I was her old Melissa, the fat baby girl who slept with her toys. She'd never know that her daughter had turned into Lissa, the warrior who would find her way to her blood-bound sister on a dark mountain.

The window was open, and I eased the satchel out and onto the ground. Putting my left leg over the sill, I held on to the frame and climbed over and out. Taking a deep breath, I held it there until I felt brave and steady, picked up my satchel and shouldered it, and stepped away from the house. I looked back to see what it looked like in the dark of night. It was lonely looking, and dull and plain, but also safe. I'd never thought of that before, how safe I was in my house.

I turned my back on it, and began hurrying to the mountain. The night was cool. Frogs croaked along with other insect and animal sounds. Far off, I heard a howl and I wondered if it was Sweetie. I knew how sound traveled in the mountains, how something close could be far, or something that sounded as if it came from the south or north could be coming from the east or west. At least to me.

I hurried my walk to a run, hoping that none of the neighbors were up late. A dog barked when I was three houses down from mine, but no one seemed to notice that a girl was out in the night. When a cool breeze hit my face and pushed back my short hair, when the night creatures sang their tunes, when the mountains rose up and up and up, while I took all this in as I ran, for just a minute, I forgot about finding Sweetie and instead thought of how good it felt to be out alone, running towards the mountains that rose up blue-black against the sky. I was free.

The moon was almost full, and would help me find my way. I tried to stay in the shadows while I was in the neighborhood, but knew once I was on the mountain; it would be darker than the darkest of nights. I shivered, forced myself to shake it off into the wind.

I ran almost all the way to Whale Back, except in the places that were too rough. The moon didn't leave me until I was there, but once on the trails, I'd had to use Father's flashlight to see. At Whale Back, I searched the ground for a message in the dirt. There was none, so I beamed the light in the bushes and brambles, hoping. There was no moccasin note under the rock. I shone the beam in the bushes, and as I walked, I yanked the yarn away. Every piece of it I could find, I tore off and stuck into my pocket.

While climbing up the little hill from where her cabin stood, I put the flashlight in my satchel and let the moon guide me. Behind a clump of thickets, I crouched down and watched as the moon spread out and over Sweetie's place. There was no movement, and all was quiet and dark. I stood to go inside.

I was maybe twenty steps from her door when I heard someone behind me.

"Well, well. Seems someone else snuck out to look for Sweetie Pie. I didn't think you had it in you."

I turned around.

He shined his flashlight at me. "What's in that bag you got there?"

I held it close to me, looked around to see if he was alone. He seemed to be.

He stepped closer and I hoped he didn't see how hard my heart was beating. I imagined Peter's shirt moving with every thump.

"Don't come near me, T. J.. I mean it."

"Awww, what's her gonna doooo? Hummm? Her gonna butt me like a goat again." He spat on the ground, wiped his mouth with the back of his hand, and asked, "W-w-where's y-y-your f-f-friend?"

"I don't have time for you. Go run and play now." My lips were quivering, but my voice sounded almost strong. I squared my shoulders so I'd look taller and called up the fire Sweetie said was inside of me.

T. J.'s eyebrows shot together. "I asked you a question, bitch."

I turned away from him, even though my back tingled and my heart thumped harder. My mouth dried to a crisp.

When he stomped up behind me, I remembered Peter saying that the one who had the surprise was the one who had the upper hand. I remembered the television shows we watched together and how he'd show me how the good guys got one over on the bad guys.

When T. J. was so close I imagined his hot wheezy breath would soon scorch my neck, I turned and swung the satchel as hard as I could and hit him on the side of his head.

He fell to the ground with a grunt, his flashlight flying off into the woods, the only light then coming from the moonshine. "*You bitch.*" He began to get up.

"I'm warning you to stay down." My heart was on fire. Barns on fire. Barns on fire. Warrior of the creek. *Lissa, show him your fire inside.*

"You made a big mistake, Melissa."

It was the first time he'd used my name. I was winning. I was strong. I was the warrior. I lunged and hit him with the satchel across his head, then whirled and hit him on his chest and shoulder. He dropped down and curled up into a ball. I hit him two more times, once again on his head and once on his back. It almost scared me how I could have kept hitting and hitting. I didn't want to be like T. J.'s father. I remembered what Sweetie said about worms under dirty feet.

I backed up. There was that show where the good guy beat up the bad guy and then he'd asked the bad guy if he had enough. He had talked quietly to him just as if he were asking him what time it was. I remembered how I thought it the perfect thing to do. I asked, "Had enough, T. J.?" I took out my flashlight and shined it full on his face.

He was breathing hard. His face was so purple-red, I thought his head may explode. There were cuts and reddened skin across his face and arms. "Don't hit me again, you hear?" He wouldn't look at me, and I liked that more than I should.

I spit on the ground, said, "Get up nice and slow. No sudden moves."

T. J. sat up, and rubbed his head.

Swinging my satchel, I stared him down. "If you bother me again, I'm telling the whole town you let another girl beat you up, and when they find out it was me, well, how's your posse going to feel about that?"

He made a growling noise.

I tossed the flashlight down, and reached in the satchel to pull out the knife wrapped in the towel. I put the satchel across my shoulders, and slowly unwrapped the knife, happy that I'd taken the mean-looking one that Mother used to cut beef. Keeping my eyes right on T. J. the whole time, I said, "Well, lookie here what I got, T. J.." I thought the knife looked scary in the moonlight.

He said, "You're crazy as a loon, as crazy as that girl and her crazy mama."

"Her name's Sweetie! And she's not crazy!" I stepped one step forward. "I could bury you in the hole we dug for her mother. I think you'd fit just right. What do you think happened to that boy they never found? He didn't fall off the ridge. Sure didn't. He tried some funny stuff, just like you're doing, so Sweetie and Miss Mae killed him with witchcraft spells and threw him over the ridge to make it look like an accident. I like that idea. I like it a lot."

I lunged forward, thrusting the knife towards T. J..

Then he was up and off, running into the woods faster than I'd ever seen a person move in my life, other than Sweetie.

All my years of sitting in front of the television eating candy finally paid off. I wrapped the knife back in the towel and slipped it into my boot, picked up the flashlight, hitched up my satchel, and went inside Sweetie's cabin door.

I checked Miss Mae's room, and up to Sweetie's room. I asked into the darkness, "Where are you, Sweetie?" The house looked just as it did when I was there earlier. I looked inside my satchel and sighed. Peter's picture frame was busted up and I picked out the glass, tried to straighten the picture. The banana was mushed, and the candy bar didn't look much better. I cleaned out the satchel, re-wrote the banana guts note to Zemry on another sheet of paper. I unmashed the candy bar as best I could and left it on the table.

With the flashlight, I studied Sweetie's maps again before starting out to Zemry's place. I shined my flashlight here and there, worrying about hungry animals, about the mountain spirit being angry with me and carrying me off into some strange place. At first, the sounds of animals screeching and limbs cracking sent me scurrying to hide behind bushes, but I made myself stop. Morning would soon come and I'd be able to see better.

When I at last found his place, no Miss Annie trotted to greet me. I pounded on his door in the case he might be there, but he wasn't home. I knew he'd forgive me for going inside without him being there, once he read that Sweetie's mother died and Sweetie ran away before they could take her. Without Zemry, the inside of his shack was a bit scary. The masks stared at me. The bed was empty. The doll wasn't there.

I took one of Zemry's effigy masks off the wall, and stuck the note on the nail so he would see it. He'd understand that I needed to borrow the mask. I held it against my face and waited to feel the spirit of the wolf. I needed it to help me find my way, and to be brave. I wanted to be a wolf, wild and free, running through the forest, sitting on a boulder howling. If I had magic, I'd put on the mask and turn into one, and I'd run through the woods to find Sweetie and use the magic on her so she could be a wolf with me. I put the mask in my satchel and left Zemry's place.

Sweetie wasn't at Whale Back Rock, she wasn't at her cabin, and she wasn't at Zemry's. There was another place she could be.

An owl hooted, and I said to it, to the moon, and to the night creatures singing, "She wouldn't go where her grandfather used to go to smoke, would she? She promised her mother she wouldn't." And the night whispered right back at me, "But her mother is dead now."

I put my hand in the satchel and touched the mask. I checked my watch to see how much time I had before light, and it wasn't there on my arm. I must have left it on my dresser. My arm was naked. I couldn't remember a time when my watch was not on my wrist. It didn't matter, Sweetie never wore a watch. She'd tell me time was just what it was and staring at my watch all the time didn't change a thing, it only made a person worry about time. Time was endless. Time didn't mean anything to me anymore.

I flipped through the diary, through pages of our writing, looking for a map. There, where I almost missed it, on a page almost at the end of the diary, past empty pages filled with only promises, was a map leading up to a ridge with what looked to be barbed wire and a sign with a skull and crossbones. On top of the ridge was a figure, arms out, legs spread out, long hair blowing, and behind her, a man standing in the same way. Maybe it was a drawing of Sweetie and her grandfather.

The way to the ridge was hard, and I had to use my flashlight most of the way. The trail up was thicker and steeper. I gritted my teeth and kept going. I wished for fireflies to come gather together to light up the path for me. I should have gone to the ridge first. Sweetie would figure no one would look there. Everybody stayed away after that boy died. I couldn't help but imagine his busted body being eaten by animals, the piece of his shirt torn on a branch and the stickers nearby with skin still stuck on them, and the bloody fingernail where he'd scratched at the ground so hard it tore off, and the tooth they'd found.

Mr. Mendel the Janitor told us kids about the landslide that happened there after a big storm roared over and down the mountain. How that boy was standing on the ridge one second and the next he wasn't. He said the boy haunted that part of the mountain, and pushed off other kids to their deaths, if they were foolish enough to go up there. Mr. Mendel the Janitor liked to tell it bloody and scary, eyeing us all cockeyed, while we snickered on the outside, but trembled on the inside. All the kid's parents said the mountain was steep there, and unstable from the slides. The sheriff had put barbed wire and signs to warn people, especially kids and tourists. The sheriff said everybody sure better take heed or they'd be bear food and bobcat food and no telling what all. He'd said they suspected two other missing kids, a little kid and a teenager, might had been fools and gone up there, too.

I stopped to wipe spiders' webs off my face, put on the mask and howled at the moon, hoping Sweetie would hear me. From above me, I thought I heard a howl answer back, but it could have been just the wind through the trees, or maybe an echo off the mountain. I had to put it back into the satchel, but I kept my hand on it to feel strong as I ran as fast as I was able, up to the ridge, where the haunted boy and the angry mountain spirit, and maybe, my blood-bound sister Sweetie were.

TWENTY-FOUR

Everything was different. Everything had changed over one little summer. It was as if my brain and body were trying to keep up with each other, and my heart was somewhere in the middle of the two, ripping open and apart. The ground under my feet vibrated up through my whole body and made me feel like the rocks and the boulders and the North Carolina earth full of things I couldn't see and didn't always understand. I wondered if all the ancient women of all the ancient times were standing in the mists watching me, telling me, *Run. Find her. Be a strong warrior.*

As morning came to the mountain, the mists hovered. Where the ridge lifted up to the steepest area, where I knew everyone was supposed to stay away, I shone my flashlight, and there in front of me was the barbed wire fence. I thought about all the Indians Zemry talked about. I thought about the boy lost forever. I thought about Sweetie's grandfather smoking kinnikinnick and denying God. I thought about Nonna. I thought how the mists could be their ghosts coming to help me find Sweetie, or to lead me to her. All the spirits surrounded me and I felt their cool hands on my cheeks so I would stay brave.

I shined the flashlight right and left. There, farther down, was a sign that read, "Danger! Keep Away!" Someone had drawn the skull and crossbones over the sign.

I called out, soft at first, then louder, "Sweetie! Sweetie!"

It was getting lighter, and the mists glowed even more, so I put away the flashlight, pushed apart the barbed wire, and squeezed through. A piece of Peter's shirt tore off and I had a moment of worry that he'd be mad that I ruined one of his favorite shirts. I was sure going to make a lot of people mad for the things I had to do. Peter's boots slipped in the damp grass and dirt, and my satchel hooked on brambles and branches. I pushed and pulled and climbed, sweated and grunted.

"Do not come up here, Lissa."

I was so surprised, I slipped and fell, caught myself on a branch, and held on until I could get my footing again. I took out the mask and put it on, looked up at her, said through it, "I got the spirit of the wolf."

"Lawd, you should see yourself." She cackled, standing on the ridge with her hands on her hips. She wore the army jacket, and it was torn, smudged with dirt, leaves stuck here and there.

I reached into my pocket, pulled out the carved wolf and held it out in the palm of my hand. "Remember, like Zemry said about me when he made this."

"Look at you. Climbing up here like you got a fire in your belly."

I put the carving back into my pocket, turned the mask around and looked at it. "I wish we were wolves and could be wild and run free."

"Sure sounds like a real nice way to be."

The ground where she stood looked mushy to me. There was dirt, rocks, and a few small tree roots sticking up all around her. A big tree lay on its side, its roots reaching for the ground that no longer hugged it safe to its home.

I put Zemry's mask back into my satchel and used both hands to climb up closer to her.

"You will not come up here. I mean it."

"Then you come down."

"Nuh uh."

"I'd rather be at Jabbering Creek with our toes in the water."

She rose up on her toes and swung her arms in a pinwheel, a dreamy look softening her face until it turned hard again.

"I'm scared, Sweetie."

She looked down at me. "Nope, nuh uh. You are not scared. I can see inside you. You were just used to being scared all your life before."

"Remember what they said about that kid? You want someone to find your skin and tooth and nail scattered all over creation?"

"I feel fine up here. Nobody will come get me and make me go to no orphan house with bars on the winders where they's no mountain or critters."

"I told you. You can stay with us. I talked to Father." I stood up, but had to drop down on my hands and knees and crawl like a baby.

Sweetie laughed, then said, "That sure looks funny."

I stopped, hanging on to a tree branch, my boots digging into the ground, breathing hard enough to feel dizzy.

She stopped laughing, said, "Miss Lissa. You surely know your mama would want to make me wear fancy clothes and stay home all'a time. Nope. Besides, you know your mama don't want me any more'n I want her." She crossed her arms over her chest and tossed her head. "And your daddy won't stay here. This here is my *Home*."

It was eerie the way the mists curled up around Sweetie and hugged her, whispering it seemed to me. Whispering to her things like, *come with us, stay with us, don't listen to her, she doesn't know you like we do.*

"Father can stay here and write his books. That's what he wants. And you and me can stand against the Circle Girls and all of them. You and me, Sweetie. Blood-bound sisters." I steadied my feet, found a grounding in the dirt, my arms felt stronger than they ever had. I *was* stronger. "You and me, Sweetie."

"That sounds like a pretty picture. But it don't always work out in ways we wish."

"What about Zemry? You could stay with him."

"Zemry's a old old man. He don't got time to worry over no kid. He's got to go off sometimes, like he did this time. He got a wandering soul."

"Like your father."

Her mouth turned down to a frown, then she said, "I saw him."

"Who? Zemry?"

"At the tent."

"Who?" I slipped a little, dug my boot, Peter's boot, into the ground, held on. "Who, Sweetie?"

"We got the same eyes. It was him." She rubbed her arm. "And when I was hiding up in the woods, when you was setting on the log with your daddy, I saw him again."

"*Who?*"

"That green-eyed man what smells like pipe smoke. Them stories about my daddy I needed. But that green-eyed man is the truth."

"The green-eyed man at the tent is your . . . he's your father?"

She looked up at the sky, then over her shoulder, then back to me. "I will hide up here, and when they's all forgot about Sweetie, I will come back down and live with the critters. You come find me when things get safe. I will wait for you forever and ever until you can come back. I will. I promise."

"Forever and ever?"

"I will always be here. Just you wait and see." She stepped back a bit, the ground under her shifted a little, and rocks and dirt began tumbling down toward me. She laughed, then said, "Watch out! That mountain spirit is ornery today."

I crawled, holding onto roots and vines, finding my voice between my huffs and puffs. "If green-eyes . . . is your father . . . he'll take you in . . . and everything will be good."

"Nuh uh." She bent and picked up a stick, and waved it in the air like a sword, or a magic wand.

I grabbed and pulled, but slid back for every bit of ground I made. How had she climbed up there? She had because she was Sweetie. "Everybody dies, Sweetie. You can too." I didn't want to think about falling to a horrible bloody death, and so I kept my eyes on Sweetie. "I'm dragging your silly butt down here whether you like it or not. I promised Miss Mae! I promised!"

"I got magic, remember? Don't worry over me. You best stay back. I am not fooling."

The wind blew and it, too, sounded like whispers, like those in the mists. The whispers grew louder and louder, until my head was full of voices. I wanted to clamp my hands over my ears, but the voices sounded as if they were more inside my head than outside. I wanted to scream. And then I realized I was, yelling at Sweetie and beating my fists on the ground. What I yelled didn't even make sense to me, sounding like snotty gorbles and garbles.

All the whisper voices whispered lower, lower, lower.

I looked up at her.

Everything became still. Silent. She said, "You are my friend. Don't forget me. Come back to find me. When it's safe. When they's forgot about me."

The whispers began again. As if they were chanting songs.

Sweetie rose up on her toes and held her arms in the air. Her hair blew all around her. Then from behind her, I saw a man standing the same way, ghostly, like the mists, but he was there. I saw him. Sweetie closed her eyes, two high spots of color on her cheeks. She looked as if she'd aged and aged, as if she wasn't twelve but a hundred and twelve.

Below, in the woods there was rustling, my name called.

She looked down at me, capturing me with her eyes just as she did the first day we met and became fast friends.

The whispery voices on the wind raised and raised, wind through the trees, branches rubbing together, and whispery sounds like women cooing to babies, chanting like women before a barn on fire. And within the sounds were voices that sounded real.

I scrambled, held out one hand to her, while the other held onto a clump of vines. The mists floated in and out. My teeth chattered from the morning chill and my sweat. The sky peeped through the trees, turning all kinds of shades of red and orange and yellow that swirled together and made me dizzy. The whispering started up louder and louder until I thought I'd go insane.

Over all the whispers, the pumping of my blood, over the sudden call of the hawk, and then of men shouting, I heard Sweetie say, "Nothing ever got to hurt, if you set your teeth to it."

I blinked away the dirt falling down from where she stood. I blinked, and when I opened my eyes, she was gone.

When the sheriff found me, I was at the top of the ridge where Sweetie had stood, screaming her name and I couldn't remember how I'd climbed up there. I was on the ground. The ground was wet and cold. The sheriff grabbed me, held on, and pulled me away from where Sweetie had been. The sheriff and another man from town carried me back over the barbed wire and down the mountain. Father was at the switchback of the trail, wringing his hands, my note to Peter sticking out of his pocket. When he hugged me, he squeezed so hard I couldn't breathe. He kept saying, "Oh Princess. Princess."

I was limp in his arms. I didn't care about anything. I'd never care about anyone or anything. Ever. Again. I was so sleepy. So tired.

TWENTY-FIVE

Father later said that some of the men from town went back with ropes they tied to trees, and worked their way to the other side, just as they had years before when that boy went missing. They searched hard for Sweetie, but the woods were thick, and they didn't see how she would have survived the fall over the side anyway. There was talk of bears carrying her off, or that she just kept falling and rolling down too far in the woods for anyone to see. There was talk of how that haunted, lost boy picked her up and took her to his spirit cave to be his ghost bride. They only found the army jacket, ripped and hanging from a branch, but no other sign of her.

The women in town gathered at their churches and took up money to give Miss Mae a proper burial. I sat in the church, where the new preacher, Reverend Joseph, talked about Miss Mae as if he knew her. Reverend Seth had left town in the dead of the night. I sat at the end of the pew and stared at a spot on the wall until the funeral service was over. As the townspeople walked by me, they placed a hand on my shoulder and squeezed.

I asked Father to take me to Zemry so I could tell him, and he did. Zemry took me in his arms and held me as if he was my grandfather. He stroked my hair. He said, "Don't you worry. Don't you worry one bit. Don't you worry." He wouldn't say anything else and then he stepped back, turned, and walked into the woods. He looked so very very old.

***

Nothing was ever said about Sweetie, and once Miss Mae was in the ground, she faded away, too. After Mother boxed up Peter's clothes for the church to have, she hauled me to town to buy better clothes, ones not made for running free on mountains. I thought I saw the green-eyed man, but then I guessed I really hadn't at all.

I tried to paint Sweetie's face, but all I could do was stare at a blank canvas, as if she were a ghost I couldn't capture, a dreamy dream. I put away the paints and decided right then and there that I'd never paint again.

In the ice cream shop, Mother bought me something sweet. Deidra and T. J. sat with their milkshakes. They wouldn't look at me, no matter how hard I burned a hole into their backs. It was as I didn't exist, either. As if I was nothing but a dream. As if they didn't know who I was.

No one asked about Sweetie. No one said anything more about Miss Mae.

When Sweetie disappeared, she never existed at all.

***

Mother packed up her last wine glass in newspaper and dishcloths, and dusted her hands together. When she went outside to order the movers around, I went to the box, opened it, and broke every one of her wine glasses with Father's ball peen hammer. The ping and crunch felt good, *tap tap tap tap tap . . . tap tap.* I heard whispers telling me, *Ha! That's it! Break em all! Good warrior. That'll show her.* But it was just my own mean voice.

We followed behind the moving van in our car and I watched the mountains disappear.

I was Melissa again. Nothing but a biological machine.

In Ohio, Father found a job at a private high school, and he sold his first novel called, "The Lost Last Years of a Last Lost Girl." It was a familiar story. That was all it had ever been, one of Father's stories. I'd just been too caught up in it. Of course.

Mother joined another ladies' club and didn't read Father's book.

Peter visited me on my thirteenth birthday, and at Christmas, and Thanksgiving and at Easter. Or maybe I only dreamed him, because sometimes that's just how fast things came and went and were forgotten. And after a time, as we moved again, and then again, new towns replaced old towns and the dream faded . . . faded . . . faded.

I set my teeth against any pain. Pain was biological, whether it was from the inside or the outside. Everything can be controlled, and if not controlled at least explained. But I knew, still, that pain on the inside could hurt in a much different and worse way than anything on the outside.

One summer. One dreamy summer. The only thing real is what was happening right at the moment it happened. That was what it meant to grow up.

My parents finally divorced. Father lived with his off and on women, grew his hair even longer and with it a beard, ate sushi, and traveled with his restless feet taking him here and there and everywhere. And Mother married a man who gave her what she needed, loved her. The change softened her, made her into someone I could, and did, like. How funny the way things happened in life.

Miss Lissa fell asleep, as long lost dreams make reality forgotten.

Until . . .

TWENTY-SIX

And this is not the end . . .

. . . the memory box. Release of the long sleep of denial.

Wake up.

I stopped at a rock that looked like it may be Turtlehead Rock. I knew I was on the right old log trail. I took in air, deep into my lungs, and let it out.

"Sweetie? Sweetie?"

The wind blew against my back, pushed me forward. I went forward.

Old whispers drifted on the wind. How familiar they were.

When I came upon it, my skin tingled. My heart pumped blood through my veins. My synapses fired, *onesies twosies threesies, five-thousand.* The scientific biological body knew what to do. The woman who was me, a fallible creature, knew not what would happen next.

Whale Back Rock. I placed my palm on the rough lichened surface, closed my eyes, opened them.

I climbed on it, as we had when young, and looked around. It all looked the same, felt the same.

Surely, a biological machine, a woman such as me, can live here for as long as her body allows, as long as her heart beats, and then she can die here when her heart stops beating and let her cells decay here. Can one day have her ashes scattered here. There is everything I need here. This is Home. It's been waiting for me. Just as Sweetie is waiting for me, as she promised.

I pressed my face on the warm rock, the heat spread from my cheek to my entire body, then I climbed down and lay face up on the Western North Carolina earth. It thrummed with life and stories, both ancient and new. Everything, all of it, the entire summer, all rushed back, as if I was hurtling through space and time, forward then backward. In a real-time dream. I said, aloud, "I want to paint again." And right then and there I could feel how my hand would move against the canvas; I would paint her face. That's what I'd do.

I woke, from my dream, to a familiar whisper on the wind:

Sweetie. *Wake up, Silly Brains. No time for sleeping. We got things to do, inneresting things to show you. Hurry before we get to be old granny women.*

How real my dreams were. How the sleep seemed like waking and the wake seemed like the dream. I turned my head, still lying upon that throbbing heart of the mountains. Turned my head and squinted my eyes against the tears rising up as little storms. Something . . .

. . . something fluttering in the rhododendron bushes.

A feather? A flowered vine hanging down? I crawled on my hands and knees, weak and shaky, for a closer look. There, within the branches. I reached out my trembling hand, touched it, pulled it free, pressed it in my hand, opened my hand. Red in the palm. A piece of bright red yarn. How? How could it be? Because it could.

She'd said she'd wait for me. Had I believed in the magic in her, buried deep inside of me?

"Sweetie? Sweetie? Are you here?"

From the trees above, I heard laughing, tree branches shaking. I knew those sounds. I remembered them. Not a bird, or squirrel, or chipmunk. Not the wind through the trees. Not a ghost. Not a memory. Not a thought, wish, or dream.

I stood, stared into the trees, searching, the red yarn soft in the palm of my hand, soft and light as a baby bird, as if it wasn't even real.

"I don't need the yarn, Sweetie. I can find you."

Laughter. Shaking branches.

"Sweetie. Come down. Stop teasing me." Not the wind. Not the critters. Not a ghost.

The mountain spirit claimed what it wanted. Without arrogance, without need. But sometimes the mountain spirit gave back instead of taking away. Because it must. Because that was how the magic worked. That was how friendship stood for all time. Even Steven. Forever.

She'd waited. No kind of sleep broke the bonds—just as Sweetie said.

"Sweetie! Sweetie! I see you! Come down!" I ran then, to the base of the tree, laughing, laughing, hot tears rolling.

Real. Not the wind. Not a ghost. Not a dream. Here. Now. Solid. A scientific woman would not lie.

I reached out and touched her scars. Ran my hands along her arms. I licked salt from my mouth. I caught up my sobs. I kissed her and her lips were spread in happy laughter.

And we were off, running, running, as if young again. We ran through the forest, laughing, laughing, laughing. Blood-bound sisters.

Beautiful biological wonders. Scientific anomalies.

. . . and did I ever want to leave her again? Did I ever want to forget again? Did I ever again wish for the long unknowing sleep? No. Never. Never. Ever.

THE END

Sweetie

Reader's Guide
By Mary Ann Ledbetter
Baton Rouge, Louisiana

EPIGRAPHS

Magendie's epigraphs offer intriguing possibilities for interpretation. How does her quotation from Ovid speak to the issues of affliction and friendship in the novel?

Explore the novel's motifs of death and illusion as revealed by the old mountain song which is Magendie's second epigraph.

SYMBOLS

Blood

Blood is one of the most powerful symbols associated with Sweetie. Her faded yellow cotton dress is "scattered with once-bright roses that had turned the color of old blood." Think of her torn finger, her slashed palm, her bloody handprint on the white robe. Discuss blood as a revealing symbol of Sweetie.

Birds

Throughout the novel, Sweetie is also closely associated with birds. What might the bird symbol mean in Sweetie's life?

Scars

Sweetie's external scars likely mimic her internal ones. The narrator sees "the scabs marching across her knees, the puckered skin racing up her right arm, the reddened zigzag that ran from her ankle up her thigh . . ." Think about the issue of emotional scarring in children.

THEMES

Sense of Belonging

Sweetie tells Melissa about the necessity of replacing the baby bird in its nest, "It belongs where it belongs, right? And where something belongs is where it's got to stay, right?" How does her statement pertain just as strongly to herself and to Melissa?

Friendship

The narrator speaks of the bond of friendship as ". . . water finding water always. Like finding like. Need finding need." Melissa's father says, "It's at times irrational, but our instincts to survive and to form community and to bond with other human beings are quite strong." Explore the ideas of survival, community, and friendship. Why are these concepts so crucial in the novel and in our own lives?

Maps

The grown narrator wonders if Sweetie had drawn maps "only for young me" or for her adult self. What might maps as symbol mean in the narrator's life as both child and adult?

The Supernatural

Discuss belief in the supernatural as held by Sweetie's grandfather, the granny woman, and Sweetie. Remember Sweetie's magic tea and her mountain spirit, for example.

Destiny

The grown Melissa describes herself as "a scientific woman, a biological machine, made of fallible parts and calculating synaptic brain . . . A woman who believed only what science showed her and not what was felt with the heart." How has her destiny followed that of her father? What do you imagine will be her new destiny?

Exclusion

Discuss the significant increase in today's culture of the bullying of children. Think of the mean-spiritedness of T.J., Beatrice, and Deidre. What comment does Magendie seem to be making on this phenomenon?

Sweetie's Affliction

What would it be like never to feel pain? According to Sweetie, is her affliction completely advantageous? What sorts of precautions must she take to maintain health? What is Magendie saying about pain of any kind?

Romance vs. Realism

Explore the dichotomy of Sweetie's parents—her romantic mother and her realist father. Remember the mother's hilarious food poems, strange menus, forced manners, European wine glasses, inflexible rules. She seems to deliberately mis-pronounce Sweetie's name as "Sweet-tea." Her father discusses slaughter houses at the dinner table, says there is an answer for everything, and writes novels with unintentionally funny titles. What is their marriage like? How does Melissa interact with them? Why do you think they eventually divorce?

Emotional Instability
How was Melissa's physical and emotional being shaped by the transience and discord of her home life?

Secrets
Melissa writes of Sweetie, "She trusted me with the part of herself she'd hidden from the world, and in her way, presented back to me the gift to see what I had hidden inside myself." What does she mean? What parts of themselves had each girl hidden?

By the end of the novel, does Melissa achieve further self-insight? Explore the apparent ambiguity in the novel's conclusion.

Death
Analyze Magendie's treatment of death. Discuss the dignity and beauty of the funeral rites performed on Mae by Sweetie and Melissa. How do they contrast with the traditional American way of death? Discuss any blessings to the bereaved that descend upon the girls as they minister to the body of Sweetie's mother.

Religion
What is Magendie saying about the vulnerability of naive people to manipulation by religious con artists?

STRUCTURE
Explore the structure of Magendie's novel. What is gained by her use of two narrators, both the grown and the young Melissa?

SETTING
"Oh, North Carolina. What mysteries and secrets you hold," Magendie writes. Her setting functions almost as a character in the novel. How has Magendie enabled the reader to experience the mountain where Sweetie and Melissa ran free? What might Magendie mean by her vivid

portrayal of such an Edenic existence? Discuss Magendie's use of sensory images in her description of the Smoky Mountains.

CHARACTERS
Why is Sweetie's "affliction" so troubling to Melissa? How do the other children and townspeople view Sweetie and her mother? How does the fake healer use her affliction for his own purposes?

Discuss the troubling image of the burning barns in Grandmother Rosetta's paintings. What do they seem to symbolize?

Trace the progression of Melissa's physical and emotional development during her mountain summer with Sweetie. How does she mature?

What coping mechanism has Peter used in his relationship with his family?

Zemry embodies the wisdom of his native people. What lessons does he teach Sweetie and Melissa?

Author's Note:

I wanted to mention this to you, Dear Readers, and it is the truth, as real to me as I am real sitting here typing this author's note. One beautiful Smoky Mountain morning I was walking in the woods, and this blonde-haired girl appeared to me, an apparition, standing with feet rooted in the grass on this rich Western North Carolina soil, her feet bare, her thin dress blowing in the breeze, her eyes steady on me, and she said to me, "You got to write up my story." And I answered, "I am writing something . . ." and she said, "No, you got it all wrong, this here's how it is . . ." and when I returned from my walk, Sweetie began to emerge fully and wholly as if she'd revealed something to me in a way I do not understand. I have not encountered her spirit in this mountain cove at Killian Knob again—she rests because her story is now told.

About the Author:

Kat lives in Maggie Valley, North Carolina, in a little cove at Killian Knob with two dogs, a ghost dog, a GMR, a mysterious shadowman, and many wild critters. She is co-editor/publisher of the Rose & Thorn. Visit her at kathyrnmagendie.com.

Photograph by Christy L. Bishop